CW01208934

COVEN COVE

The Curse of the Crescent Moon

David Clark

1

"Relax!" shouted Jack. He had both hands up, ready to either restrain or attack me. It wasn't his brightest idea considering how our sparring usually faired in Mr. Helms' class.

Nathan grabbed for my hands, but I yanked them away. The others parted like the Red Sea, clearing a path between Clay and me. Nathan made another grab, and I avoided his grasp. His arm wrapped around my waist, and I felt the taut muscles in his forearm twitch and strain as he tried to hold me back. There was a light glow in Jack's hands. Did he really want to do this?

"Larissa, he is fine. He's clean. Your runes blocked Jean for good, and Mrs. Tenderschott cleaned the love spell."

Clay held his hands up, like a criminal held at gunpoint. He wished it was only a gun pointed at him. I could do so much worse than just splatter a bit of him against the wall of the hall. Having him, a creature under Jean's control, in this house was vile.

"Larissa, it's true. He's clean," Nathan said. The physical strain of holding me back was clear in his voice, but it still sounded sweet, and that backed me down a notch. I thought I even heard two sighs of relief as I rocked back on my heels.

"Larissa, I am fine now, and I am so sorry."

"Sorry? Clay. I've heard apologies from you before."

"Remember, you were in my head. You know what created all this. That's not me, but if you don't believe it. There is one way you can be sure." With that, Clay held out his hand. It trembled. I knew what he meant and pushed Nathan's arm from my waist. Jack moved aside, and I walked cautiously down the hall past the others. Each looked on fearfully.

"Stand still, or so help me God. You will end right where you stand."

"That honestly doesn't sound that bad," Clay said. The remorse in his voice pulled me through the pain of the memories his presence caused.

"Just stand still," I said, a little less intensely than before. I reached my hand out, but I was hesitant to make contact. I needed to know, and this would be the only way. My flat palm touched his, and there was nothing, and that was the happiest I had ever been with nothing, but I needed more. "Come here."

My fingers wrapped around Clay's hand, and I yanked him into the parlor and sat him down on the burgundy settee in front of the open window. The cool breeze of the southern winter night carried in the refreshing scent of honeysuckle. I had missed that smell. I knew I would smell the lilac and lavender tomorrow when the sun warmed the fields, if the plants were still there. I sat next to Clay. Nathan entered the room, but the rest still seemed a little leery of these events and stayed out in the safety of the hallway. Nathan's jaw twitched nervously as he looked on.

"Relax," I said to him, and he just shoved his hands down in his pockets as hard as he could.

"Clay, I need to check something to be sure."

"You aren't going to burn any fancy letters into my skin again?" He asked, and leaned away from me cautiously.

"No. No more letters. Just another trip into your head." Clay jerked back even further away. "And no potions either."

He almost looked relieved.

What I was about to do was something I hadn't done before. I had read about it and seen my father do it probably half a dozen times. Would this work? Who knew? With only one way to find out, I placed my hands on either side of his temples and massaged my fingers back and forth. There were no words, just focus, and at the moment, that didn't seem to be a problem anymore.

Slowly the feeling of my fingers on his skin changed, but not to how it felt before. His skin stuck to mine, then my fingers sunk into his skin each time I pressed. When all eight fingers were in and my thumbs securing his head, I knew I was in. At this point, there were two options. I could either plant a thought or read a thought. My mission was to read them. In particular, I wanted to read the thoughts of who else might be in there. I could probe as deeply as I wanted to, but the pain and unsettled feeling of the countless times I had been through this—twenty-two but who was counting—was still with me, I wouldn't do any more than I truly needed, and it didn't take long. He was alone in there. There was no one else, just Clay. A teen, who was full of emotions flashing from one extreme to the other with the moments of fear lasting longer than any of the others. This was Clay, all Clay. Before I let go, I felt one more emotion flash through and hold longer than the others, and I now knew why he came.

I let go of Clay and settled back against the arm of the settee. Clay looked at me, concerned, as did the others, which included a few who were only peeking around the door frame. "Okay," I said, and then heard a collective exhale throughout the room.

"Larissa, I am sorry." Clay turned his head toward Nathan standing in the doorway, but before he said a word, I grabbed it and turned him back to look at me. That wasn't out of concern for what he was about to say. I was no longer worried about that. I felt the real Clay. The real Clay that appeared a few times and caused me to assess him as *nice*.

“Clay, you need to stop apologizing. To me. To Nathan,” I winked in Nathan’s direction, “to everyone. You weren’t in control. And I know why you are here, or at least part of the reason.” I had to consider the possibility there were other reasons hidden behind the raw emotions I felt, but those powerful emotions told me that only one mattered. “Time for revenge against those that turned you will come. I can promise you that.” I slapped him on the shoulder and stood up.

“Well, everyone, welcome to my home.”

2

"Now that you are here, I only have one other thing to say." I walked to the center of the room and worked hard for the pleasant look I hoped was on my face. "Why the hell are you here?" I yelled. "I mean, I know why he is here," my right hand pointed back at Clay, "but what about the rest of you? This isn't your fight. This fight started long before any of you were even alive. No, that's not right," I corrected, sounding no less angry. "This fight started long before your parents were born, and possibly even their parents." Now I was pointing at them like an angry parent myself.

I was mad, frustrated, and now worried. My plan, what there was of one–which wasn't much, didn't include anyone but me. Clay, I could add in, and in some ways, he might be some much-needed help. I came down here to take care of things, which meant killing Jean St. Claire and ending that threat, and then return to what I considered home, the coven. Then, and only then, I could be together with all of them again. Of course, if Jean was still in this world, that wouldn't be possible, not without putting everyone in danger. Which, going back to the beginning. was why my intention was to come down here and deal with this *alone*, to keep them out of harm's way. My own brain wanted to scream in frustration.

Nathan approached me with his arms outstretched. I couldn't tell if they were there for defense or if he was trying to come give me a hug. "Larissa," he started, but I stopped him.

"There is no explaining this away." I side stepped him waving my arms and marched toward the others. "You guys knew better, too." My eyes locked with Gwen's. I wasn't expecting any argument from her. Her presence was a mystery. She was the unlikeliest of all allies.

"You two," I addressed Mike and Laura. Mike had his arms wrapped around Laura, holding her tight, and had since I pulled Clay into the parlor. "With all the stories and discussion about Jean and his followers, you both knew better."

Mike let go of Laura and appeared to puff out his chest a little. "You forgot what we are. We are the only ones who can help you."

I could see where he was going with that, but again, Kevin and Jennifer Bolden said more than once that Jean was someone you didn't want to mess with.

Rob and Martin stood out in the hallway, and when I looked at them, and their clueless faces, I knew they were just following the others. They were great friends, and I knew they would leap before thinking anything through. All I could do was just let out a faked sigh and a shake of my head. Both responded with a smile.

That brought me to Jack, who backed up into the hallway when he saw my focus coming his way. "And you." I was now face to face with him. I didn't need his ability to know he was scared and uncomfortable. The rapid and uneven thumping in my ears told me that. "Not only did you come here putting yourself in danger, but you went a step further and brought the others." He opened his mouth to reply, but I didn't give him a chance. "And what makes this even worse? You, of all people, even more so than Mike and Laura, know how dangerous this guy is. You felt what I felt every time he came to me, and when he came to Clay."

"Do you ever think that was why?" Nathan asked from behind. I spun around on my heels. My hair whipped around across my face before settling.

"Don't start..."

"Larissa, that was why," interrupted Jack. They were teaming up on me and I didn't like it one bit.

"Don't make this seem like some noble effort to come help me." I turned to look at Jack, but stopped at Mike. I stared at him intensely, and under the pressure of my gaze, he nodded his agreement.

"That wasn't our first thought," Jack said.

By now, Nathan had reached me, and his hands were gripping my shoulders from behind. It was not a restraining grip, but a loving, almost caressing touch. "We were going to try to talk you out of this, and have you come back with us."

"Of course, that might be a little hard now," Martin remarked under his breath. Rob jabbed him in the ribs with a sharp elbow. Seeing Laura put her hand over her face, and looks of discomfort on the others, I feared something had happened at the Coven, but how could it? I had only been gone for an hour before the others arrived. It was obvious something had happened.

"What happened?" I squawked. Panic and worry squeezed on my vocal cords with a death grip. I had focused my mind on what I was here to do, but what I had left behind was never far from my thoughts. Most of that was here with me now. The only major piece of my life missing, an enormous piece, was Amy. If something had happened back at the Coven, that would have involved her.

"Mom caught us leaving and forbade us from returning."

I turned, pulling my shoulders from Nathan's grip. "She what?"

"She told us if we left, we could not return, but I have a feeling if we returned with you, she wouldn't try to stop us." He smiled halfheartedly as his blue eyes looked into mine. That was what he believed, but I wasn't so sure. I think I had cut her pretty deep when I left, and I had doubts if she would allow me to return after I had done what I planned to do, but that was a bridge I was going to cross when I got to it. Now the others were sharing my fate.

"If you all go back now, she will let you back. I know it."

Nathan objected, "Not without you."

"Yea, not without you," Gwen said, drawing a surprised look from everyone. I was shocked.

"Absolutely not." I walked over to Jack, and stopped just inches from him, and demanded. "You will create a portal and take them all back. Right now!"

Jack peered around me at Nathan, but I grabbed his chin and redirected his attention right back to me. "You don't need his permission. You're a big boy and can do it all on your own. Or should I do it and then shove you all back through it?" Now that was an idea I hadn't thought of before. I could do it easily. Just a quick flipping of my wrist with the grand entry of the Coven in my head and it would open. A shove with my other wrist would send them crashing through, but I didn't. I couldn't. A pang of loneliness stopped me. In some ways, many ways, I was happy they were here.

"I'm not going to. Not without you, and you know that. So, you have two choices: come back with us, or let us help you." He was defiant and steady, like the craggy rocks of the cove against the raging tide. I stormed off with the rest of that raging tide, not letting on that any part of it was a great acting job.

"Well, I guess if you guys are going to be staying here, I better show you guys around." I grabbed Nathan by the hand. "This is the parlor." I glanced at Rob and Martin and added, "A really fancy living room." Rob stuck his tongue out at me.

I gave Nathan a little tug and led him out of the room. "Up the stairs are the bedrooms and the bathroom." I did a quick count of those with me and made a few natural pairings. "We have quite a few guest rooms upstairs, so there are enough for everyone."

"Do you let dogs sleep inside?" Mike asked.

I knew where he was going with this and couldn't miss an opportunity. "When I was growing up, the dogs slept out in the barn."

"Sorry guys." Mike gave Martin a firm but playful shove from behind.

"Down this way is the kitchen." I walked them past the stairs and into the kitchen, where I instinctually moved toward the table. While there was a chorus of "Wow."

Nathan pulled me close and asked, "This is where?"

I nodded and pointed to the chair I usually sat in, and then at the chair where my mother normally sat. He glanced at both, allowing his free hand to trace the top edge of the chair where my mother usually sat during our visits. There was a regal reverence to his motions.

"Is this a real wood fire stove?"

"Yes, Jack. I haven't upgraded things yet. Just some light cleaning," I said, rushing over to close the door on the large cast-iron stove that sat in the corner. We had electricity and phone service growing up. Both, I had to assume, were disconnected long ago for unpaid bills. We could have afforded an electric stove, HotPoints were becoming all the rage, but my mother preferred to cook on a wooden stove, at least until gas service reached us way out here. Something I doubted it had, even this many years later. She swore the food tasted different. Now that she mentioned it, it did.

"Whoa, check out the old crappy barn!" yelled Rob.

Feeling a little defensive about my home, I rushed over to pull the curtains shut on the window over the sink, blocking the view of the old barn. I had cleaned up the home, but hadn't touched the barn yet. Something I remedied before I let go of the curtains, revealing a red barn and white trim that looked as fresh as the day they built it. Rob and Laura both did a double take out the window at its appearance.

"The back door there leads out to the fields. Let's go out there." I ushered everyone out of the kitchen and through the door. Once they were gone, I performed the quickest kitchen renovation in the history of home improvement shows. Demolition, restructure, paint, and new appliances. All without a commercial break. Now there were modern and working appliances, and food in the refrigerator. Something I hadn't considered needing when it was going to just be me.

Now it was my time to be surprised. I expected to see other homes or buildings close by, completely expecting urban sprawl to have made its way out here, but it hadn't. Nothing but acres and acres of fields of lavender and lilac plants. They were still there, unmaintained, and wild, but alive. A few still sported their purple flowers this late in the year.

Watching the others march through the fields was something that would have sent shivers through my father. You had to walk in the plowed alleys between each row of plants, of course, those rows didn't exist anywhere but in my mind now, and I couldn't help myself and followed the others walking through the plants, with my fingers extended down to feel the plants as I did. Our movement rustled the plants enough to release their sweet and pleasurable fragrance, causing those of our party who breathed to take in a deep breath. Memories of when I did the same thing made me jealous of them.

"I used to witch-whisper from here all the way into the kitchen."

Jack took a gander in the house's direction. "That far?"

"Yep."

Now he looked at me in disbelief. "That has to be over 500 yards." Mike joined Jack and his estimation and added, "At least, probably closer to six or seven."

While out in the field, I pointed to the woods that bordered our property to the south, just beyond what used to be the sugar cane fields, which were now overrun with more lilac and lavendar. Beyond those woods, I told them, was the Mississippi River. A fact that Mike and Clay raced each other to verify. I considered joining them, but knew what I would find was not what I had hoped to. The day of the paddlewheel steamers was long gone. When they returned, the first crickets of the night sang, and I realized how much I missed this. The overcast night still had the orange hues created by the setting sun, and a layer of dew announced the beginning of the transition from a warm day to a cool night. We returned to the house, entering back through the kitchen. I flicked on the light switch by the door, surprised I could enchant the lines that quickly. The new kitchen sparkled. Stainless steel appliances everywhere.

"I don't really know how to cook," I announced, giving a little bow, "but there is food in the fridge and the pantry."

"I got this," Nathan answered to a room of astonished looks. "What? Mom taught me how to cook. Gwen, how about you help me? I know my mother taught you too." Gwen refused with a quick shake of her head with her mouth clamped shut.

"I'll help." Jack was already plundering the pantry.

I went on into the parlor with Laura and Mike. Gwen followed, but kept her distance. We sat and listened to the silence of the night. Another flick of a switch, this time from across the room, helped chase away the lengthening shadows.

"Electricity?" Mike asked.

"In a manner of speaking." I held up my hands. Sparks flew from finger to finger.

"Oh."

"So, what's the plan?" Laura leaned forward and asked. She seemed more than a little interested as her eyes narrowed, waiting for me to tell her about my master plan to take care of Jean St. Claire and return the world to a peaceful order. There was just one problem, and I was concerned admitting that problem was going to disappoint her, and the others, more than a just a little, especially considering what it sounds like they had to give up following me here.

"I'm not sure yet," I confessed, leaning back away from her. I was glad it was just us at the moment. Disappointing two people was all I could deal with now.

"Nothing?" Mike asked, slightly irritated.

"Well, I know what I need to do, but I haven't figured out the *how* yet."

Disbelief was written all over their faces.

"Look, I didn't expect anyone to follow me, and my plan — if you can call it that — was to figure things out when I got here." It was true. I had no master plan. Blame my temper. Blame my short fuse. Blame Jean St. Claire. Hell, as far as I knew, this was all part of his master plan. Push the right button and make me push logic aside and come rushing right into his trap. I needed to be careful and turn this around. Every move needed to be based on my own rules. How was still the big question. That was why I reached out to my mother when I arrived. That was why I finally broke down and destroyed her by telling her what I was. I needed her help and her guidance. I needed to know who I could trust to help me gather information. Then, I could come up with a so-called plan. "We are in his backyard, and you both have heard all the stories about how powerful he is. We need to be careful and do this with extreme caution. Rushing in and bashing skulls won't solve anything." I ended my statement, looking right at Mike.

"You never know. Catching him off guard might be the best play."

"For him, but not us. It would be a slaughter. First off, I don't even know where to find him. I vaguely remembered seeing him once at a holiday Gala in town, but that was it, and even then, it was from the other side of the room." I glossed over how the room split down the middle when he walked in, witches on one side and vampires on the other. Hissing from one side, and witches standing at the ready. Mr. Helms would have been proud of that scene. Eventually Jean left, and his party followed behind him, but that didn't mean the festive atmosphere returned following his exit. The tension of that brief standoff suffocated the room. "Not to mention dozens upon dozens of vampires that would be there waiting, and the others that live out in the city that support him." I looked at both Laura and Mike and addressed each of them gravely. "Look, I am glad you guys are here. I didn't like the prospects of being here alone, but this is really dangerous. We are literally right in his backyard. His home turf."

My hands reached up and rubbed through my hair while my head leaned down. I propped both elbows on my legs. The weight of all this was pressing down on me and inside I was cussing my on impulsive nature. The more time passed, the heavier this felt. "I'll figure out something," I mumbled toward my lap.

"We will," Laura said, and reached over and rubbed my shoulders. "We just need to figure out where to start. Then from there the next step, and the step after that. One step at a time."

I almost wanted to say thanks mom, but kept it to just a soft, but gratitude filled, "Thanks."

"I don't know what it is," Clay said as he strolled in from the hallway, "but I can't even stomach the smell of food anymore."

There was a group nod in the room that I looked up to take part in. Food, the sight, and the smell of it turned my stomach. Occasionally, the power of a memory was strong enough to block the retching, such as the Christmas tree party. The times I sat with Nathan while he ate, I had to focus on his face. Why we had that kind of reaction? That was a mystery to all of us. It was almost a cruel joke. Something that was part of our life, a source of nourishment for our bodies, and something that was central to most family gatherings and holidays, was now, well, a source of pain and disgust. Kind of reflection of our life, I guess.

"So, what is the first step?" Mike sat gingerly on a two-hundred-year-old chair that I wasn't allowed to sit in when I was growing up. His hands rolled around each other furiously, like two anacondas battling for control.

"Well, I asked my mom about any families I might be able to reach out to for help."

"Wait. I thought your mother was dead," Clay said.

"Well, yeah, she is, but I have a way I can go see and talk to her. It's a witch trick. In fact, when I do, she is here in this house. Actually, in the kitchen." I pointed toward the kitchen that was down the hallway. Clay, regarded that with a puzzled look and walked to the other side of the door, farther away from the kitchen. Every old house has to have a ghost story, I guess.

"Of course, that means that is a potential problem." They all looked at me, sharing the same puzzled look that Clay had. "Anyone my mother knew was now dead and has been for who knows how long. Probably forty years or more. But they are all witches, and witches stay connected to the same coven generation after generation. Their families are probably still in the area, maybe even living in the same homes."

Over the next thirty minutes, while the others ate whatever Nathan and Jack whipped up in the kitchen, Mike used his cell phone to search for each family my mother mentioned to me. Google was truly magical. Not only was I able to find several of the names, but I could also read what some were up to in various news reports, all good community service pieces, no axe murderers here. Looking at the maps that came up, my hunch was right about at least one of them. Two other families were still in the area but had moved closer to town. That was better than none.

3

It was well after midnight when I noticed Nathan and Gwen yawning. Remembering how good that felt for those few days I was human again made me jealous. Rob and Martin looked refreshed and had already made one run through of the property just to check things out. Martin said it was out of habit, something they did every night at the coven. I knew why they did it there, and I knew it was the same reason here, not that I minded. Knowing they had checked made me feel a little more relaxed. Jack was pretty wired sitting there with Mike watching some show on TV, one of my additions, while he worked on his fifth cup of coffee. I needed to remember that not everyone was like me.

"Why don't I give you guys a quick tour of the upstairs? There are rooms up there for everyone." I got up and headed toward the stairs. "Come on."

Halfway up the stairs, I issued an apology. "There is only one bathroom." I braced myself for a chorus of groans behind me, but it didn't arrive. Perhaps they were all too tired.

"Okay, here are the bedrooms. We have three guest rooms, down the right side. The bathroom is opposite those. My room was.. is.. right here," I pointed to the door just to my right, "and my parent's room is there." I felt my voice losing steam as I stared at the closed door to their room. Its sight, the feeling of really being here in front of it, froze me, while behind me Jack and Gwen laid claims to two of the guest rooms. Rob and Martin were arguing over the bed in the other. Jack settled it by splitting the bed in two. In the distance behind me, I heard the obligatory comment about them just rolling up on the floor like dogs.

"Larissa," Laura whispered. "Why don't you and Nathan take your parent's room? This is your home, after all."

A shudder went through my body. "No. No. Why don't you and Mike take it if you need one? I just can't." I turned away from the door, repeating. "I can't. I can't."

Laura grabbed me by the shoulders and embraced me, as warmly as her cold body could. "It's okay. We'll take that one. Why don't you take your room?"

She gave my shoulders a quick rub as I mumbled the answer, "okay."

Laura handed me off to Nathan, who seemed to understand. I just couldn't take my parent's room. I couldn't even make myself open the door. There was just something about that room. It was theirs, alive or dead. Going in there, and taking that room, just cemented that they were gone, which they were, and I knew, but it made it final.

Walking back into my old room was easier, but still difficult. It was like walking into a museum of my life before, loaded with reminders of the life I lost, and I felt it. Everywhere I looked, from my bed which was still covered with my comforter and sheets, to my dressers still full of clothes, all several decades out of date, and then the row of stuffed animals still sitting along the windowsill, just like I had with the Nortons. I had to force myself to think of the life I have now to avoid being pulled down into darkness by the overdose of nostalgia. A quick grip of Nathan's hand gave me a reminder of the present.

"So, this is your room?" he asked.

"Yep."

"And that is your bed?"

Teenage boys. Of all the things he could point out in the room, and that was what he chose. Then it hit me. We had never spent the night together, anywhere. The two closest moments we had were when I was watching over him while he was recovering, and that night on the train, which was spent most of the night talking to Laura. Neither were exactly alone, like this would be. Why did that word mean so much? It really shouldn't. Nathan and I had been alone many times, just because it was night doesn't make it any different. I could keep telling myself that all I wanted, it didn't make it less awkward.

"Nope," I answered, and with a quick point of a finger, and a shower of sparkles, it wasn't my bed anymore. It was now a queen-sized bed that barely fit, and a very neutral white comforter with probably more pillows than we needed. "Let's get some rest. It's been a long day."

"I thought you didn't sleep."

"I don't, but I would like to lie beside you while you do." His arm cradled me against his chest as I let myself lean into him. This was my safe zone. "I put some things for you over in the bottom two drawers of the dresser if you wanted to change into something comfortable." Stupid me. I should have waited a few more minutes and just enjoyed this feeling before I said anything. He let go and went to check, pulling out a pair of shorts before moving over to the bed and pulling his shirt up over his head. I reached for the door. "I'll step out while you change."

"You don't need to," he suggested in a seductive tone, tempting me to stay and read deeper into what he said. I just couldn't let it go there. There was too much going on, and maybe I was too much of a girl about this, but I wanted it to be perfect, and this moment was anything but. That didn't mean I didn't feel it and allow myself to compromise. "Okay, but I will turn around?"

"If you must," he said, disappointed.

"Let me know when you are done." I turned and faced the opposite corner, making sure that my mirror on the wall didn't offer me any opportunities to sneak a peek. There was no way I could trust myself not to look if it did. I heard him sigh behind me, a sentiment I shared.

"Done," he said, sounding flabbergasted. "Want me to turn?"

"Nah." I held my hand over my head and focused on what I was wearing and what I wanted to wear. The change was instantaneous. With a small flash, my jeans and shirt had become a t-shirt and shorts. Something cute, but not too sexy. No lace.

"Cheater." Nathan yawned and crawled into bed.

With controlled movements, human speed, I lay down on my side and scooted over close to him. I figured that might appear sweeter than a vampire zipping in. What may have just been seconds felt like hours while I waited for him to join me in the middle of the bed, but when he finally did, the wait was worth it. He wrapped a single arm around my waist. I grabbed his hand and pulled it up to my heart. It was cold and un-beating, but that didn't matter. At that moment I felt all the warmth of our love wrapping around me, and I felt a single, and maybe somewhat silly, regret that I wouldn't be able to fall asleep in his arms like so many lovers around the world were doing this very night. That didn't mean I wasn't going to lie there as long as possible.

That was what I did, and I enjoyed every minute of it. Hearing every breath Nathan took while he sank into a deep sleep. Feeling his pulse slow to a very relaxed rhythm, but most of all, feeling safe and complete in his embrace. It was then that something he said once before struck a chord. Why was I here? Why not just move forward, and leave everything, and he meant everything, behind? It seemed so simple and straightforward, and such a straightforward decision to make. They might consider, forget might, they would consider me an idiot for choosing anything else, but, and it was a *big* but, I couldn't ignore what the last eight decades had taught me. Jean St. Claire would never stop looking. A harsh reminder that came crashing in when Nathan rolled over, pulling the warmth of the future I desired away from me.

I stayed there for a little while longer, just listening, and tempted to roll over and wrap my arms around Nathan. I don't think he would have minded, but I was also concerned it would wake him, and I didn't want to do that. He looked like a god lying there asleep. The moonlight that splashed through the window highlighted the features of his chiseled face. I looked up at the clock on the wall: my clock. It was just before four in the morning. I had been there for several hours, and it was wonderful. I could be here for days, at least emotionally and spiritually. Physically, I felt the urge to move. Other than sitting down to read, I couldn't remember when I had been this still for this long.

I slid out of the bed slowly and walked to the door. A quick glance back confirmed I hadn't woken Nathan, and I opened the door to walk around my old home. Down the stairs, I found Clay, Laura, and Mike in the old parlor, talking. I remembered something Jennifer had told me about bored vampires, and knew I needed to occupy their time tomorrow with something more than just a television. Maybe a few games, or music. The TV and talking among themselves would only be entertaining for so long. I was tempted to join them, but a light down the hall drew me. It was from the kitchen, where I found Martin sitting at the table. "Couldn't sleep?"

"Rob snores," he quipped back.

"Figures."

"Nah, it's just odd being here. I am not sure how he can sleep with this hole. Rob has always been a little different."

I took the seat across from him, and asked, "Hole?"

"Yea, it is probably hard for you to understand, but when you are in a pack, you hear everyone's thoughts and feel their feelings. I can still feel Rob, and he can feel me. But Dan and Mr. Markinson are gone. It's just strange. You get so used to them that when they disappear, it is like a part of you is gone."

As if I didn't already feel guilty enough that they followed me, and Mrs. Saxon banned them from returning. "Martin, why don't I send you and Rob back? Just tell Mrs. Saxon it was a stupid and impulsive move."

"Absolutely not," he barked back, bumping the table when he did so. "Look, you may be a vampire, and a witch, and we might be werewolves, but to me and Rob, you are a sister. Dan too. We won't let you face this alone, and there is nothing you can say that will change our mind. Got it?"

I nodded.

"Plus, you are going to need some bad ass wolves to take care of those vampires."

Martin smirked, but I didn't. I wasn't in the mood. The heaviness I felt earlier was bearing down again. "Look, Martin, I don't know how this is going to go, or even end up. To be honest, I don't even know what I am going to do yet. This could go great or end up in a burning disaster. I guess what I am trying to say, this isn't just a game or some talk. This is real, and you and Rob could be hurt or even killed. I can't ask you to take that risk for me."

"And you can't deny us, either. We wouldn't listen. We're stubborn," he interjected.

"This is our war. Something that Laura, Mike, Clay, and I need to take care of. Jean is part of our world, and our problem."

"No, this is OUR problem. You don't have to ask. We volunteer, and even if you tried to refuse our help, we would stay and help anyway. You can't get rid of us. I believe Jack is the same way, even though he is just a witch, and Gwen," his eyes glance up to the ceiling, "I can't explain that one."

I leaned forward against the table and looked at Martin with all the curiosity that was the situation with Gwen. "I know. What is with that? I don't understand why she came. We aren't exactly on the same team."

"And she has been acting odd since we got here."

"I know. Maybe Jack was right," Martin wondered aloud.

"Right about what?"

"He said he thinks she came because she believes you are going to be the queen witch, or something like that one day, and needs to kiss your ass now."

Now that made me laugh, and this wasn't just a little giggle either. It was a rock back in my chair kind of laugh, and it wasn't long before Martin joined in. The thought of the queen B– being reduced to a follower, a follower of mine, was just so out there compared to how things were when I arrived at the coven. But I knew how obsessed she was with the council. Could it be true? If she thought I was one day going to be one of them, might she be laying the groundwork to be someone I trusted?

"Nah," I whispered, dismissing the idea as farfetched. How Martin looked back at me made it appear he didn't think it was that farfetched. In fact, he felt it was the reason.

"I'm going to head back up and try to get a little more sleep. What's the plan for tomorrow?" He stood up from the table, but waited to hear what I had planned.

"I guess go check out the first family. See what we can find out from them, if they are willing to even talk to us." That was a huge possibility that would be a major roadblock. I had to hope they would help.

"So what? Do we just walk up to the door and say, you won't remember us because your parents weren't even born yet when I lived here, but can you tell me where to find the vampire king?"

"First, he isn't a vampire king," that word was hard to even say. Considering Jean as a king of any kind tarnished the word. "And second... I guess, yes." I hadn't really thought about it, and now that I had, the image of me frozen on the steps while someone asked me what I wanted played over and over in my head. How was I going to do this?

"Well, I will be there with you the whole time. This will work out," Martin walked out of the kitchen, but added from the hallway, "because my awesomeness will be there."

He made me laugh, which was good, but he had raised a good question. My first thought was to go ask my mother, and I had actually relaxed my mind to slip back to go see her, but one thought wouldn't leave, and it was what Martin had said. The parents of those living weren't born when we lived here. She doesn't know them any better than I do. This was something I was going to have to solve, and as it would seem, I had a few hours to do so.

4

After Martin went up to get some more sleep, I spent the rest of the night much like I had most of the nights in the recent months. Mike pulled up some music on his phone, and we tried to make it feel as normal as we could, ignoring that we were now exiled from the coven, and in a strange place. It was at least strange for them. There were sounds and smells off and on during the night that delivered a sense of home to me. The horn of the boats passing up and down the Mississippi River just a few miles away didn't sound all that different from how they had years ago, though I didn't hear any of the steam whistles I would hear then.

Unlike those nights up on the deck, I watched the clock like a hawk. In the coven, Jennifer or her husband were the timekeepers and would remind us of when it was time to head back down, that is, if we hadn't noticed the first pinks of sunrise all on our own, which was what normally happened. I was watching it now so I could sneak back upstairs and slip into bed next to Nathan before he woke up, and it wasn't so he wouldn't know I left. Whether that would bother him, I didn't know. If it did, too bad. That would just be something he would have to learn to accept. I didn't sleep, and he couldn't expect me to lie there with him all night. No, that was not the reason. This was all about me. I wanted to know what it felt like to be in his arms when he woke up. What it was like to roll over and welcome him to the new day.

Right at 6:30, with the sky outside still as dark as midnight, I headed back up. Laura, Mike, and Clay followed. They noted the one bathroom in the house and wanted to get their showers out of the way before the others woke. I peeked inside the bathroom and wondered what the expiration date was on soap. Probably not a century. I quickly replaced it with something newer, my brands. The guys would just have to get used to smelling like a coconut for a few days until we could get supplies in the more traditional way.

Mike showed a level of curiosity about my witchcraft that he had never had before when I made the swaps in the bathroom. Normally, any conversations about this side of me resulted in a huff of disinterest, but this time he asked, "What? Are you stealing these things?" He had a devilish smile on his face when he asked. It grew with my reply.

"Yep."

"All right." He gave me a high five, Laura gave me a look of admonishment.

"Relax, it's not really stealing," I started, but I quickly amended my remarks. "I don't think. These are all my things. I can create a piece of food, or something I am familiar with, but things that are more complicated, I can't, so I am borrowing them. The soaps are from my bathroom in the coven. The kitchen appliances are from the Norton's kitchen." Come to think about it, I wasn't sure why Mr. Norton upgraded every few years. Probably just for show in case anyone ever came over so they wouldn't be suspicious. "So, they are really mine, or my stepfamily's. I just relocated them. Some of the food I borrowed from the kitchen at the coven. Everything else is just a modification of how things appear, like the clothes, and cleaning. The clothes are really all my old clothes, just slightly changed to look and fit differently." This explanation seemed to fascinate Mike and relaxed Laura.

I headed into my room, which was darker than when I left a few hours ago. I lay down and slid across, looking for my comfort zone. Halfway across the bed, I was still searching. Now, clearly across the middle of the bed, there was nothing there. I reached back with my hand to search for him but found just a pile of sheets and a pillow. I groaned. He must have woken up while I was downstairs. I missed my chance.

Frustrated and defeated, I swung my legs back to the floor and walked out the door and down the stairs to the kitchen, the logical destination for first thing in the morning. I was a little surprised that he hadn't stuck his head into the parlor to at least say good morning, but having never really seen Nathan first thing in the morning, it was possible he was not a morning person. I always was.

The kitchen was dark and empty, which had me a little concerned as I did a quick search through the bottom floor. Everywhere I looked, the parlor, formal dining room, informal living room, library, Nathan was nowhere. Going back up the stairs, I heard the thud of several doors closing over my own steps. It was probably one of the three taking their turn in the shower, but maybe Nathan had just needed the bathroom and was heading back to bed. That had to be it, and it gave me hope I hadn't missed my chance. That hope put a spring in my step as I bounded up the stairs and to the door, which I opened without hesitation.

I turned and closed the door just as quickly before sliding down the frame to the floor of the hallway. A flash of heat rolled through my body, and if I had a beating heart, it would have skipped a few beats before picking up a rapid rhythm. My hand reached up for my chest and gripped at where my heart was, and nothing I could do stopped the embarrassed chagrin from growing across my face. My other hand fanned myself to help with the second flash of heat that rolled through me.

Laura stepped out of my parent's old room, obviously on the way to the shower with a towel and a fresh change of clothes in hand. She stopped and asked, curiously, "Larissa? You okay?"

"I just saw Nathan naked. I think he just got out of the shower." I had. Right when I walked in, I saw all of him, or all of his backside. His back was to me, and he didn't see me, but there was no doubt he heard me slam the door shut as I spun back out into the hallway. The image, the glorious image of the bulges on his back, all the way down to his... Just thinking about it brought another wave of heat through me. My pale skin wouldn't give away its presence with any flush of color, but I felt it.

Just then, the door behind me creaked opened, and Nathan stepped out wearing a clean pair of jeans and a long sleeve knit shirt. "Morning Ladies," he said, giving a glance down at me, sitting there crumbled on the floor. He stepped by and down the stairs. My head leaned back against the door frame.

"Maybe he didn't notice me." I hoped.

"Oh, he knows," remarked Laura. "What's the big deal?"

"I..." I started, feeling more than slightly embarrassed. "We..." I couldn't make myself say it. Not even to Laura. I had talked to Jennifer about this just a few days ago. Why couldn't I now? Probably because then there were no images of Nathan's perfect Adonis backside dancing in my head when I talked to Jen. Another flush of heat came over me, and I struggled to string enough words together to make a sentence, but I did the best I could, "I've... never... seen... a... guy... naked... before."

"Never?" Laura asked, stunned.

"Never," I shrieked, and clamped my hand over my mouth to muffle it. Before I explained further, I took a second to compose myself. "I'm maybe almost a hundred, but remember the life I lived. I was never around anyone, and before that, I was sixteen, living back in the early 1900s. Things were different back then."

"Well honey, you picked a magnificent specimen to make your first." Laura bit her bottom lip.

My hand whipped out and slapped Laura on the calf, and she laughed all the way to the shower, leaving me there embarrassed.

5

I walked into the kitchen, timidly, and gave Nathan a little kiss on the back of his shoulders as I wrapped my arms around him. He stood at the counter, spreading peanut butter on two pieces of bread. I could smell it, and had to fight against the turning my stomach did inside.

"Morning," I said.

"Morning," he replied before running a finger through a dollop of peanut butter that fell off the edge of the bread and then licked it off.

The coolness of the winter night had settled in throughout the house, and my hands felt gooseflesh as they rubbed down Nathan's arms. Luckily, the first trick I ever learned, and then learned again in the coven, was how to set something on fire. That was a skill I had used more times than I could remember now. I also had a knack for setting my own life on fire. Now I just hoped I didn't do the same to those that followed me here. This time, I only used it to light a fire in the fireplace. Its heat wouldn't warm the entire house, but it would knock the chill off downstairs for the others who weren't immune to a cold morning.

Over his shoulders, I saw the first glint of the sun coming up in the east, over the fields covered in the morning dew. It wasn't cold enough for frost, but it wasn't far away. He finished fixing his peanut butter sandwich and proceeded to the table.

"Why don't you take it into the living room or parlor? You'll be closer to the fire. I know you're cold."

He stopped just before his butt hit the seat and stood back up. Before he left the kitchen, he gave me a little kiss on the forehead. I followed him into the formal living room, which had a fireplace. It was a room about twice the size of the parlor. There was a coffee table, plain wood, in front of a large green sofa that sat against the wall opposite of the fireplace. A smaller one was against another wall, with a few chairs scattered around. There were two large archways on the other walls, one leading to the parlor and the other leading to the library. I didn't have the same fond memories of that library as I did the one at the Norton's. It seemed there was always something else to do other than read, not that I didn't take advantage of it from time to time. Maybe a few lazy afternoons out in the field reading Twain.

I sat on the chair next to the sofa Nathan sat on. Even though I didn't feel cold, I had to admit there was something comforting about the crackle of the fire and the glow of the flames. The long shadows of the furniture it cast up against the wall were familiar old friends that I had spent many a night watching dance.

"So, see anything you liked?" Nathan asked before taking another bite of his peanut butter sandwich.

I about fell out of the chair, and he about choked on his sandwich when he started laughing mid-bite.

"If you choke to death on that, it serves you right."

"Hey," he mumbled with a mouthful. He worked it over violently in his mouth and swallowed. "I'm not the one that barged in on me after my shower." He smiled widely.

He had a point, but I had a card I could counter with. "It was my room."

"Ok, good point." The last word muffled through the bread of another bite.

We both giggled and smirked. If I had been a human, I would be fifty shades of red now, but I wasn't. But that didn't stop me giggling like a little schoolgirl while I tried to hide it behind a hand.

"So, how does it feel to be back here?"

"Good, to be honest. It strangely feels like I never left. I keep expecting there to be a reminder here and there of what happened, and there are, but not as bad as I thought."

"Your parent's room?" He asked.

I nodded grimly. "I just couldn't open the door. It just felt if I went in there, things would be final." It was how I felt. "It's silly," I said, and pulled my knees up to my chest. "They're gone. I know that. There are no grand illusions that they are going to walk in through the door. I just couldn't." Just the thought of opening that door and going in created a cold hole in the pit of my stomach.

"No more bad memories. What is your best memory here?"

That was a great question, and a great time for Nathan to ask. Just thinking about last night sent me down a cold, dark chasm. This question was the opposite. Instead of a cold spot, warmth radiated throughout me. When it reached my face, a smile crept across my face as so many wonderful memories competed for the honor of being the best. There were so many to choose from. Each had their own merits, but there was one that kept bubbling up to the top.

"I was eight. Not quite old enough to have chores out in the field yet, but that didn't mean I wasn't out there alongside my parents while they worked. My mother and I had a little routine where, while she worked, she would quiz me on schoolwork or a spell here and there. Looking back on it, it was probably just a way to keep me busy and out of her hair, but I didn't care. It was great. They had stopped for the day, and my father was putting things away. I could hear him and Harley, our foreman, off in the distance pushing things into the barn. My mother and I were lying down in a patch of weeds full of dandelions. I remember lying there, bathing in the sun's warmth, while looking at how beautiful my mother is. Hoping one day to be as beautiful as she is, to be the witch she was. To live up to her example. I remember telling her that and she reached over and brushed the hair out of my face, tucking it behind my ear. It was always a mess when I was running around the fields. She told me she knew I would, that I would even exceed what she is." The misty start of a tear formed in the corner of my eyes. "I didn't understand it then, but I do now. That is the hope of every parent. For their kids to be better than they were." This is something I would have never thought about if Amy hadn't come into my life. So many of those kinds of thoughts had occurred to me since she arrived. God, I missed that little girl. I sure hoped she was all right.

"That's beautiful," Nathan whispered. If I wasn't mistaken, I watched him just brush the corner of his eye during a yawn. Was he getting teary eyed during my story? I was going to let it go this time.

Gwen walked into the living room and took a seat in the other chair. I quickly wiped my eyes to remove any remnants. There was no way I was going to let her see me all weepy eyed.

She all but ignored me, and scooted her chair closer to the fire. It was clear she was cold. Nathan and I exchanged a look. Neither of us seemed to believe Gwen was a morning person. Though we were in a strange place and who knew how that impacted everyone's behavior. I didn't know if Nathan was an early bird either, but here he was up before the sun.

"Morning Gwen."

She answered with a diminutive, "Morning." She finally looked our way. There was something off about her appearance. Her shoulders were slumped, and her hair was a mess. She wasn't wearing any makeup sitting there in a pair of gray sweatpants and just a plain wrinkled t-shirt. I seriously doubted she would roll right out of bed and come out for everyone to see her that way, especially Nathan. It was so unlike her. She looked at us from across the room, her gaze locked on what remained of Nathan's peanut butter sandwich.

"Gwen, are you okay?" I asked, looking for a reply or response that was more Gwen like, but it didn't come. She only nodded. This new Gwen was unnerving. I would have felt a lot better if she had sniped back, "Of course I am, look at me." Of course, at the moment, she wasn't much to look at. Her eyes stayed glued on Nathan's sandwich. Could it be she is this way because she feels like a guest here? Gwen has never been one to be polite. Not in a way that wasn't dripping with acidic sarcasm. It was possible, I guess. "Gwen, feel free to make yourself at home. Help yourself to anything in the kitchen, and if we don't have it,... well, you know."

There it was, another shy nod while her eyes stayed focused. I could see the hunger in her eyes, and this wasn't the normal hunger she looked at Nathan with.

She wanted that sandwich. I got up and walked across to Gwen. "Gwen, if you're hungry, why don't we go to the kitchen and get you something?"

She stood up, and for a briefest of moments, she reached out and took my hand.

"I can do it," offered Nathan. As he got up and headed down the hallway, there was something strangely familiar about how Gwen walked beside him.

6

"Larissa." Martin ran his hand over his face as a reminder.

"Oh yeah." I did the same while a shower of glitter rained down over me, giving my cheeks and eyes life. If we were going to go up and knock on a door, they couldn't come out and see me in my natural form, even if they were who I think they are and would be familiar with the sight of a vampire. It wasn't the first impression I wanted to make. That was why I asked the others to stay behind. A suggestion that Mike fought hard against. He wanted to come for protection and took several opportunities to remind him of a point I had made last night. *This was Jean's territory. Members of his coven could be everywhere.* Which they could be. So, I compromised and allowed Rob and Martin, who appeared normal on the outside, to accompany the four of us. Mike suggested I find a few more werewolves to substitute for him.

The four of us stood on the sidewalk at the opening of a little white picket fence. According to our map application, we were only four miles away from my home, but the walk felt longer. Not that it took a physical toll on me. I couldn't speak for the others, though. It was the mental gymnastics my brain did about what to say when I knocked on the door that made the trip drag, and even then, I wish it had taken longer. Here we were, only thirty feet away from the front steps, and I still didn't know what to say. If I stood here any longer, I was sure someone was going to shove me from behind. So here it goes. It was time to just wing it.

I walked up the walkway, trailed by Nathan, Jack, and Gwen. Rob and Martin agreed to stay by the road. Jack and Rob had heard tales of some witches being able to sense their presence. No need to set off any alarms at hello. I ascended the steps alone and glanced back at the others before my hand made a weary knock on the red wooden door. As the time passed, I half hoped for no answer, but that hope disappeared when I felt a strange pulse behind the door, and then it opened.

"May I help you?" asked a man in his early thirties with a creole drawl that fit right in with how I remembered everyone in these parts sounding. He had neatly combed blond hair and wore a red sweater to battle against the chill of the winter morning. There was a friendly demeanor to him, but I felt dejected just by the sight of him. I was hoping for someone older, much older. Someone that might have heard the story of my family. Someone that might remember things. He must have been at least two or three generations removed. The chances of our tale making it down the family tree that far.

"Mr. Bergeron?"

"Yes, and you are?"

"Umm." *What a great start there, Larissa.* If only I had thought about what to say. Oh wait! I had. A lot. I just never came up with a good opening. "I am Larissa Dubois. My family owned the plantation down the road a few miles. Are you familiar with it?"

"The farm with the two-story plantation house?" He asked while giving the rest of my party a once over. So far, he was staying cool. Nothing had made him worried or concerned, yet.

"That's the one."

"Yes. I know it. What can I do for you, Miss Dubois?"

"Well." My mind was racing a thousand miles a minute. How should I call him out and tell him you know what he is and then tell him what you are too? This would be so much easier if everyone wore some kind of uniform, or at least a common team t-shirt. Of course, I would need one that was split down the middle. Vampire on one side. Witch on the other side. "This might sound a little nuts, but do you know the story about what happened to my family a long, long time ago?"

He looked at me curiously, a few extra beats of his pulse, and then again scanned the others. "I know the house has sat empty for the last several decades."

"Do you know what happened to my family?"

With that question, he clammed up, and went as frosty as Antarctica in the dead of winter. The door was already closing when he said, "I'm sorry I can't help you, and this isn't a good time. I am really terribly busy." His pulse raced, and he pushed the door closed. It was just about closed when I played a card I wasn't sure I would have, or even should have.

A large gust of wind pushed the door back open against the straining man, and with it open enough for him to see me again, I whispered to him, "I know what you are. I am one too." The man gave up his fight against the door and allowed it to open. He stood there slack jawed while the inflatable frosty the snow man danced behind me. I didn't realize Jack added his own touch and had the grapevine wreath that hung on the door floating over us. With or without his help, this seemed to convey my message adequately enough. Mr. Bergeron ushered us all, including Rob and Martin, inside the house. He gave them a little sniff as they passed by him.

"What do you want?" he attempted to ask sternly, but his voice was still lacking some of the strength to deliver each word with the weight he wanted. His body was erect, almost vampire straight, standing in front of us.

"Do you know what happened to my family?" I asked again.

He swallowed hard, and his pulse was still slightly elevated, and I could smell the scent of sweat. He teetered back and forth from one foot to the other. "I know the story of your relatives. We all do," he squeezed out before taking another big gulp of air.

"Can you tell me?" I asked, needing to make sure he wasn't bluffing before my next step.

He took two steps back. His hand searched for the back of the red leather easy chair that was in the room, which appeared to be a collection of mismatched, worn furniture. Rather shocking, considering how nice the outside of the house looked. The rest of the room matched what you would find in most two century old colonials down here: wood floors, plaster walls, and wide crown molding. "They were killed."

"Do you know by who? And why?"

"I do," he answered after another large gulp. I watched fall down his throat. "Why do you want to know?" he croaked. "It is something I am sure you can find..."

"I know," I interrupted. "In the archives or any number of other sources." At this pace, it was going to take all day just to tell him who I was. Not that I didn't believe this wouldn't be a lengthy process, but this constant question-and-answer ping-pong was frustrating me. Time to be more direct. "Do you know what happened to the daughter? She would have been a young girl about my age then."

"She was killed too," he reported, now holding on to the back of the chair with both hands.

Nathan had to have sensed what I was about to do. He reached forward and grabbed my hand. When I looked back, he asked, "Are you sure?"

It didn't matter if I was sure or not. There was no easy way to do this, and it had to be done. "Mr. Bergeron. What if I told you she survived and is still alive?"

"I would tell you that is impossible."

"They never found her body. It says that in the archive reports."

"I am well aware of that, and Miss Dubois, I am not sure what you are getting at. She died that day; she was just never found." He paused in thought for a moment. "Even if you are correct, she would be almost a hundred now."

"Try ninety-six, and she is standing right here in front of you." With a chorus of voices inside my head screaming no, I dropped my little illusion and let my real self show. Before I saw his reaction, I felt it in the world's vibration around me. He was pulling something deep, ready to either defend himself or attack. And why wouldn't he? There was a vampire standing here in his home. "Mr. Bergeron. I am not a threat to you. I just need your help. I am that girl. Larissa Dubois..."

Before I finished, something slammed me in the chest, forcing me out the door and down the stairs, lying on top of the others. Sorry Mr. Helms, I wasn't ready for that one.

I was back up the stairs before he had the doors closed. I saw what he was trying to do and remembered what Master Thomas and Mr. Demius had said about the old ways still being taught here. I carefully executed a tug and pulled his hands apart to keep him from forming the shape of several runes. He was strong. It took a lot to hold them out away from his body, which also thwarted his attempt to launch a few attacks.

"I just need your help..." I started again.

"You need to leave, you vile creature. I will not allow you to be here." His right hand was pulling hard against my control. I had to loop another imaginary string around it and yank it back down. The vibrations between us tightened.

"Look, I'm not like the others. I'm a witch too." The struggle told me this was going nowhere, and this was as far from how I wanted this to go as I could have imagined in my worst dreams. My best hope was we would all be sitting down at a table drinking tea or coffee while Mr. Bergeron told me what he knew about what happened, and what he knew about Jean and his coven. Not a struggle to make him listen, while having to avoid being harmed. I closed my eyes, keeping a tight grasp on the magic strings in my head. The vibrations around the strings were fast and strong. Something I hadn't seen since I first noticed the vibrations. Could this be evidence of the power struggle between us? That was the only possibility I saw. I went deep into my mind and then attempted to go deep into his. "You are going to help us."

"Don't waste your breath. That works on the weak minded. I am much too strong for that, and for you."

His ego was a little too strong for me, too. His words and actions dripped of male machismo, and he felt he had the upper hand. The grin on his face was a confident and proud one. Even his pulse had calmed down. The vibrations between us hadn't. They had increased and appeared to swell around him. Something big was coming, and I wasn't about to wait around to see what it was. I had another plan. Brain over brawn. I reached out and looped around the tattered red leather chair and gave it a yank, losing focus on the ones around his hands, but only for a second. The chair hit him from behind, just at the knees, sending him buckling backwards. He was startled, and vulnerable at that moment, and he knew it. Seeing me standing there in a fighting stance, both hands ready to launch any attack I wanted faster than he could blink, hammered it home for him.

"Look, I just came here to ask some questions to see if maybe you can help. I didn't want things to end up like this. I assure you I'm not what you think I am. Well, I am... but I am different." Well, that sounded half crazy. "I was raised like a normal person." I give up. There was no way to calm someone down about this that would come close to sounding rational. I needed to just skip that. "I need your help. Jean St. Claire is still after me, after all these years, and he is torturing someone very dear to me. I need to know everything you know about him and his coven so I can find him and stop him. I won't be able to live a normal life as long as he is around."

And there it was. I laid my situation out before him in a massive plea for help. Now I stood there waiting, and watching, for any sign he would lend a hand. At first there was nothing, but then his body relaxed. He didn't slump in the chair, just a minor loosening of the tension in his neck that most wouldn't notice, but I did. Most also wouldn't notice his pulse slowing down just a beat. In a sign of good faith, I did the same, and lowered my hands. Maybe by lowering the threat level, we could have a normal conversation. That image of sitting down at the table drinking tea and coffee while he tells me everything I need to know might not be that far-fetched anymore.

It wasn't until something pushed us back out the front door, sending us tumbling down the stairs, that I considered the possibility that there was another family member home. A wife, perhaps a child, like the young boy who resembled a ten-year-old version of his father, who now stood next to him proudly in the doorway.

"I wish you well, Miss Dubois. I can't get involved in this and attract the attention of your kind." With that, the door shut and I saw a quick, but familiar shape, glow on the door. Master Thomas said they still taught the old ways here. It would appear he was right.

7

"I don't get it," Jack said as he kicked a small pebble in the gravel walkway that led up to my porch. "You went through Mrs. Saxon's runes like they were paper. You could have torn that door down if you wanted to."

"Could I? Yes. Should I? Absolutely not," I explained to the assembled group standing out on the porch. "What good would it have done? The door would be down, and we could walk right in, but then what? Do you think that would make him more likely to help us? I can tell you if someone broke through the door and entered my house, they would walk into a war. Especially if one was a known vampire." It was how I would have reacted. In fact, it was exactly how my mother and I reacted when they walked into our house. "I always knew this was a possibility, but we had to try. We have two more families to check out. Hopefully, they will go better than that."

"Hopefully," muttered Mike as he passed me and walked up the steps. "Should have taken me with you."

I wasn't in any mood for his macho attitude. The brawn over brains approach never succeeded at anything. His tone set me off, though it didn't take much to push me at this moment. "Yep, your presence would have been so helpful. He would have felt the presence of a vampire and sealed the door before he ever opened it."

"But..."

I stopped him there. I stopped them all and stepped up onto the porch. Like a general taking the stage to talk to her troops. "Look, there is something you all need to realize. This isn't the coven. We are in a place where harmony doesn't exist among our kinds. Everyone fears and hates vampires." I made eye contact with Laura, Mike, and Clay. They needed the reminder. "Werewolves, witches and vampires are mortal enemies." Martin and Rob stood there; stern faced. "And you two," I turned to Jack first, and then Gwen, who was sitting on the old porch swing next to Nathan, way too close for my comfort. What I was about to say was probably going to break more than one of the council's rules, but they had to know before they underestimated anyone, or overestimated themselves. "The magic you know, isn't the same as what the witches down here do. They are more powerful than anything you have ever experienced. What you know is just kid stuff. Just stay behind me, so you don't get yourself killed."

The normally talkative bunch went quiet and solemn. They appeared to take my warnings to heart, at least for the moment. I only hoped they remembered them tomorrow, and the next day, and every day we were down here. This was the real world. Not the protected confines of a magical building built to give us everything we want and protect us from every threat out in the world. A place where we are all family with those we should be at war with.

I turned my attention to the porch swing and grabbed Nathan by the hand and yanked him up to his feet, away from Gwen, who was now snuggled against his shoulder. "And I appreciate you being here, but keep your hands off my boyfriend." Nathan let out a groan as I yanked him even harder through the door and down the hall.

"You could have put a stop to that."

"Sorry, I saw nothing wrong with it."

I stopped and spun around so fast I almost whipped him right into me. "Nothing wrong with it? Did you really just say that?"

Nathan stood there locked-jaw, and a little fearful. Good, I guess my message got through to him loud and clear. I started toward the kitchen again, still towing Nathan by the hand. "Look, we all had a hard day. No need to make it any worse."

That stopped me yet again. This time I didn't turn. I didn't whip him into me. "Really? You think we had a bad day? I'm not sure how it could have gone worse, and worst of all," I felt myself wilt on the inside. I was about to admit something I had been hiding since we left Mr. Bergeron's doorstep. Something I had hidden the entire walk back, and during my little speech outside. The frustration and anger I felt then were gone, almost like how adrenaline wears off, though I didn't I no longer experienced that in my current form. "I... I don't know how to avoid this happening again with either of the next two families."

Nathan reached forward with his free hand and attempted to rub my shoulder. His way of comforting me. I shrugged it off and let go of his hand.

"You'll think of something."

"If I was going to think of something, I would have already thought of it," I replied, deflated, discouraged, and disheartened. All three were states I wouldn't let the others see me in, but Nathan, on the other hand, I didn't have any issues with exposing my vulnerabilities around him. I wanted him to see me, all of me. To know me. To accept me. To love me.

"Larissa."

Hearing Jack's voice snapped me back. Well, not really. I pulled myself together to put up a strong exterior. A case of self-doubt run ruined my insides amok.

"What was that you said about what we know is just kid stuff?" There was an air of disgust in Jack's question, which wasn't all that surprising. Without the context, which I had and couldn't share without breaking a few rules, it probably sounded like an insult of sorts. Hell, they already consider me a rule breaker. What was one more, no matter how stiff the warning? He and Gwen both needed to know this to avoid getting into trouble. In fact, all of them did. Mrs. Saxon and the coven had sheltered them in ways they didn't know.

"Bring everyone into the parlor and I will explain it." It was against the rules, and while I didn't think there was anyone around us that would hear me, I took that precaution anyway, no matter how feeble it may be. "You need to hear this too," I told Nathan while Jack went to gather the others. "Then I want you to meet my mother."

He gulped. "Your mother?"

"Yes, I met yours. It's time you meet mine. I'm going to go visit her to ask for advice. Why not bring you with me?"

"You can do that?" There was another gulp as he thought about it. In his mind, I was taking him to go visit a ghost. In my mind, she was still alive, just some place different.

"I think so." I hoped I could. It was another thing I hadn't tried before, but in theory it would work, or should work, I hoped. I just didn't want to tell him what it involved yet. He might turn it down flat if he knew how bad the potion was going to taste.

The noise of the others coming in summoned me to the parlor. Nathan followed and stood behind me at first before I reached back and pulled him into the room. The others took seats on the settee and other chairs in the room. Jack and Clay stood against a wall.

"What I am about to tell you is forbidden by the Council of Mages and will undoubtedly get me in trouble if it ever gets out, but what's new?" A nervous laugh slipped out. "Jack, you and Gwen could get into trouble for even knowing about it."

Jack seemed entertained at that statement, and Gwen was... well, silent.

"Where to start... I guess with the basics. There is a lot more to magic than what Mrs. Saxon was teaching us, and it's not just her." I spewed and watched several jaws drop. "It's the same in all the covens around the world. There is a whole other world of magic out there that some call old magic. It's full of runes and elemental symbols. That is where true power exists. I know of them because my mother taught me when I was a little girl. A few members of the council were helping me to remember them." I left the names out here to avoid any implications, but didn't doubt that a few might make the leap that this was what my tutoring sessions were about.

"Now, the harsh truth. They don't allow these skills to be taught. That lets them control who becomes powerful enough to be on the council." I paused, expecting a challenge from Gwen. I'd just impugned the righteousness of her precious council, but much as she had been since she arrived, Gwen was quiet. "The same families stay on the council for generations. Each generation handing down the forbidden knowledge, so they keep the edge, and keep a stranglehold on their council seats."

I waited again, knowing I made them just seem like a hostile dictatorship, but there wasn't even a huff. At least not from Gwen.

"And they think we are devious and deceptive," uttered Laura.

I knew where she was going with that. She was well aware of the issues the council and I had, and the concerns they had about me. The irony of this revelation wasn't lost on her, just like it wasn't lost on me when I first heard it.

"We are in a place that loves its old history. Many still long for the old days, and the old ways. It will be safe to assume that every witch we run into down here was taught those by their parents, just like I was."

"What exactly does that mean?" Jack asked.

It was a great question. It was something hard to explain, so I believed an example was in order, and with a big sweep of my arm, there was a flash followed by a shower of golden glitter. It was beautiful and mesmerizing to everyone. Little did they know. This wasn't the trick. Then, in the center of the room, it started. The shape of all the all-seeing eye drew itself over and over in fire. Each incarnation was faster than the prior, creating multiple copies of itself each time. I sent one copy into the forehead of each of them and then pulled it through back through their chest. It happened so quickly it was doubtful that anyone but the vampires saw it. Clay flinched, understandably, and tried to avoid it, but I still hit my mark. I chanted.

"See, but not be seen."

"See, but not be seen."

"See, but not be seen."

Then, with a second flash, we were standing in Jackson Square under the bright sunlight of midday. All three vampires ducked, holding up an arm to shield themselves from the sun. Not that they would turn to dust, a myth in modern literature, but it burned slightly. Purification of an impure soul if I remember how the description goes.

"Relax, the sun won't hurt you. Neither will anyone that is walking around. You are here, but not here."

Right then, a man, out on a daily run, trotted through Gwen, and then passed through the left half of Rob.

"Whoa!" Rob screamed as he backed away from the man.

"Like I said, you are here, but not here. You can see and hear everything around you. You can even walk further into town, but you really aren't here. We are all still back in the parlor."

Nathan was the first to take a stroll. He tested a theory as he passed me and reached out with a hand which went right through my own. He passed it through again and seemed amused.

"I have to admit, this is a little unsettling," Mike said as he watched a couple walking hand in hand, pass right through Clay. He didn't see them until they came out and walked past him.

"Larissa, how did you learn how to do this?" Jack rushed up to ask me. "This is some next level shit here."

"My mother taught me." Which wasn't a lie. It just wasn't a lesson she taught me until just last week after I saw Mr. Demius and his counterparts in their meeting, and I asked my mother how they were able to do this. She didn't hesitate to tell me. Whether she knew it was against council rules to teach such magic, I didn't ask.

"Can you teach us? He asked while regarding Gwen, who stood well behind him, looking around at Jackson Square.

I waved my arm around, and we returned to the parlor. Everyone still sitting or standing where they were before. "That might be a problem." Jack opened his mouth to protest, but I stopped him with a single finger. "But I will consider it. All right?"

He agreed with a nod.

"Now, I needed to tell all of you that, so you understand what we are going to run into. Does everyone have it?" I again stopped a response, but this time it was a hand held up and not just a finger. "And before there is any comment. I would assume the vampires and werewolves we run into are stronger. Remember our brief encounter with Reginald? He came from this coven. This is the real world, guys, not our coven."

I grabbed Nathan by the hand and left the room, letting my warning sink in. "Come on. It's time."

8

"Are you sure this stuff is safe?" Nathan asked, looking at the cup of brown tea with orange flecks.

"Yes, I have had it a few times. It's perfectly fine."

Clay snickered from the doorway, prompting Nathan to turn around.

"Do you mind?" I warned. This was a private moment.

"By all means. By all means." He turned and walked down the hall.

"Don't leave me Clay," Nathan screamed.

"You're on your own, Romeo," he screamed back. "Try not to throw up on the first sip. I almost did."

I rolled my eyes and made a mental note to thank him later in a not-so-subtle way. "It's safe," I reassured Nathan.

"I mean for human consumption." He gave it a cautious sniff before putting it back down and sliding it to the center of the kitchen table. I reached across and shoved it back in his direction.

"Go ahead. I made the necessary alterations for a human."

"And you are one of Mrs. Tenderschott's best students? I hope." His hand reached out and grasped the cup, but didn't pull it any closer.

"I am, but she didn't teach me this one. My mother did, just for this purpose. Using her old stash of ingredients, and wait...," I interrupted a mounting objection, "before you ask. These never expire. If I did it right, you will join me and my mother right here in the kitchen. If I did it wrong, you will grow hair all over."

Nathan didn't appear to appreciate my wit or the humorous smile that accompanied it. There was a tremble in his fingers when I placed my hand over his empty one. I closed my eyes and let the image of my normal human form consume me, but I didn't change entirely. Just my arm and hand so he could feel some warmth to help comfort him.

He shook his head. "The real you, please. This is too much magic for one day." There was a shiver when my normal icy touch returned.

"One more trick, and then no more magic for today." I grasped his hand that held the cup and urged it in his direction. "Trust me on this. The love potion I gave you didn't kill you, did it?"

His eyes looked up from the cup. "So that is how you did it?" Now it was his turn to give me a humorous, yet nervous, smile back.

"Drink up." He did, only coughing or gagging twice after he drank it all down. I knew I wouldn't have long, so I grabbed his hand to keep his astral self from wandering away without me. He would need a guide, and that was me.

"So, this is the young man you have been telling me about?" asked my mother. We were both seated at the kitchen table. Me next to Nathan. My mother sat in her common seat across from me.

"Yes mom. This is Nathan Saxon." I put my arm around him to hold him up straight. "Normally, he is a little less woozy." Nathan looked like a drunk that had had more than a couple-too-many drinks. His eyes couldn't focus on anything and just wandered around the room. It took everything I had to hold him up here. In this world, I was human. No super strength or extra vampire abilities here.

"He is handsome," she said, studying my wobbly boyfriend. "He's not a witch or vampire, right?"

"No, mom. He's human."

"That explains the..." her hands waved around in front of him erratically. "It will wear off soon." She sat back in her chair with a bemused look on her face. "He is cuter than..."

"Mom, stop that."

She giggled. "Oh, all right, but you know he resembles your father. He was an attractive man."

I was dying on the inside, while my mother appeared to be enjoying this little episode, but I would be lying if I said there wasn't a part of me that was enjoying it, too. This was another of those mother daughter moments taken from me by what had happened.

Now it was Nathan's turn to giggle. He was a little steadier and found the table with his arms and propped himself back up. "Now that, I find funny."

"Welcome back to the living. How do you feel?" I asked, running my hand through his hair.

"Nothing is spinning anymore."

"Then this is your first potion. The first is always the worst," my mother said.

"Yes ma'am, that was my first, as far as I know."

She looked down her nose and studied Nathan again, and I knew we were now entering another one of those moments I had missed, and I am sure Nathan would have preferred I never had the chance to experience. The interview. "So, your mother is a witch?"

"Yes ma'am. Mrs. Rebecca Saxon. She is the headmistress at the Ipswich Coven."

"Ipswich Coven?" she asked, now looking directly at me. "That is a long way from home. How did you end up there?"

"It's a long story."

"It's also an incredibly old coven. Probably older than ours here. Nice. Now, back to you, my dear boy. What about your father? Was he a witch as well?"

"No. He was a human. At least that was what I was told. I never met him. He died when I was young."

"Oh, I am so sorry to hear that." She stood up and walked toward the sink and stood there looking in our direction, but not at us. Past us. Her mind was a flurry of thoughts that I could see turning around and around behind her eyes. "Saxon? Do you know the name Douglas Saxon?"

"Yes ma'am." Nathan said. The last ill effects of the potion had now completely worn off, and the previously intoxicated boy that sat next to me had given way to the person I knew. "He was my great-grandfather on my mother's side. I never met him, but I have heard a lot about him from my mother and grandparents."

"So those Saxons? Very noble family. Nice Larissa."

"Mom!" I am sure in this version of the world I had already turned beet red, but Nathan so far had held his cool against my mother's interrogation. I am not sure Todd Grainger could have held up as well. Not that I ever wanted him to have that chance, no matter how much our parents pushed back then.

"Great family," she repeated. "So, Nathan, what are your intentions toward my daughter?"

Well, Nathan holding his cool only lasted so long. We both about choked with that question, which was right out of the 1920s. Which, yep, that was when I was from. I gave my mother a death stare, that I know she picked up. Her grin grew as I intensified it. She was enjoying this too much.

"You don't have to answer that," I said, and reached up on the table and laced my fingers through Nathan's. His other hand laid on top of mine.

"Actually, my intentions are to spend the rest of my life with her. I couldn't imagine life without her."

Now I had to be blushing. My cheeks were flush with heat, and my palms felt damp. Was that sweat? Oh my god, how embarrassing. I wanted to pull my hand back, but Nathan gripped it even tighter to keep me from getting away. A light mist formed in the corner of my eyes as I wondered, did he just propose to me? If he did, he better do it again and better than that. Then my thoughts went to Amy. If he was going to do this, I wanted her here for it. It was a thought that made little sense, but the yearning was strong and undeniable. If anything, it cemented thoughts I had had days before.

"Good answer. Now, when you are ready, I will be here to talk about giving you my blessing to take her hand." Nathan's hand jerked. And now it was my time to hold on, which I intended to do so until my dying breath. "Now, I am so glad Larissa brought you here to meet me. I expect you to both visit often."

"We will," I promised.

"How are things going with your little activity? Have you attempted to find any of the families?"

Nathan and I both let go of each other's hand and leaned back. The glow I felt a few moments ago left me like a rapidly deflating balloon. I probably looked like one slouched down in the chair.

"I will take that as a yes you have, and it didn't go well."

"We went to visit the Bergeron's," I reported. "And no. It was a disaster."

"Was Gertrude there? She would have been about eight when we were attacked, which would make her eighty-three now, or thereabout. She should still be alive." Upon hearing that name, I remember exactly who my mother was talking about. How could I not? She was my shadow. I was the older witch that lived just down the street, so that meant I was the de facto person for her to look up to. That freckled faced raven-haired girl with brown eyes. Of course, my mother and father, being who they were in the coven, probably had a little something to do with why she was always hanging around. I used to tease Todd that she had a crush on him. Which I honestly believed she did. I even made him dance with her once at the coven ball.

"No. If she was, we didn't see her. It was just a man, probably in his mid-thirties, and what looked like his son. I am guessing he was her grandson, maybe." I shrugged.

My mother walked back to the table and had a seat. "Then either they are gone, or they moved away, leaving the family farm to the younger generation. Which could make sense. Even her parents would be up in their fifties or sixties by now. That is unfortunate. I was counting on her to be there. She would recognize you, which would go a long way with getting anyone to believe your story."

"That is the problem," added Nathan.

"Of course it is. The minute you tell anyone you are a vampire; they aren't exactly going to be welcoming. Not down here. Remember how we treated the vampires that entered our house?"

Oh, I remembered painfully and vividly. "Yea, but they were here to kidnap dad, it's a little different."

"True, but they don't know you, and to be honest, your story is quite fantastic." She rubbed her forehead and sighed. "We need to find an opening, an icebreaker."

"What if I or Rob and Martin talk to the next family?" offered Nathan. "I am human, and they are not vampires or witches. Or even Jack and Gwen. They are just witches. Would that help?"

"Absolutely not," I stated.

"No," agreed my mother. "The story is still out there, and it could put you at even greater risk. You can't defend yourself, and from what Larissa has told me, the other witches aren't ready. It has to be Larissa. I am banking on familiarity here. That is the only way. Who's next?"

"Landry, I found them in Audubon, just like you said they would be."

"Good. I doubt they will ever leave that huge Greek mansion. It was a little gaudy for my liking, but Sylvia just *loved* showing it off every chance she got. You are looking for Clarence Landry. I am sure if he is still alive, he would still live there. There were so many wings in that damn house you could house several generations without stepping on each other... Anyway."

"Mom, he would be almost my age though," I stopped and corrected myself. "My actual age."

"He was three years younger, so that would put him at what?"

"Ninety-seven," I answered quickly.

"Yep, ninety-seven." She looked at Nathan and teased. "You sure you want someone that old?"

I elbowed him and gave my mother that death stare again. This was not the time for jokes, but I had really missed her sense of humor, and her laugh was infectious. Nathan had caught a good case of it. He was about to add his own comment when a second elbow made him think the better of it. "Mom, let's stay on task," I barked, sounding a lot like her when I was younger.

"Right. Gertrude was really our best chance, but this is what I believe is our next best."

"But I wasn't that close to Clarence. I wouldn't really call us friends."

"I know, but he knew you, and you knew him," my mother replied, and she was right, but that was about as far as it went. We knew of each other. Maybe we had a few conversations, but that was it. Forced engagement because our parents were socializing. Nothing more. I had to work to even picture his face, chubby as a cherub as it was.

"If I had to bet, Sylvia would have hosted our memorial. She always thought she and I were best friends. That would have made a lasting memory of Clarence. Enough of one to spark some recognition when he hears your story."

"Would he even remember that?" I asked in disbelief that he would. "Over the years, how many other memorials have there been, and for people, which meant more to him than we did."

"Larissa, I know, but this is all we have to go on. It's shaky. There is really nothing else besides reaching out to the council, which you said you didn't want to do."

"Absolutely not." I threw both hands up as big stop signs to keep either of them from going there.

They both ignored me. "But you have some friends on it," Nathan pointed out.

"Ha. I wouldn't really call them friends. They put me through the modern-day Salem witch trial." I knew I was being a tad over dramatic, but I felt it made my point accurately.

"What about Master Thomas, and that other one that has come a couple of times to help?"

"No. No way." I waved that suggestion away. Master Thomas and Mr. Nevers, not to mention Mr. Demius, were already risking enough to just teach me, I meant refresh my memory. I would not drag them into this and cause problems for them. Not to mention the greater charge they had given me, which went way beyond this rather personal mission I was on. If I were going to reach out to them, it would be for that, not this. This was not the time to use that card, especially when I felt it was one I could only use once. "We are on our own here, and we will do what we have to make it work."

My head drooped down to my hands. The desperation and lack of hope I felt about our plan drained me. This had to work, but the more I thought about it, the more I knew it wouldn't. No one was going to remember me, not from that long ago, and not a soul that did would believe my story enough to risk their own safety to help us. I knew the story in and out; I lived it, but even I had to admit it felt like the work of some great fantasy writer. It was the farthest from anything believable. I couldn't turn back. That fact tore at me from the inside. "We have to. For our own safety and to help Mrs. Norton. I can't leave her there to be tortured by Jean. Not with all that woman has done for me, and how she treated me like her own daughter. If it wasn't for her and Mr. Norton, I wouldn't be here."

"Have faith Larissa. This will work out." My mother looked on with that pleasant and confident expression she often did when I was just moments from giving up on a spell or a trick.

"There is another option no one has mentioned," Nathan started. "Vampires live forever. Are there–"

"Absolutely not," my mother blurted defiantly. "Vampires can't be trusted." She regarded me with a sheepish look before correcting, "Well, some can."

I knew Nathan meant well, and he had a point. It was more likely to find some of them that might have been around back then, but my mother was also right, at least as far as I knew. I mean, I knew there were exceptions to every rule. Take the Nortons, for example. I knew I could trust them. I trusted them with my life and would again if I had the opportunity. That was why I had to do everything possible to help Marie Norton. Beyond them, I couldn't remember any vampires from then I would even consider the possibility of approaching. The ones I knew were directly involved in the attack. There was also another side to Nathan's point. Ones that might recognize me would still be alive. We would have to be extremely careful, especially as we moved around New Orleans.

"I guess it's Clarence," I admitted reluctantly.

"Clarence," my mother agreed with a nod.

"Is there anyone else?" I asked, already thinking past plans b and c, which was the Mallory family, Ben Mallory to be exact. I think I met him once.

"I'll think about that. Maybe I can look through some of the old picture books we had."

"You can see those?" Nathan asked.

"Yes, Nathan," I answered before my mother had a chance to. It was a knee jerk response to what I believed to be a reminder that my mother was indeed dead. Something that when I was here, I chose not to believe. To me, she was alive, right here. That didn't stop my mother from admonishing my abruptness in a way only a mother could.

"Nathan, this world is an exact copy of the one I left. Everything I remembered or had is still here with me. From my kitchen to the deck of playing cards the girls and I played bridge with every Sunday afternoon while our husbands told stories out on the porch, and the albums." She reached over and grabbed Nathan's hand. At first, he jerked it back, but relaxed when hers touched his, and he felt the same thing I did each time she hugged me. She was just as real as anyone alive else was. "Don't think of me as being dead, or some type of ghost. I have just moved on to a different place." She let his hand go, and his eyes stayed glued to her hand as it retreated across the table.

"Can I ask a question about this... place?"

"Of course, if I get to ask you a question in return."

Nathan nodded, and then swallowed hard. Whatever he was going to ask appeared to be caught in his craw, and it took a few more swallows and a cough to get it out. Upon hearing the question, I understood why. "When my mother dies, will she come to a place like this?"

"Yes, and no," answered my mother. Nathan's head dipped at the latter of the answers. My mother saw this, stood up from the table, and moved to the chair right next to him. With a delicate touch, she reached under his chin and propped his head up. While looking directly in his eyes with as compassionate a look as I have ever seen in my life, she completed her answer. "She is a witch. When she ceases to exist in the world of the living, she will move to another place. In some ways, it will be like this place, but it will be all her own. A place that is familiar to her."

I immediately thought of the marble cathedral that was her residence in the coven. Spending eternity in there helping others while watching over all of us through those enormous picture windows that look out on the pool, woods, and off in the distance, the cove. It seemed fitting, at least to me, but I also felt she would be happy with it, too. I would have to make sure Nathan visited her, with my help, of course. If she ever forgave me. One thing at a time, Larissa. One thing at a time. I needed to take care of Jean first, then worry about repairing the damage I'd done.

"Now my turn to ask a question." She paused and let out an enormous sigh. Probably releasing the weight of the last few moments, I had to imagine. I even felt them. "So, where is the wedding going to be?"

Without a second thought, I said, "The coven." Much to the surprise of my boyfriend and the amusement of my mother. My mother got me with that one.

9

The visit took a lot out of both of us. Nathan just sat there by my side on the porch swing, almost shell-shocked. I leaned against him as we watched the last of the day's sun dip into the bayou, leaving behind the perfect shade of purple painted across the sky. A prelude to another night that the crickets were already warming up to welcome. The others were inside. Jack was feeding those that needed to be fed. He'd announced dinner was ready just twenty minutes ago, but Nathan didn't move. He stayed there, solemn and quiet. Probably still trying to process the experience he just had. To most, it's not normal to have a conversation with someone who was no longer alive.

Underneath the crickets was the murmur of their conversations from inside and whatever they were watching on the television, or the DVD player Jack swiped from his room in the coven, a trick he had learned from me. I told him it was some of the forbidden magic. It wasn't, but it satisfied his curiosity for now, albeit probably temporarily. Gwen didn't seem that interested in learning. She actually didn't seem that interested in much of anything besides Nathan and me, which was why seeing her emerge back out on the porch didn't surprise me. She kept her distance, but she was never far from me, or us. I had given more thought to Jack's theory. Could this new demure version of Gwen be her trying to serve me? It couldn't be. Something didn't fit. She wasn't trying to serve or help. She was just there.

"You know this kind of reminds me of sitting out reading to Amy." Nathan finally broke his catatonic trance and spoke, and what he said floored me in a way that was both deeply personal and emotional. The thought of that little angel sitting out at the table by herself broke me. Or even worse, her sitting at the window of her room looking out at where we would all sit. A tear rolled, and another followed it. Before I wiped them away, others joined it, and I pulled my arm free from Nathan's doing my best to hide my face. I turned away from him and wiped the ones that were there away. It didn't matter. Others replaced them just as fast.

Nathan placed his hand on my shoulder, and I didn't wait for him to pull me toward him. I spun around and buried my head in his chest and let them roll. Why hold them back? I missed her. I deeply missed her. There was a connection like no other. It differed from the one I shared with Nathan. In some ways deeper, as was the grief of not being with her. While my tears rolled, I heard a sniff, and I knew it didn't come from me. I pulled Nathan closer and tighter and glanced up, but he wasn't crying. The sniff didn't come from him. There was a second very wet sounding sniff, and all at once we both looked at the only other person on the porch with us. She hid her head behind her hand, but there was no doubt she was crying.

I pulled back from Nathan and looked at her. This was very un-Gwen-like. I couldn't even comprehend it. It was like she was a much younger Gwen, almost childlike in how she pulled her legs up in the chair, making her look like a little ball.

"Gwen, are you all right?" I asked, knowing full well the answer was going to be no, even if she said yes, but I wasn't expecting her to give me an answer that was neither of those.

It was a very muffled, "Uh-huh." She didn't even look up from her knees.

"Something is off," I said to Nathan, but I said it loud enough so that Gwen could have heard it, hoping to arouse a reaction of some type. There was one, but not the glare I expected or wanted. This, again, was a very childlike glance in our direction with a single eye over her knees. It was odd enough for me to get up and go check on her.

"Gwen?" I called, in a soothing sing-song voice. What I wouldn't give for her to snap at me right now. I might even thank her for it. Again, there was a great big heaping helping of silence. Not even a look this time. I did it again, with the same result. When I was right in front of her, I knelt down in front of her. I went to call her name again, but she shot forward with a speed that even caught me off guard and wrapped her arms around my neck and her legs around my waist. Tears flowed from her eyes and her breath shuddered. Only one person had ever wrapped herself around me like this, and it most definitely wasn't Gwen. My heart knew what was happening before my head did.

"You got to stop doing this, little girl." My hand stroked her long, blonde hair. If Gwen saw this image, she would die a million deaths.

"You know?" a voice that wasn't Gwen's asked.

"I do," I confirmed, and pulled her closer. It all made sense now. Her hovering. The lack of snide remarks. The overall lack of talking in general. I was sure Gwen was only quiet when she was asleep. "Why don't you change back, and we go sit with Nathan on the swing."

I felt it happen when she was in my arms. She went from the seventeen-year-old young woman who despised me to the young girl I knew and loved. Nathan's gasp confirmed when it was complete. I stood up easily with Amy draped on me and walked over to the swing, where I placed her next to Nathan, and I sat next to her. Tears still ran down her face, but they had slowed. I wiped them away and wrapped my arm around her. Her head snuggled against my side. Her hand holding on to Nathan's.

"Amy, why did you follow us?" I asked, already knowing the answer I was about to hear.

She pulled away from me and looked up and whined, “You left, AGAIN!” I knew I was going to hear that, and it was a fair answer. We did.

“Yes, we did, but this is dangerous. We are here taking care of something so everyone can be safe. We were coming back.” That was the plan, and we were going to come back. The only question that remained was whether we were going to be allowed back in. Again, we would cross that bridge when we came to it.

“But you left,” Amy repeated, looking up at both Nathan and me. I could see where this was going. To Amy, it didn’t matter why we left, it only mattered that we left.

“We did,” I gave in and agreed and pulled her in close again. “But you need to stop sneaking out to follow us, and no more using your ability. Just be you. Agreed?”

“But you are using magic. You use it all the time.” Children and their insane ability to point out the obvious truths.

“Busted,” remarked Nathan. I gave him a you’re-not-helping look, which tempered a little of his own amusement at the moment.

“It’s not the same thing.” I felt like a complete hypocrite. It was totally the same thing. “I’m not hiding and sneaking around, making people worry about me.” An even bigger hypocrite there, but isn’t that what a parent does? Do as I say, and not as I do, and all that jazz? My father said that to me. Even Mr. Norton said it. I wondered if they sat next to me, hoping as hard as I was now that I would just accept it and not ask why or anything else. “I bet Ms. Parrish is worried about you. Not to mention Mrs. Saxon and all the others.”

She looked up at me with her big blue eyes that were as big as saucers. There were still moist spots on her cheeks that hinted at tears that flowed moments earlier. “I don’t care about none of them, just you and Nathan.”

Dammit girl, you may not be magic, but you seem to know how to cast the most effective love spell of all. I melted down next to her and nuzzled her against me. Nathan collapsed on us both, and that was how we stayed for what felt like the longest time.

“I have one question. Why Gwen?”

“Don’t know. I guess I kind of like how she dresses.”

That caused me to let go of Amy and sit right up, holding her at arm’s length. “I am going to ignore that you just said that.” Then I laughed as I pulled her back in, realizing I’d better get used to pinks, purples, and other fluorescent colors. I was sure I could whip something up, even if the thought made me nauseous.

“The only thing missing is a book,” Nathan said.

“Well, I do have a library.” I had barely finished the phrase before Amy was bolting in through the door and down the hall, heading for the library. From inside, I heard shocked reactions from the parlor as she sped by. I stood up from the swing and looked back at Nathan. “Wanna go help her find a book? I think I need to go explain things to the others.”

10

"I thought we talked about this. I wanted you to be you." Nathan huffed toward the door of my old room. He looked back a few times at me, standing there brushing my wavy red hair. The perfect frame for my pink cheeks and green eyes.

"Yes, and when it is just us, I'll be me, but I can't go out like that."

"I guess," he begrudgingly agreed. Not that it really mattered. I wasn't about to walk out with my pale skin and dark eyes. Yet alone go up and knock on the door at the Landry manor. That would be a suicide mission. Not that there wasn't a chance this was one as it was. Which led to the other probably that was pouting on the bed behind me.

"Look good?" I turned around and asked Amy.

"Yes," she said over a bottom lip that was stuck out so far, she risked tripping over it. We had spent the better part of her breakfast and then some, fighting about her not going with us. I get it. She wanted to be with us every minute of the day. I wanted that as well, but—and this was a huge but—I couldn't bear to risk it. There wasn't a chance in the world I could.

"Look, you will stay here and have fun with Uncle Mike and Aunt Laura, and we will be back soon." Both had eagerly agreed to babysit for us. Though Nathan had his reservations, which was a little surprising at first, until I finally figured out it wasn't with Mike or Laura, it was Clay. He was still a newborn and could be rather impulsive, but Mike said he would watch things. Martin had overheard the conversation and volunteered to hang back as well and keep an eye on things. I reminded him that if Clay really went off, he or Mike would be hard pressed to hold him back. That was when Martin again pointed out his previously disproven position of being faster than a vampire when in wolf form and promised to grab Amy and give her the ride of a lifetime away from this place and Clay. It was the best we could do. The danger in taking her with us was far greater than what Clay posed.

Everyone gathered outside. Those that were staying watched from the porch as I spun my hand around in the air, imagining a spot Mike had shown me on a map on his phone, Gumbel Fountain. I had never been to this place. They built it years after I left, but I didn't believe that would be an issue, and it wasn't. It wasn't more than a few moments until the simple concrete fountain and its aged copper patina statues came into view. It was just as the picture on the phone showed. A man standing on the top of what looked like the earth in the center, and on either side along the outside walk, two boys rode on the backs of large turtles. With a quick wave to Amy, I grabbed Nathan's hand and stepped through.

No one was there, but the street, St. Charles Avenue, was busy. A city bus rattled by, leaving a trail of noxious diesel fumes. A far departure from the clear air around the coven and my family farm on the outskirts of the city. Other cars sped up and down both sides of the street. We walked out through the opening of the park and blended in with the others walking. Some, residents I guessed, appeared to have some place to be based on their pace. Others, tourists, took in the sights of the crescent city. Here there were parks and buildings that belong to Tulane University. All displaying Civil War era or older architecture. What we were looking for was a few blocks down.

To some extent, the four of us were tourists too. Jack, Nathan, and Rob had never been here before. I had, but it had been years. The homes and the streetcar rails were familiar to me, but not much else was. I remembered begging my mother many times to go for a ride on a streetcar when I was younger. "Walking is good for us", she would always say. That didn't cure my fascination with them, and in my mind, I could almost see a car coming now, with the bell clanging as it got closer. It was so real to me. It was real to everyone else too, because it was there. Something else as old as I was, still moving.

I never knew the actual name of the street the Landrys lived on until Mike looked it up, but I really didn't need it. I recognized the arches at their corner without fail. They were what my father called pretentious arches. A phrase he muttered under his breath every time we came to a visit, which was never really our own choice. It was always for some social function or other. Sylvia would talk of my mother like they were best friends, and my mother would tell you they were close, but not that close. They were familiar acquaintances, which was also why Clarence and I didn't really know each other that well.

Being the same age naturally put us together to entertain each other when our parents were socializing, which were really boring times from what I remembered. I had nothing in common with a chubby boy who always dressed like he was about to welcome the King of England. I doubted that he ever ran through a field chasing fireflies or anything a normal child would have done. Always dressed up in a suit and sat in a chair like some perfect little doll. So, we spent those afternoons with me running around the yard like a normal child, while he sat there prim and proper on the steps, much like how our parents probably were sitting inside. I often wondered if my mother was as bored as I was.

As we grew older, we talked some about things from the coven and our classes. He struggled with the most basic of things. A problem I blamed on his parents for giving him everything. They even hired a tutor for him, of all things. My mother scoffed at that the entire way home after she met him, Mr. Linder.

"The struggle is the most important part of learning," she said more times than I could remember when I was learning. Looking back on it, she was right.

"Here we are," I announced, standing in front of the monstrosity with white fluted columns lining the front.

"This place? The freaking White House?" Rob asked, leaning back to take in the place's grandeur. "Does the secret service know we are about to burst in on the President?"

"No, and they absolutely don't know we brought a werewolf with us. So, hang back here on the sidewalk, if you will."

There was no objection to my suggestion, and Rob stayed right there while Nathan and I walked up to the steps. Jack stayed as well. He said something about this place made him feel off.

It is amazing how simple things can take you back. Walking past the large holly bushes and toward the door with a Christmas wreath that looked exactly like the one I remembered being on it, the red bows tied around each column, all of it had me thinking I was back there walking up the walkway with my parents. It all seemed so familiar, and gave me some hope that maybe, just maybe, this would work.

At the door, I didn't hesitate like I did at the Bergeron's and reached up and grabbed the brass knocker. I gave the door three good raps and stood there confident and patient; exactly how I wanted them to find me when I opened the door. It was the opposite of how I felt. This seemed hopeless, absolutely hopeless, and that tore me up inside. Every failed attempt doomed Marie Norton to more suffering and was one step closer to robbing me of any type of free life. It was a thought that constantly had me on the edge of taking off on my own to save her and face Jean. Of course, I didn't know where they really were in the city, thus why I needed help. Even now, standing there before the large red door, the thoughts of her were what consumed me. The only image that played over and over in my head was the one of her chained to the wall in that dank dungeon looking room. As it tore my psyche to shreds, my outside threatened to crack, and I quickly reached up and wiped away the start of a tear from the corner of my right eye. Nathan rubbed the center of my back, just as the lock of the door clunked on the other side.

"May I help you?" The elderly African American man stood there wearing a black suit, white shirt buttoned up to his chin. I felt a little of my mother coming out in my thoughts as I considered how pretentious it was to still have hired help in this day and age, but that was the Landry family that I remembered through and through.

"We need to speak to the man or lady of the house," I said, remembering my manners. "Is Mr. or Mrs. Landry available? This is a rather private matter." Without a word, he backed away from the door and motioned with his arm for us to come in. It was like stepping through a time machine. The entry hadn't changed at all. Not a bit in almost a hundred years. The white speckled marble tiles formed a perfect circle around the gold star inlaid in the center of the floor. Pictures of the previous generations, each with their own gallery style light, were hung on the dark paneled walls. Most of them I recognized, including one that had a young Clarence Landry in it. Next to it was another one, with a much older Clarence, and what appeared to be his family. There were two more next to that one.

"Wait here," he requested, and then disappeared through a door that blended in with the wood-paneled walls. I knew that was the servants' door. I once got in trouble for going through it. Not with my mother, but with Sylvia. I moved to the left of the star and pulled Nathan with me. I knew whoever was coming to see us would either come down the spiral stairs from the living area, or from down the hall that was now directly in front of me. They chose the stairs, and they didn't come down.

"What is this about?" asked a female voice from the landing up on the second floor. She hadn't stepped onto the stairs yet. "And before you start. I know what you are, and what those waiting outside are, but..." she took a single step down on the stairs. The heel of her shoe clicked on the wood stringer. "I also know what you aren't." She took a few more steps down. The woman, in red heels and a matching red pants-suit, looked like she belonged on the cover of a fashion magazine. She wore bright red lipstick which offset against her pale complexion; framed by raven black hair. Her features were striking, sophisticated, and memorable.

"Mrs. Landry?" I presumed.

"Yes," she answered, but she didn't look in my direction. Which sent a feeling of relief through me. She focused on Nathan. "You are human," she wondered out loud.

"Yes ma'am."

Now she regarded me with a curious gaze. "So, he knows what you and what your friends are?"

No need to sugarcoat things or come up with an elaborate story or excuse here, just let the truth fly. "Yes, his mother is a witch, and she actually runs a coven in the northeast."

"Huh," she said, and stepped down off the bottom step, and walked around us, studying us. With each step, her gaze became more curious, and I worried if she was feeling what I also was.

"Mrs. Landry, I am Larissa Dubois, and I was wondering if Clarence Landry is still alive."

This broke her from her obsessive studying, and she jerked straight up, vampire straight. "Clarence? My husband's grandfather?"

"Yes ma'am. He is a friend of my family's. I need to speak to him. It's an urgent matter."

"Concerning?" she asked. There was a curiosity in her expression again, but her tone was defensive. That told me he was alive, and the hope that roared inside me almost convinced me to just blurt out why we were there. Luckily logic and restraint won out. Telling her I was also a vampire was probably the best way to ensure I would never see Clarence Landry, and unlike at the Bergeron's, I didn't want to chance any use of force here. From what I remembered, the Landrys were quite strong, even though Clarence never applied himself. And even though she was only a Landry by marriage, I doubted the latest generation would have stooped so low and allowed anyone beneath them to be part of their family. The vibrations in the room confirmed my belief.

"It's a private matter," I said.

She broke her stiff posture and leaned toward us, hands on her hips, and an absence of amusement in her expression that caused my stance to crouch slightly. "Look. You can't just walk in here off the street, ask to speak to my husband's grandfather, and only give me that. You need to give me a little more to work with. So, what is it, or should we just show you the door now?" Her right hand pointed to the door in a flash.

I could see her point, and I was sure if she knew the truth, she would see my point about why I couldn't tell her everything. I needed to speak to him. He was the link, I hoped. I made another attempt, again being as vague as I could without appearing so. "I am here looking into a family matter, and I was told he knew my," I almost said parents, "family when they lived here, and he might be able to fill in the missing pieces. I am sure you understand how important our ancestry is...," and then it hit me. A little white lie, which I could dress up in some truth, and might tug on the string of any witch rooted in tradition, which I felt this family was.

"I can't visit them. There is something blocking them from being there for me. I owe it to them to find out what happened that is keeping them from taking their place and being a part of my life. Mr. Landry may remember details about what happened."

"Oh, I see."

I hoped she did, because I was officially all out of ideas.

"I hope you haven't come a long way. I'm afraid Mr. Landry is old, and his mind left him many years ago. He hasn't spoken in some time. I'm not sure what help he would be," she apologized. Her defensive tone was gone, as was any stress or tension she had in her body. I felt her pulse relax. It was nice being a human lie detector of sorts.

"I know a few spells. Maybe I can bridge the gap." I went back to the Bolden's class and altered my tone slightly to convey more emotion. Which normally wasn't a problem for me. Though most of those were of the teenage variety. Now I needed to implore her to help. "It is very important." I took a step forward toward her.

"I'm really sorry."

"May we just see him? Sometimes familiar faces, or even fresh faces, can spark someone. That happened to my grandmother. A new nurse or doctor would come in and she would speak for the first time in months. Something about stimulus, I believe." I looked back in astonishment at how smart my boyfriend was.

What Nathan said really had her thinking. She even started pacing while she looked down at the floor, and a hand rubbed her chin.

"Even just for a moment. If nothing sparks, then we leave," I added.

"It's that important?" she asked.

"Yes," I said, doing my best acting to put urgency behind it. Even though that didn't really require much. I felt that urgency and then some every second of the day since I saw Marie Norton tied up there. This was our best bet. Even if he was how she said he was, I could probably try to reach his mind. I just needed to be near him. Mrs. Landry was teetering on giving in. I could tell, with how she kept looking back at us. I needed something to push her over the edge. "It really is. I ascended, but my family wasn't there to answer."

She stopped straight with a gasp. "How is that even possible?"

I shook my head. "I don't know. I am kind of stuck in the middle. If I can clear what is blocking them, then I can go to them and complete the ritual."

She stepped toward me and grabbed my hands. Luckily, thanks to my current state, they felt as warm as anyone's would. "You poor child. Let's go see what we can do. Maybe you can reach him, or fresh faces would help like your friend said. If not, maybe what you are looking for is somewhere in some of his old journals. Follow me."

She led us down a hallway lined with the same tile and wood-paneled walls. I had been here before. The door out to the garden was down this hall, as was his father's study and library. He was an attorney when he wasn't being a high-ranking witch in the New Orleans coven. Also, down this way were a set of stairs that were closest to Clarence's room. That was where we were heading. I even pulled Nathan toward the door before Mrs. Landry opened it.

At the top, it was just a few steps and then to the right, through the open door. The room looked unfamiliar, but also familiar. It was no longer the room of a young boy in the 1920s, but it still smelled the same. His bed was in the same spot. Right between the two large windows at the end of the room. Though the hospital bed and the carts of medical monitors took up more room than his old single bed did. At first, I couldn't see him over the mound of covers that laid across his midsection, but as I followed Mrs. Landry around to one side, I saw the young boy I knew in the old man that laid before me. It was the eyes and the cheeks. Even in a sea of wrinkles and age spots, they were all still him. I felt myself want to say hello, but I held back.

"He hasn't responded to anyone but his nurses in years. Even then, it is only to their touch as they guide him when feeding or bathing him," she explained in front of him. She turned to him and stroked his forehead. Clarence stared straight up at the ceiling. There wasn't even a twitch in his face or eyes in response to her touch. "Mr. Landry, this is Larissa Dubois and," she stopped and looked at Nathan at the foot of the bed rather quizzically. "I didn't catch your name."

"Nathan. Nathan Saxon."

She nodded and turned back to Clarence. "And her friend Nathan. They have come a long way to ask you some questions about a family you might remember from a long time ago." She backed away and motioned for me to take her place at the head of his bed. I did and looked down at my old friend for any sign of life in his eyes. They were dead. Just brown lifeless marbles lying in the sockets of his skull.

"Mr. Landry, can you hear me?" I figured I would ask to see if my voice triggered anything, but there was nothing. I leaned a little closer and played my hand to see what would happen. "Clarence, it's Larissa. Do you remember me?" Slowly, his eyes turned in my direction, and then a gasp escaped his lips. Then a gasp escaped from Mrs. Landry.

"How does he know you?"

"It's a long story," I started, but then there was another gasp from Clarence, and his hand reached out from beneath his covers and pointed toward a bookshelf against the far wall.

"Oh my!" exclaimed Mrs. Landry. "He hasn't done that in... well, I can't remember when. When he lost the ability to talk, he would point at the book on the bookshelf he wanted."

The hand dropped and slapped against the mattress of his bed and then shot up again with urgency. A single extended finger shook as it pointed out, and he grunted. His eyes were straining to look in the direction he was pointing, but his head would not cooperate and lift up to give him the view he desired. I reached down and lifted his head and pillow up, folding the pillow to prop him up.

His granddaughter-in-law attempted to follow the path of his point and walked to the bookshelf. There she ran her hand across the books that sat on top of the cabinet that made up the bottom half of the bookshelf. Clarence pointed more intently, trying to urge her toward the book he desired. When she wasn't close, the hand shook violently, and the grunting turned more primal. It was obvious whatever he was after wasn't on that shelf. She moved up to the next shelf, and more of the same. Now she was really having to reach up to the top shelf that was filled with old dusty books stacked on top of one another. It was obvious those hadn't been touched in many years, if not decades.

A long book with a red cover shook on the shelf. When she touched it, the grunting and pointing stopped. Clarence held out a flat hand, waiting for the book. She pulled it out from under those that were on top of it and delivered it to his waiting hand. Clarence took it and placed it on his lap, and eagerly flipped through the pages. It was pages upon pages of pictures, snapshots, glued or taped to the page, and these were old and yellowed. His eyes were alive again as they scanned each page as he flipped through them. Then he stopped, and a finger, and his gaze, focused on a single picture. The three of us all leaned over the bed and looked down at the picture. I immediately knew why there were two others now looking up at me.

Clarence's stare stayed on the page, but his finger lifted and pointed right at me.

Mrs. Landry spun the photo album around and studied the photo, and then studied me. "How can it be?" she gasped as she looked back down at the picture of Clarence and me sitting in this very room. Next to it was another picture of us out in the garden, with our parents behind us.

"That's my grandmother." I explained, hoping she would accept this bald-faced lie.

The I-wasn't-born-yesterday look said she hadn't. "It is not just a resemblance. It IS you. That is why he recognized you. Care to explain?" She spun the album around on Clarence's lap, giving me a perfect view of the picture and what they wrote under it. Landry and Dubois, Easter 1934. Mrs. Landry always put on a big Easter feast, and like so many of the day, she wore an enormous hat, what she called her Easter bonnet. She had it on in the picture. I remember that thing and wondered what would happen to her if a big gust of wind came up. The thought even tempted me to send one just to see what would really happen.

I stood there and looked over at Nathan. He looked worried, and I felt the same. The pit of desperation in my stomach was growing miles in depth by the moment. Telling someone the truth hadn't gone so well the first time, and I didn't have any delusions it would this time either.

"Are you going to tell me? Or shall I find out on my own?" She had backed away from the bed and started for my side. I kept reminding myself to not run and stay cool. All the while the motto of Mr. Helms' class played in my head. *Your enemies are everyone and everywhere.* She passed Nathan without a glance and reached for my hand. I saw the all-seeing eye flash in my mind, and a tingle of electricity ran up my arm. "Reveal!" she proclaimed, and then it happened. The illusion I cast of who I was crumbled away in a pile of glitter to the floor. I stood there, pale skin, cold, and black eyed.

Mrs. Landry gasped and released my hand quickly before taking several steps back.

"Relax, I know what it looks like," I said. "Let me explain."

"You have 10 seconds before I show you what we do to those of your kind that wander out of the swamp." Blue orbs were growing in her hand. I hadn't seen that before, even long ago, and wasn't really interested in finding out what that was all about.

"I am Larissa Dubois. The girl in the picture there with Clarence. Jean St. Claire attacked my family when I was sixteen. My father and mother were both killed, but I survived. Two vampires protected me and hid me from him. A few months ago, Jean sent Reginald Von Bell after us, and killed who I thought was my father and now has the woman I considered my mother imprisoned. I need help to locate him and finding out anything anyone can tell me that will help. I need to save her and end him if I am ever going to have peace in my life." It took over ten seconds she allotted me to explain, but I think she stretched it a bit to hear me out.

"I have heard that story before. The farm outside of town? That was what? 1936?" The rotating blue orbs in her hands disappeared.

"1939. I was 16. I was 11 when that picture was taken."

I watched as she absorbed the story and details. She was reconciling it with whatever she had heard. Probably a story handed down about what happened to that poor family outside of town, which served as a warning of why you never crossed vampires.

"And you are?" she looked at Nathan curiously.

"I am seventeen, and human."

"Okay. Good," she said, as if trying to assure herself that not everything was out of sorts.

"I was really hoping Clarence could tell me something, anything, that might help me. With who this family is, they would know. Plus, his mother was one of my mother's closest of friends." She wasn't, but from the Landry point of view, she was.

"I am sorry to disappoint you. What he just did now was the most Clarence has done in years. His mind started going on him, leaving him like this," she explained, now standing at the foot of the bed with Nathan. Probably because she felt better about standing next to a human than a vampire.

"But he recognized me. That's something."

"He did, but as you can see, all he did was point. He can't really communicate."

"Not verbally," I suggested, hoping she would take the hint.

She did and pondered it while staring at her grandfather in law. "I don't know. Plus, my husband would freak if he knew you were here."

I knew she meant my kind, and not me personally, but I let it go. "It won't take long. No potions or anything."

"Are you going to do one-mind?" she asked, but before I could answer, she posed another question. "Are you even able to? You are a..."

I stopped her there with a raised hand. "I can, and have done it many times. My father showed me how. Just because I am a vampire now doesn't mean I am not also a witch. I remember everything and can still do everything I could before." Just for show, I levitated the album back to the shelf she retrieved it from, turned myself back in to my more publicly presentable self, and threw a few symbols around just to make sure she got the message. Then, to settle any lasting doubts she had, I added, "I have even ascended, with the help of a council member." I wasn't about to give out his name.

"Oh," she said, and went back to staring at Clarence with a life-or-death intensity. "I don't know."

"It's perfectly safe," Nathan said, and I wondered if he even knew what we were talking about, but I appreciated the support all the same.

She let out a deep breath and took a step closer to me. Or make that closer to Clarence. "Okay, but you will stop when I tell you to. Agreed?"

"You are coming in with me?"

"Yes," she said, and grasped Clarence's hand between her own.

I reached over and put my hands on either side of his head. "One mind. One thought. One mind. One thought. Open your thoughts to me. Guide me through your memories. Un esprit. Une pensée. Montre-moi."

We both appeared in the garden in the backyard of Clarence's house. The rose bushes stood high, like I remembered, a hint, I hoped, that we were back at that point in time. Though this could be any time in Clarence's memory. I called to the one member of our party we needed that was absent. "Clarence, where are you?"

It wasn't too long before I heard the giggling of a child, and Clarence came running around the corner of the bushes. The same chubby faced eleven-year-old I remembered from that Easter picture. He didn't stop when he reached us, and just whizzed by and around the other end of the line of bushes.

This time Mrs. Landry called for him, and again he came running around the bushes. But just like before, he didn't stop, and flashed by. This was so odd. He never ran around.

"I think we should follow him," suggested Mrs. Landry.

We ran around the end of the bushes after him. On the other side, I stepped back into a surreal scene that was almost too much to take in, and I felt my body perform a reflexive gasp. Sylvia Landry, and that hat, was trying to organize us all for the photo. Clarence, her husband, and my eleven-year-old self, standing there in front of my mother and father. The ultimate out-of-body experience.

"This makes sense," Mrs. Landry said. "This was the photograph. The memory that sparked inside of him."

We stood there and watched Sylvia straightening Clarence's suit so he would look exactly right for the picture. When that was done, the adults went inside, and Clarence and I took his normal seat on the steps where he always sat while I ran around. I, my eleven-year-old self, rounded the bushes again, and then headed off away. Clarence stood up and followed, but at a much slower pace. I knew where they were heading, and without a word to my passenger, I headed for the small koi pond on the other side of the courtyard. Both of us, well, my younger self and Clarence, reached into the old burlap sack and pulled out handfuls of fish food that we threw into the pond to start the feeding frenzy at the surface. That was where we would stand for the next few minutes watching the orange and white fish come up to the surface to grab a pellet or two of food before they disappeared back into the depths of the pond.

I stepped to the edge of the pond, putting myself between my younger self and Clarence. Little Larissa was focused on the fish and didn't notice me. Clarence glanced in my direction when I bent down. "Clarence, do you know who I am?"

He nodded and threw another handful of pellets into the water.

"Do you know what happened to me and my family?"

This time he didn't look in my direction and stayed focused on the surface of the pond several feet away from the bank, but he did nod. It was a slow and pained nod.

"I need your help. Can you tell me about those that did that to me?"

The world exploded, and we were no longer at the pond, but I knew exactly where we were. My mother had been wrong all along. Sylvia didn't have the wake at her place. She had it at ours in the parlor where I was standing. In front of me was a large walnut casket. It had to be my mother's. Sylvia was holding court at the door behind me. I could hear her greeting people as they entered. Off to the side, in the corner of the parlor, stood Clarence, in a black suit and black bowtie. He stared at the casket. Pure fear dripped from every pore of his soul.

Seeing the casket ripped at me. This was his memory of this moment. It was as it had occurred, and in there I knew was the body of my mother. Where I was, I didn't know. Probably not even awake yet, still going through the turning process. Were we already in Virginia, that far from where my mother was being remembered and laid to rest? I felt like I needed to apologize to her.

"You okay?" Sylvia touched my arm, pulling me back from the rabbit hole I was diving into.

"Yep." I shook it off and walked over, and leaned against the wall next to Clarence. The heaviest of what and when this was stuck with me as I asked Clarence, "Do you know what happened to her?"

The young boy nodded, but still didn't say a word. I needed more out of him. I needed him to engage with me, talk to me, or even show me.

"Clarence, can you tell me who did this to her?"

The boy looked at me. The irises of his eyes shook in their oceans of white. He slinked away from me, attempting to cram every inch of his chubby body in the corner. His hands pulled in tight against his chest, and the room grew dark around me. I stood up and looked around, hoping this was his way of showing me since he couldn't tell me. What I witnessed was a nightmare mesh of every memory Clarence had stored in his head, all in a random order, only interrupted by primal screams of pain and helplessness.

I turned back to the boy, and he was gone, replaced by the old man I saw laying in the bed. He was sitting there in the corner with the same fearful look on his face as the world spun and screamed. Every once in a while, I thought I heard a voice, "please help me." As soon as I thought I heard it, an ear shattering yowl in that same voice replaced it.

"Can you slow it down?" Mrs. Landry asked.

I looked back at Clarence in the corner, then closed my eyes and focused on the screams and pleas. I was right. They were all him. All at the same time. "I can't control the flow."

That kind of control didn't exist here, because that kind of control no longer existed in the man. His mind was a jumbled prison. Trapping him inside, with no hope of ever controlling it or exiting. I felt a great sorrow for my old friend. Standing here, in his mind, I could feel his presence. The more I listened to the screams, the more the mental anguish he was under was clear. What was also clear, he may know what I needed to know, but it was buried somewhere in here with no hope of ever retrieving it. My presence today helped spark that one memory he had, and that was it. Something new. A new face that triggered something from long ago. I even feared we were making it worse. Did he know what I was asking? Did he want to help us, but couldn't? That had to be pure torture to someone who lived so long, being a confident, competent member of our community, now unable to control his own thoughts. "We need to go."

With that, I removed my hands from the side of Clarence's head, and we were once again back in the room beside his bed. Clarence appeared unaffected on the outside. He lay staring up at the ceiling, but I could still feel him. I knew our presence in his mind disturbed him, but our departure did even more so.

"You were right," I said, still looking down at him. "His memory is shot. He can't remember anything. I think seeing me sparked that one, but the rest of it is all jumbled around." The remorse for the pain we caused him overshadowed my disappointment at not finding what I needed.

"I am truly sorry," she apologized unnecessarily.

"Maybe you can help?" I walked away from the bed, feeling I needed to leave Clarence before I caused him more pain. I stopped by the shelves and read across the covers of many of the books. There were literary classics, as well as a few witchcraft related books, which it surprised me to see them so out in the open. "I need to know where Jean and his followers live, how many of them there are, and anything else you can tell me."

Her hands fidgeted as she stepped away from the bed herself. Nathan flanked her, but kept his distance. I felt her heart flutter several times, which told me even today Jean's darkness still cast a shadow over life here. "I honestly don't know where they are or any of that," she said apprehensively. Her eyes avoiding any direct eye contact with my own.

"You do know who I am talking about?" I asked, feeling confident she did.

"Yes," she answered abruptly. "And that is why I don't believe we can get involved and help you."

That punch hurt. "I am only looking for information," I assured her. "I am not asking you to join me in my fight against him. Just information."

She took a few more steps closer, and now looked up directly into my eyes. "Are you really intent on starting a war with him? You know that is a fool's errand. A death sentence. It doesn't matter who you are. He will kill you and then go after anyone that helped you." She turned and glanced at Nathan. My big brave knight in shining armor swallowed loud enough for it to be heard over the beeps of the medical devices hooked to Clarence.

"He already started the war by killing my parents," I corrected.

"I am sorry to hear of your family, but in the grand scheme of things, that is just an insignificant event in the course of the cosmic universe. There is so much more to lose, not just for you, but for all of us, if you do something stupid. Think beyond yourself. You, and everyone else, would be better served if you just let this go, and go on with the rest of your life."

"Has she told you he is still trying to kill her?" Finally, my knight showed up to my defense.

Mrs. Landry first looked at Nathan, and then back to me.

"Remember, I told you earlier. Just a month ago, he sent Reginald after me. In fact, Reginald bit Nathan, but we reversed it."

She stood there, still confused, looking back and forth between us.

"I would be more than happy to just ignore him and get on with life. Leaving that terrible chapter behind me, and getting on with my future," I felt Nathan would appreciate actually hearing those words come from my mouth. "But it isn't that easy. Jean is not leaving me alone. He wants what I am." I watched the light flicker in her head, and then flipped the switch on the rest of the way. "He wants to have the ability of a witch that will live forever. If he could ever get that, he would be unstoppable."

There was the big click. She finally realized everything and backed up and sat on the foot of the bed before falling to the floor. "He can't can he?"

I reached up and held out my blood charm. "He could. He also has the woman who raised me as her own imprisoned. She is being tortured, and I need to save her."

There was silence in the room for what seemed like ages, but it was probably only seconds. This was beyond an uncomfortable silence. This was torturous. When it ended, she looked at the floor. Her hands wrestled with one another nervously as she murmured, "You need to leave. We can't help you."

I was about to make another plea when she sprung up and walked toward me. "You really need to leave," she said more forcibly. "We can't be involved in this. This is too dangerous." She avoided eye contact with Nathan and me as she passed us and walked out the door of the room. "In fact, you need to forget you even came here. No one can know of it." She said from the top of the stairs, where she waited for us to follow.

Out of respect, and against my first instinct, we did. Nathan attempted several times to get my attention, but I kept walking, knowing he would follow. She remained quiet right up to the door, that she opened herself, and then closed it behind us as we exited.

Halfway down the front walk, Nathan grabbed my arm and spun me around. "Why didn't you try harder?"

"Trust me. It wouldn't do any good," I explained. "You saw the fear in her. I felt it."

11

To borrow Mike's term, we were striking out more than a baseball player not on steroids, and that had me more than a little desperate. I had even considered taking a page out of some books I had read and movies I had seen, and become the dramatic hero. Sneak out under the cover of darkness and walk into town with my arms spread open, showing I am not a threat, hoping to give myself up, and perform some Hollywood-esque feat of combat while rescuing Marie Norton and killing Jean. The movies made it appear so easy, and I was running out of options. We were down to one family, and I didn't think that had a snowball's chance in hell of that working. In fact, I think the snowball stood a better chance of surviving hell than The Mallory family being my saving grace.

I knew I owed my mother a report, but I couldn't bear to tell her about another failure. At least not yet. I roamed the quiet halls and rooms of my old family home in search of an answer, or something to feel good about. I found it in the library where Amy had fallen asleep in Laura's lap. I offered to take her, but Laura told me she was fine. I had to admit there was a glow to her there with Amy with her. It seemed almost a natural picture watching her stroke her hair. Outside of that, the house felt so gloomy, or that was my mood. I heard the boys watching what sounded like a football game from the whistles and Rob yelling, "he should have had that." I poked my head into the parlor and saw exactly what I expected. All of them standing up watching a college bowl game, much like Mr. Norton did this time of year. They adorned the score at the bottom of the screen with green holly leaves hinting at the holidays that were coming up in a few days. I looked around at our entry and the staircase again, and I realized what was missing. What would make this place seem livelier, even if I didn't feel it?

With a single sling of my arm, that all changed. A long piece of garland wrapped in red ribbon appeared on the stair railing. A large tree in the corner by the door, complete with decorations, just as I remembered them. We didn't have lights back then, but I created some twinkling ones to keep up with the modern traditions. It didn't take long for the boys to notice. Martin was the first one to emerge from the parlor and look around. He reached out and touched the garland.

"Feels as real as it smells."

"So that was how you knew it was out here?"

"Yep, that and the pine odor from the tree. I knew either you brought a tree in or hung up one of those cheap air fresheners from a car wash." He chuckled at his own joke. "Looks great Larissa."

"Figured, we are here, and it is the holidays. Might as well." It did at least lighten the house, even if my mood was still as dark as the deepest cave. "Just don't eat it." I said with a nudge. I followed him back into the parlor with the others. All except Clay and Rob were sitting now, and I found my way over to Nathan and sat on the floor, leaning back against his legs. His hand tousled my hair. I hoped just the feeling that would make everything feel right with the world, but it hadn't. Not even close.

When the game ended, the television went off, and everyone retired to their room. Everyone that needed sleep did. I again went and checked in on Amy. Laura looked down at that young angelic girl that was sound asleep on her lap. There was a motherly look to her at that moment. "Do we have another room? If not, she can have the one Mike and I are using. We don't really need one."

"I'm going to put her in bed with Nathan up in my room."

"And I bet you are going to snuggle with both of them."

I couldn't deny it. That was absolutely what I intended to do when I took her upstairs and placed her in bed. I needed it. "Just like you are going to snuggle with Mike."

She smiled. "We might do a little of that. Don't you and Nathan want some private time?"

I shook my head. "No," and then cautioned her with a wave, "Don't start. That's the furthest thing from my mind at the moment. There is just so much going on."

"Understandable. Just don't forget to live in the moment. Even though we live forever. Moments don't."

"Laura the philosopher," I teased, but understood what she said clearly. She was absolutely right. We may live thousands of years and never have another chance at a missed moment, or at one that was even close.

"Something Mrs. Bolden told us. Never take today for granted when tomorrow is guaranteed. It took me a while to understand it, but now I clearly do." She looked down at Amy and rubbed her back ever so gently. "Here, why don't you come take her and get her settled? I am sure Mike is missing me now that his game is over." She reached down and cradled Amy before handing her to me, and then left the room, but not before lingering at the door looking back at me.

I took Amy up the stairs to my old room, where Nathan had already passed out in the bed. I laid Amy down in the center next to him, and then crammed myself in beside her. With one arm, I pulled her close and felt her body nestle against me. She knew I was there. It wasn't more than a few moments before I felt Nathan's hand reach over and cover my own. He knew we were both there. And there it was.

Another reminder of why I should take the advice someone gave me before, and then again today, by Mrs. Landry. Just let everything go and get on with the rest of my life. Who wouldn't want this life? It was, dare I say it. Perfect. If only it were that simple.

Over the next several hours, I debated with myself if it could be, but each time I came back to, after eighty years, he was still searching for me. This... this perfection, wouldn't be able to exist under those circumstances, and if it could, I wouldn't let it. I couldn't put them at risk. My mind again raced to what were my next steps, already assuming defeat in my planned visit with Ben Mallory tomorrow, if he was still alive. There were no next steps.

That wasn't entirely true.

There was one.

One that came to me in one of the more heartbreaking moments of the night while I lay there holding the ones who meant more to me than anything. It was another scene out of a Hollywood movie. I could just walk away, disappear into the world, far away from Nathan and Amy, leaving them, and everyone else, safe.

After that thought, I got out of bed to keep Amy or Nathan from finding out I was crying and sat outside the door for a while, listening to them breathe. Each breath I heard reminded me of why I couldn't do that. They were all that completed me. Without them, so much was missing from me. I might as well be that empty, soulless creature that pop culture had cast us as. I kicked myself for having the thought, and for being that weak to even consider it. There was no place for mental or emotional weakness here, but as soon as I chased it away, I felt it creep back in. There were so many reasons for it to do so. Nothing had gone right and there was so much at stake, not just for me, but for all of us. And there it was again. I had resolved myself to push it back, but again, it came in just as quick. I was never the type to give in so easily. Maybe it was the darkness that was around me. If I went downstairs with the others, it wouldn't have as much of an opportunity, much like those nights out of the roof deck back in the coven. They were all simple moments, but I now completely understood why. Moments alone with your thoughts, especially when you are already in a dark place, were hard to fight. So many thoughts can race across your mind, and not just the type of world domination. It could really shape a person, make them into something they normally wouldn't be. Dare I say it? They could become the monster the world considered us to be.

I went down and found Mike and Laura in the parlor watching an old holiday movie. It wasn't one I had seen before, surprisingly, but it had a great deal of singing and dancing. Clay was out on the porch. This was not like the jovial nights on the deck. My mood and my failures had dragged everyone else down. I was thinking of ways to help, when I heard Mike get a little snippy when Laura moved and caused him to have to move his arm. This was more than just moods. I counted back the days and factored in the stress we had all been through. That was when I remembered back to when I had felt like this before, and times when I had snapped at Mr. and Mrs. Norton. The answer was simple. Weak body, weak mind. That was what Mr. Norton always told me when I tried to stretch out my feedings. All of this had taken a lot out of us, and we had missed something.

"It's Friday," I said. That was when I saw Mike working it out in his head. He perked up.

We were on a schedule that our bodies had become used to, and this wasn't the time to stretch things. I, we, needed to have both a strong body and a strong mind. "We are pretty far from anyone. I am sure there is some wildlife out here." If I listened close enough, I was sure I could hear them from where I was.

"Larissa, are you sure?" Laura said. "We don't want to cause any problems and can stretch things out." She had one hand on Mike's chest as she sat next to him, as if to signify she was speaking for both of them. From all appearances, he didn't agree.

"This is no time to try. I used to stretch things a lot before, but I can even feel it. I guess I have gotten used to the regular weekly hunts. We need to keep up our strength. It should be safe if we stay close to the farm. The best place is probably the woods out by the river."

There was no further debate before Mike moved Laura's hand and stood up. "I'll get Clay."

"Are you sure?" Laura asked again.

"Yes, it's fine. We are going to have to at some point, and really, we are way out, away from everyone. So, it is ideal." I went upstairs and retrieved my shoes before I met the rest of them out on the porch. From there I pointed at the woods to our south, reminding them it was all woods between there and the river. If we kept to that area, we would be fine.

"Why don't you and Laura go together? I got Clay," remarked Mike. Clay gave him a look of disappointment. "Hey dude. Just in case. All right?"

Clay agreed, and they were off in a flash toward the woods. Laura and I followed through the clear, crisp winter night. It felt wonderful sprinting across the field for the woods. Once we were there, we both stopped and let our senses take over. There were dozens of smaller animals around. We could both sense it. While that might work, it wasn't the best. There had to be something bigger. Something that wouldn't take multiples to take away the thirst that burned in the back of my throat from the anticipation of drinking in the fluid of sustenance. I both felt and heard something to our left, and I grabbed Laura's hand and pulled her in that direction. This wasn't an enormous animal, but the pumping of heart I felt told me it was large enough for us.

We caught up with the black bear on the shore of the river. It was a majestic-looking animal sitting there drinking from the river while being bathed in the moonlight of the clear night. We were on it and doing what nature intended. Before it knew we were there. The burning in my throat subsided, and my body and mind instantly felt clearer. This was exactly what I needed. Gone were the days of stretching it out for weeks.

Laura finished first and sat in the low brush while I fed. Two hands grabbed us and yanked us back, covering our mouths. Another creature grabbed our meal and threw it out in the center of the river some two or three hundred yards away and then joined the other and pulled us back into a brush.

"Quiet," Clay's voice whispered from behind us.

I stayed quiet, but reached up to remove his hand, and froze when he tightened his grasp and he pulled us back further into the darkness of the woods and under a large bush. I was about to reach up again when I saw nine dark figures moving along the bank of the river. All but two were men. From what I could see in the moonlight, the men were all dressed in dark suits. The women wore dark dresses with skirts that went all the way to the ground. Easily a century out of place. The dark colors of their clothes were a contrast to the pale skin of their faces. They talked and laughed loud and jovial, not making any attempt to hide their presence. Seeing them like that brought back the memories of all the times we would be in town at night and see people that looked like that walking up and down the street. Each time, my father moved us to the other side of the street and made sure he was between them and my mother and me, or, if needed, he cast a spell to keep them from seeing us at all. I never asked what they were, but I knew they weren't human, and they weren't good. That scared me at that age. My mother eventually told me what they were. Sitting here now, seeing them walk out in the open, and this close to my home, sent that same frightening feeling through me. They never stopped or gave any other sign they knew we were there. Just continued on their nighttime stroll down the Mississippi, talking and laughing as friends. No concerns about being out at this time of night where a predatory animal, or human, might cause trouble. Of course, they wouldn't be worried about that. They were at the top of the food chain.

Clay waited until they were way down river from us before he removed his hand. It was a good thing we didn't need to breathe.

"Clay noticed them when we were finishing up. I didn't want them to catch you," explained Mike.

"I just can't believe how open they were. They didn't keep to the shadows. Anyone coming down the river would have seen them," Laura said, still looking in the direction they walked.

"They don't hide in the shadows like that down here. They move around at night, but they don't hide. The locals know to stay away," I explained.

"They know they are vampires?" Mike asked.

"Maybe," I said. "Remember where we are. This is the home to voodoo, black magic, and old beliefs. Not only is this stuff accepted down here, but they also take pride in it. So, I am sure some locals know what they are. In fact, I am sure of it, and they know to avoid them. Others probably just think they are ones that love the old dark mystique of this place and enjoy dressing up."

We returned to the house, looking behind us several times just to make sure nothing followed us. Seeing them that close gave me a fresh worry. Home wasn't as safe as I thought it was. Something I shared with Rob and Martin when they woke up early in the morning. The six of us agreed to do patrols like those at the coven. Except now, they would do theirs before dusk, with the vampires taking care of anything at night.

12

It was still dark out when I crawled back into bed next to Amy and Nathan. Amy had stretched out on what used to be my side, but I still had room to lie there and rub her back and brush through her hair as she slept. A long hot shower had removed the evidence of my night's adventure, and I felt renewed, body and spirit. Even the discovery of our visitors didn't pull me down as much as it probably should have. I believed we had a plan, just like we had at the coven, and that had worked well so far. The biggest difference here, we wouldn't fight. If anyone showed up or got too close, I would just open a portal to another place I knew and take us there before they even knew we were there. Probably Virginia or the beaches of North Carolina where we went a few times during the summer just to get away, though we never really went out in the sun or on the beach.

Nathan was the first to stir and open his eyes. "Good morning," I whispered.

"Morning," he replied and then regarded Amy lying next to him. "Want the shower first?"

"Already had one. You go ahead."

He slipped out of bed, watching to make sure he didn't wake Amy, and then left the room. I stayed right there. I wanted to be the first person she saw when she woke up. With how deeply she was breathing, she still had a way to go before that happened. Nathan returned from his shower while I still lay there. As he threw on a shirt over the pants he took with him to the shower, he looked at the two of us lying in bed and smiled. I wondered if he thought the same when I looked at him and her.

"I'm heading down." Nathan motioned toward the door.

"'kay. Can you fix her something when you are down there too, please? I'm not going to let her sleep too late."

"Sure," he replied, and then headed down.

The sunlight of the morning crawled across the floor of the room. I could see little rainbows right in the aura's edge. It looked magical, but to me, what was really magical was lying there with her, in my old room, in my old home. It again pulled at a yearning I had never thought of before. Well, I had, but that was a long time ago, before I became what I am now. What little girl doesn't dream of having one of her own one day? Seeing Laura with Amy last night reminded me I wasn't the only one facing the harsh reality of a dream that would never be fulfilled, but if this was the closest I ever came to it, I could live with that.

"You're still here," her voice squeaked.

"I told you. I am never, ever leaving you again." I reached down and kissed her forehead and hugged her. She threw her arms around my neck and squeezed. "Come on with me. I have a surprise to show you." That word was the trick. She was up on her knees in a flash, and on the floor in another. She even beat me out of bed. I walked her to the door and said, "Now, close your eyes." When she did, I opened the door and walked her out to the banister on the second floor landing. "Okay, open them."

"Wow," she gasped. Her head moved to take in every inch of Christmas magic I had decorated the house with overnight. "Did you do all this?"

"Yep. I made it look exactly like it did when I was your age." That seemed to fascinate her. "Now, go scoot to the bathroom and get yourself a shower. I'll lay some fresh clothes out for you, and Nathan is fixing you some breakfast downstairs." She did exactly as she was told, and just in time, too. Laura and Mike were both emerging from my parent's old room. They were smiling and giggling, and Mike was still playing grab ass as he followed her. They both straightened up when they saw me, but both fought smirks as they passed on their way to the stairs.

"Have a nice nap?" I asked with my signature sarcasm.

"Yep, it hit the spot," Mike said with a stretch.

"I'll take care of the laundry today," Laura offered, which created a vision that turned my stomach.

In the entry way below, Rob and Martin came in through the front door. "All clear," Martin reported. Which was what I expected, but we needed to be careful.

"Thank you," I said from up top, overlooking the events below. They headed down the hallway for the kitchen, no doubt with a hearty appetite created by their morning patrol around the area. I went to the bedroom, to lay out Amy's clothes, and then went down to join the others. Everyone except the vampires was in the kitchen. I focused myself on the smell of the bacon Jack and Nathan were cooking to steady myself against the other fragrances. It helped, but didn't stop the retching completely.

"So, Ben Mallory today?" Jack asked.

"Yep. Ben Mallory. His family still owns their home on Coliseum Street. It is deep in the city, so we will need to be really careful."

"I'm coming, so you will all be safe," bragged Rob.

"I want to come," begged Amy. "Please."

"I'm sorry. Not this time. You will need to stay here with uncle Mike and Aunt Laura."

The spoon she was using to eat her cereal clanged down on the bowl. A few drops of milk splashed out on the table, which Nathan promptly wiped up while Amy sat there and pouted.

"I'm sorry, sweetie. Maybe another time. I promise you I will show you the city, but right now it is too dangerous. Just stay here, have fun with Clay, Mike and Laura. They will keep you safe, plus I think there is a box of decorations in the hall closet that still needs to be put up. You guys can all do that together." I made a note to myself to put a box of decorations in that closet before we left. I looked at Martin, who had a piece of bacon hanging from his mouth. "I need you to stay here, too."

"I get it. I will keep a watch."

"Good. I'm going to let you guys finish up, and we will leave in about an hour. Sound good?"

There was a chorus of nods around the table. Well, all except from the little girl who was still pouting over a bowl of some sugary cereal Nathan found in the pantry. A product of Jack doing a little shopping my way in the coven's pantry.

"Just curious. How well do you know Ben Mallory?" The question Jack asked was that one I had hoped no one would.

"We knew each other," I replied, and then felt a wave of guilt about what I wasn't telling them. They had to know. I grimaced and added, "Barely. We were in classes in the coven together. Our parents were friends."

There was a shared groan around the table. "So, if this guy is alive, not much of a chance he will remember you?"

"Not on a personal level, but" just as I started I thought of a single and indisputable point, "we all remember those strange families and odd house and events that happen around us don't we?"

A few heads nodded, which was enough for me to continue my point with the hope it would register and give everyone some confidence that today's outing might be the one. "Well, we were that family. We were the ones attacked and killed by vampires. He and I were classmates. I am sure that would make me memorable. Wouldn't you remember someone from your class if vampires murdered them?"

No one said no, but they didn't exactly say yes. I accepted the lack of protests as a positive even though my brain was telling me that the hopes he would remember me were hanging on by the frailest of threads. This was it. The last chance. After this, I didn't know. Maybe it was back to the idea that came to me during the night.

Just like before, the four of us gathered outside, and I opened a portal to a park that I remembered close to Coliseum Street. Close was relative, as Jack reminded me. To me, it was the closest and safest area for us to enter from, but Jack noted the sixteen blocks we would have to walk. I pointed out appearing in their living room might be a bad thing, though with how everything had gone so far, I am not sure it would change the outcome all that much.

What I didn't expect on the walk was feeling stings, and punches to my side as we passed various houses. The first time it happened, I grabbed my shoulder, wincing in pain. For me to feel pain was as equally as odd as me showing it outwardly, which caused a lot of concern among the others. I even knelt right there on the sidewalk for a moment just a few feet away from the black iron gate that led to the walkway up to another large mid-1800th century white house. It sported both the American and French flags, one on either side of the door. As the pain dissipated, I stood up, and Jack pointed out something in the brick column that held one side of the gate in place. Just barely visible, and diminishing quickly, like an ember giving off its last light, a rune glowed underneath the old dirt, mold, and vines that covered the structure. I didn't have to read it to know this wasn't one that was kind to vampires.

"We might be in the right neighborhood," remarked Jack.

I advised Rob to walk closer to the road, and I did the same. I didn't know if we would come across anything that was meant to deter a werewolf. I felt a few more, each time forcing myself to walk through them or around them once the first pinch or punch hit me. Two of them packed quite a wallop, and I knew an enormously powerful witch lived there.

After a painful and tiring trek through a briar patch of runes, we reached our destination just after eleven. The house was a two-story white house with large columns outside. It wasn't huge, by any standard, and rather modest looking from the outside, as many in this neighborhood appeared, but that didn't distract from their historical significance. Most had signs outside that denoted the year they were built. Almost like a badge of stature. They built the one we stood in front of in 1823 and it still looked every bit of that age except for the new roof and recent paint job. There was a cobblestone walk that lead through a black wrought-iron fence which showed a buildup from the multiple coats of paint which documented its battle against time and the elements. A simple set of stairs led up to the front porch. As was common in many of these long but skinny two-story houses, the front door was not in the center. It was off to the side, leading into the living area right in front of the stairs that would lead up to the second floor. Not that I had ever been in this house before. Ben Mallory's family never had us over. When his parents socialized with mine, they did it out at our farm.

I checked for signs of runes before Nathan and I made our approach. Jack came this time, something he insisted on no matter how hard I tried to talk him out of it. Using the brass knocker, I gave the door three good raps, and waited. I heard footsteps echoing inside. Someone was coming down the stairs. I felt them as they approached. Relaxed, but curious. I steadied myself and thought—this was going to go differently than before. It had to. There was no more beating around the bush. Something Jack and Martin convinced me of. This time, I just needed to let them know who we were and why we were here. All agreed I could leave out the details of what I was, partially.

The door handle turned, it opened, and my heart jumped with hope. A woman, probably in her eighties, stood there. She looked at us welcoming, but curious, as most probably would when unexpected guests arrived at their door.

"May I help you?" Her accent was thick and smooth. Reminding me a little more of Clay's than my mother's. This next bit would probably be a lot easier if our kind walked around with identification cards or something.

"I hope so." I held out my hand palm up, and created a simple snow globe, complete with a skater circling a pond, and snow falling all around him. "Can we come in? We have a question that you might be able to help us with."

She backed away from the door and let us in.

"A snow globe?" Jack whispered forward.

I didn't respond. It was better than the dancing flame we originally thought of. I felt that might appear to be threatening. There was nothing threatening about what I created, and I didn't break any rules.

"Have a seat," she said, surprisingly calm considering what had just transpired on her porch. "I need to tend to something in the kitchen." She walked back to the back of the house, and I looked around the room. It was setup exactly like I expected. We were in the main living area, or family room. Typical furniture with a television mounted over the fireplace. A design element the original architect hadn't considered in 1823. There were plenty of places to sit, but we all opted to stand.

From the kitchen I heard her say, "Now keep rolling and cutting them out. I will be back in a bit, and we can put them in." There were a few other voices that responded, young children. Three of them, from what I could tell. When she returned, she apologized. "Sorry about that. My grandchildren are working on some sugar cookies. So, what can I help you with?" She moved to a rocker in the corner of a room. "Sit. Sit," she urged, and waved her hands. We did. Jack and Nathan took the couch, and I took the leather easy chair that was directly across from her. I felt looking at her head on would be easier with what I had to say.

"Well, I am Larissa. This is Nathan and Jack. We are looking for Ben Mallory. He was a friend of my family's from some time ago, and I need to ask him a few questions to see if he can help us."

Her hand reached up and rubbed the back of her neck and looked around at each of us grimly. "Well, I'm sorry to tell you this. Ben died nineteen years ago, heart attack," her voice cracked.

"Oh." My disappointment escaped my lips before I could contain it. "I am so sorry to hear that."

"There isn't a day that goes by that I don't think of him, but I know he is still with me." She looked up toward the ceiling solemnly. This was a woman that missed him, and her heart still skipped a beat when thinking of him, but this was also a woman that had come to terms and moved on. The old saying is wrong. Time doesn't heal all wounds. It just helps you learn how to live with them, and Mrs. Mallory appeared to be a woman that had learned just that.

"You said he was friends with your family. What family is that? Perhaps I can help you. Ben and I were married for almost fifty years."

"Dubois, we had a farm outside of town. He knew them when he was very..."

She gasped and then covered her mouth with her hand. "How?" Then she waved her hands to dismiss that question. "I don't want to know. You are that family.. but that means..." she sounded flustered, and I watched as she put two and two together, and I felt she was about to come up with four, which I didn't know how she would react to. "... They found the daughter alive! She was your mother!"

Now that was a conclusion I hadn't expected her to reach, but it was one I could work with. A little white lie that was less alarming than the truth, and for once maybe our luck was turning.

"Yes, she was my mother." I looked around at Nathan and Jack to make sure they knew to go along with it. There didn't seem to be any question.

"That is so wonderful. What happened to your family was a tragedy. I was too young then to know anything beyond something bad happened, but Ben later told me he was in class with your mother, and then told me what happened."

"And you know who did it, right?"

"Oh yes, Jean St. Claire and his horde of demons," she spat disdainfully.

I sat on the edge of the chair and leaned forward, looking right into her eyes. "Then, Mrs. Mallory, maybe you can help us. I need to know some information about him. Like where he is."

"What for dear? You are safe. Your mother got away." Now it was Mrs. Mallory that was leaning forward.

"Not quite. He has people chasing us. He has my whole life. I need to stop him."

"Oh." She collapsed backwards in the chair, causing it to rock a little. Her stare left me and went to an empty spot in the room. "I can't believe, after all these years... his ego. It has to be."

I was sure that was part of it, maybe a small part, but I damn sure knew it wasn't the real reason he was after me, and I couldn't tell her what was. Not without telling her my other secret, and I finally had someone talking with me. This was no time to screw it up with the terrifying truth.

"Do you know how to use spells to alter your appearance? If not, I can teach you one."

"Yes, I do," I answered, sitting there looking as human as anyone, thanks to one I had mastered quite well by now.

"Then that is what you need to do. Hide yourself, and he will lose track of you. That is the best advice I can give you." Her eyes left the empty spot and rejoined mine. There was a concerned wrinkle on her brow. "But you don't intend to do that. You are going to try to stop him." Then she looked at the others. "You all are?"

There was dead silence in the room as she waited for our reply, but the upturned frown told me she already knew the answer before I uttered, "Yes."

"Scratch that idea right out of your heads. You can't. He is too powerful and there are too many of them. You best just hide."

"I can't do that. We have been hiding, and he still finds me, and we have others here to help. Do you know where we can find him?"

"No, and it's a good thing, too. That would be your death. If he has been after you like you say, just you being in this city is dangerous. He will find you, and you won't stand a chance," she warned harshly.

I knew that was a fact, which was why each of our little trips out and about were in the early morning hours, limiting those possibilities. Though, running into him on the street might not be a bad thing. He would be alone, or somewhat alone. That would be better than walking right into the middle of his world and trying to take him. Of course, that didn't help me find Mrs. Norton. "I really need to know," I countered.

"You don't and I'm sorry, even if I knew I probably wouldn't tell you. It's for your own good. This may seem noble or something," she said, addressing the others, "but you don't know what he is. He is not to be messed with. That is one thing I am certain of."

"What do you know of him?" Nathan asked.

"He is pure evil. The devil, and no one, and I mean no one, crosses him. If they do, they don't survive." She looked back at me with an admonishing glare. "You, of all people, should know that. Your grandfather crossed him, and you saw what happened? All because of some curse he put on the area. One that we could have dealt with, but your father wanted to take a stand, from what I have heard."

"Wait. What curse?" I asked, and sprung to my feet with amazing speed. Jack urged me to sit back down, and I did.

"You don't know what caused the fight between your family and Jean?" she asked in disbelief.

I didn't. This was something my mother had never shared, just that my father and Jean had some run-ins, and with who my father was, he became a target. A casualty of the ongoing war that Master Thomas hinted at once before.

"Grandma, we are done cutting the cookies out," called a young girl from the kitchen.

"All right," Mrs. Mallory answered back. "Excuse me for just a second."

At this point, I didn't believe there were any more family secrets I wasn't aware of. I remembered everything, and my mother had told me so much more since.

Nothing about a curse ever came up. I had to wonder what other secrets there were, and that was more than slightly unnerving.

"What curse?" Jack asked, and I shrugged in response. It was all I could do.

"Why don't you three come back here? I need to watch the stove," Mrs. Mallory called from the kitchen, and we headed to the back and joined her around the simple breakfast nook in the corner. Through the windows I saw her three grandchildren, two boys no older than ten and a girl probably about Amy's age, playing on a swing set. "We have about fifteen minutes before they will come rushing in for a fresh cookie."

"Mrs. Mallory, what curse?" I asked, eager to know.

"The curse of the crescent moon. You never heard of it?"

I shook my head.

"Well then, it seems I know something about your family that you don't." She said with a wry smile, adding some levity to the serious topic that cast a dark shadow over our conversation. "Remember, I was very young, so this is just what Ben and others told me, but Jean had enlisted the help of several witch doctors and priests that specialized in voodoo to even things up. They would do his dirty work in the magic world, while his hordes attacked and picked off members of our community in the New Orleans area, creating a reign of terror that stretches far beyond this area, as it appears you are well aware of. They have done everything from casting curses to kill off entire crops of cane and other crops to even cursing whole families for generations to come. Anything he could do to make life difficult, unless you were on his side. If you were loyal to him, you were protected from that. The coven and many other native creoles fought back, with counter spells and hexes. Undoing what they could. Sometimes it worked. Sometimes it didn't. Back in 1937, or was it 8, he cast a spell causing a great flood during every crescent moon. Oh, the floods were horrible. I remember a few of them. Water out of both the Mississippi River and Lake Pontchartrain, up over the levies, and through all the streets. Washing away homes and entire farms. It was deep, well over my head, I reckon. We stood on that very porch outside, watching it go by. By the next morning, it was over, and the water was gone. For the next week, people walked around carrying beads, idols, and all sorts of other voodoo related relics telling us we were worshiping the wrong god. That we needed to give ourselves over to the immortal one. Most dismissed them as crazy old coots, but others, like my parents, knew exactly what they meant. It was Jean reminding everyone whose city this was. Your father finally figured out how to undo it, and also figured out who cast the curse and brought them to justice before the council. That angered Jean to no end. The counter spell your father cast also blocked the floods, stopping Jean from just having anyone recast, but that didn't stop him from casting a new one. Every waxing and waning crescent moon, everything that is dark in this place, comes out. Vampires, demons, beasts from the underworld. Most of the disappearances that happen around here occur during those two phases. What I was told, your father was about to spoil another of Jean's curses when the attack happened. Since then, many have tried, but none have been able to counter it. In fact," she got up from the table and walked over to a calendar hanging on a single nail in the old wooden door of her pantry. "The waning crescent is in just four days."

"So that is why he came after us?" I asked myself.

"Yes dear. One of many reasons I surmise. Your family was pretty important and powerful back then. They offered both of your grandparents spots on the council, from what I heard. Your father never backed down from doing what was right. I imagine that put him on a collision course with Jean." She reached over the table and placed her hand on mine. "I'm sorry dear. I wish I could be more help. Most of that happened before I was old enough to remember anything. Much of it was what I heard from others, but I trust what they said, and you know what they say about the oral history of its people. It's important to hand down. I hope hearing that helps you understand more about your relatives and why it is too dangerous for you to go against Jean. Trust me, it would be best to just disappear. You have that power."

"Thank you, but I need to know where he is."

She stood up from the table in a huff. "Even if I knew, I wouldn't tell you. That would be like sending you to your death, and you seem like nice kids. I can't do that. Now please, give up on this."

"Would anyone else at the coven know where he is?" Jack asked assertively.

"Oh, I am sure someone there would, but I wouldn't know who to send you to talk to. I haven't associated with anyone there in almost forty years." She sat back down at the table.

"You aren't part of the coven?" I asked.

"Not presently." She looked out the window at her grandkids running around the backyard. "My daughter was born human, nothing at all. At that moment, Ben and I swore off magic and lived a human life." She turned back to us, stern. "It was a good life. Don't think we were turning our back on who we were. It wasn't like that. Living the dual life was just too much, and we needed to be parents more than we needed to be witches. I hope that makes sense."

"It does," I agreed honestly. It made sense, as did her concern, that we might think she was turning her back on being a witch. I had the same fear when I focused so much on magic. Was I turning my back on my other self? I didn't think so, but that didn't mean I wasn't concerned what the others would think.

"Now, I really need to stress. Gather your things and get out of town as soon as you can, never look back, and stay away from Jean. Hide. That is your only way to survive. I am not sure what you have been through, and maybe you have battled a few vampires in the past or something, but whatever it was, they weren't like Jean." She reached over again and grabbed my hand. "Promise me?" she pleaded.

I looked around at Nathan and Jack, searching for some guidance. They appeared about as lost as I was. She didn't have the information we needed, and again was one of many people telling us to go the other way. Maybe they were all right, and we were stupid to be thinking this. God knows I have the tendency to be a little impulsive. I always knew there was going to be a time where I bit off more than I could chew. Was this that time?

"Larissa, promise me?"

"Yes, ma'am. We will."

13

"You lied right to her face," Jack complained as we walked up the steps to my porch.

"Not exactly. One day, we will gather our stuff up and leave, never looking back. Just not right now. Not yet!"

Martin and Clay were in the parlor as we passed, and both joined in the line that went straight into the kitchen.

"So, what did we find out?" Martin asked.

"Nothing. Not a thing." Jack complained with a quick slap of the counter. "Ben Mallory died years ago, and his wife isn't even a practicing witch. She knew nothing about Jean St. Claire other than to be terrified of him. Oh, and there is some curse that brings everything evil in this city out during the crescent moon, which the next one was in what..." He searched for the answer, but Nathan never gave him a chance to come up with it on his own.

"Four days."

I elbowed Nathan from participating in what I felt was a moment of hysteria. As long as no one asked now what, I would be fine.

"Now what?" Laura's question from the doorway, where she stood with Amy, caused me to cringe. I need a little more time before someone asked me that. I had survived the walk back without it coming up, and really just needed maybe another twenty minutes or more to talk to my mother about any other ideas she had.

Now I was even wondering if Nathan had been on to something. Were there vampires in the area that might have been a little less than loyal to Jean? Maybe even friendly to witches? That would be the easiest. The other option in my mind is one I had dismissed many times before. I was running out of options, and at that moment, I was considering a change of plans.

The thought tore me to shreds. It pulled at every emotion and threatened to remove any semblance of stability, both inside and out. But was there any other way? No, there wasn't. I had to remove the variable that kept this cycle going. I could send them all back to the coven. Mrs. Saxon couldn't really stop me from doing that, and I knew she would let them stay. Then I would make myself known and let him come to me. Jean would take me back to wherever he lives or stays. Probably that dark, stale dungeon with the mold covered stone walls that I have seen so many times in his unwelcomed visits. Then I would flash open a portal and throw Marie Norton through it. She would be safe, objective two. The third objective, Jean's demise, would no longer be necessary. Everyone would be safe, and my third act would ensure that. There were very few ways to kill a vampire. There were the physical ways, removing of the head and a stake through the heart. Neither of those I felt I would have the opportunity to do, not to him. Even if I could lay a hand on Jean, I would be dead in an instant. Which wasn't the worst outcome. My capture would be the worst, so I had to keep that from happening. Luckily for me, I knew half a dozen or more magic or metaphysical based ways to create life, and how to take it from the universe. This seemed to be the only way, and as I realized it, I had to lean back against the stove to steady myself. I knocked two pans to the floor as I did so, and Nathan reached over and caught me before I slid off it and to the floor.

"Larissa, are you okay?" he asked, concerned, laying me down on the floor. "You..." He looked back at Mike and Laura. "Can vampires faint?"

"No," replied Laura.

"I'm fine." I stood up, shaking off his help. "Just something I was thinking of got to me."

"What?" Nathan asked. His arm clamped around my waist. It was a forceful grip, reminding me of every moment he had supported me from the first moment we met, even though I was unconscious then. And there it was. The reason I couldn't go through it. The other was running across the kitchen, sliding the last few feet, clamping herself to my other side.

"Nothing to worry about." I lied. I was sure this thought would come back. Would I ever go through with it? I was running out of options.

A knock on the door startled everyone into dead silence. I motioned for Laura to come in from the doorway quickly to avoid from being seen from the front door. Then debated going to check the door or ignoring it. No one knew we were here. Well, that wasn't true. Three families knew we were here.

"Who is it?" Rob asked.

"How the hell would we know? We are all in here," Martin said with a slap against his brother's head.

"Shhh," I shushed them as I peeled Nathan's arm off of me, and moved Amy around to his care, before I walked across the kitchen to the door. The main front door was closed, and the leaded glass distorted the view. What I could tell is there was a single person on the other side, and even more calming, they weren't a vampire. Their pulse gave that away. There was a familiar beat to it, which eased the tension I felt. With my hand on the door now, I only hesitated a second before turning it and pulling the door open.

"There is a rumor down in the coven that someone with the last name of Dubois is going around asking about the whereabouts of Jean St. Claire," he said as he burst through the opening. "That isn't exactly real smart in these parts."

I exploded forward and hugged Master Thomas. Multiple heads poked out of the kitchen entry and looked on with concern. The first to emerge from the door was Jack, who walked out cautiously. Mr. Helms would be proud, but this was no enemy. I let go of Master Thomas, but not before I spun him around to face our crowd.

"Jack, this is..."

"You don't need to tell me who he is," interrupted Jack. His cautious stance disappeared in an instant and he rushed forward to take the hand of our visitor. "Master Thomas, it is an honor to meet you, sir. I have heard so much about you."

Master Thomas looked at me, and I knew what his concern was. His involvement in my little sessions was kind of a secret, since what he was doing was slightly against the rules, depending on how you looked at it. "Not from me," I said, to calm his concerns. "I will explain later." I wasn't too sure how he would feel about all the idol worship that occurred up on the witch's floor, Gwen's book, and not to mention her little crush.

"Jack, it's just Benjamin. Larissa won't call me that, but I insist."

"Yes sir, Master Thomas," replied Jack. Master Thomas smirked, and I held back a laugh. The man was a legend in our world. There was no way any of us would feel comfortable calling him by his first name.

"Come to the kitchen. Let me introduce you to the others."

I led him back and one by one, the heads left the doorway and returned to where they were sitting before I left. I walked in and instead of the grand introduction that someone of such esteem deserved, I said, "Relax, everyone. He's a friend. He's on our side." He walked to the center of the room and bowed before I could continue and complete the introduction. "This is Master Benjamin Thomas. My defender in the great inquisition and a member of the Council of Mages."

I went around the room, giving an introduction of everyone, which included what they were, so he was aware. It felt strange doing that. They were just *who* they were to me, not *what* they were, but I felt it was a necessary step. He was here to help, I hoped, and he would need to know everything. When the introductions hit Nathan, the handshake between the two men lasted longer than the others. Almost like a moment of respect. Maybe he felt any man that could put up with me was worthy of a high level of respect, but his next comment dismissed that thought of fancy.

"Mr. Saxon. It's an honor. Your mother is one of the finest members of our community, and I have heard wonderful things about you from both her and Larissa here."

"Likewise, sir. My mother talks of you often, and Larissa never stops." His little snipe prompted some looks from around the room, and I made a note to ensure he paid for that in some not-so-subtle way later.

"Well then," he slapped his hands together. "How is your little search going?" He looked around the room and each of the expressions that were welcoming just moments again became glum. "That bad, huh?"

"I'm afraid so. We have learned a bit, but not about what we really need to know." I reported.

"Well, perhaps you are asking the wrong question. What are you in search of?" He looked around the room wide-eyed and cheery, like a game show host that had just asked the grand prize question.

"Where we can find Jean and how many..."

"Wrong," he interrupted with another slap of his hands. "That is the problem. You are asking a question that will get you killed. Either by witches that want nothing to do with anyone that might bring the attention of Jean's coven their way, or by his coven. Why are you here? Why do you want that information?"

"To stop Jean St. Claire," answered Martin.

"A noble cause, but again, wrong. There is a deeper why." This time, he looked right at me. "There is always a deeper why to everything."

"Perhaps we should talk in the library, there is a lot I need to bring you up to speed on," I led him out of the kitchen and then called back, "Nathan, Clay, why don't you two join us too." Clay was as much a part of this as I was, and Nathan, I just wanted for moral support.

Over the next half hour, Clay and I told Master Thomas about the attack on Clay, the planting of him in our coven, and Jean using him as a door to get to me. Nothing we told him surprised him. He cautioned us that revenge was a dangerous why, and one that never ended well. I brought up my safety, and the safety of anyone that I had a future with, which he dismissed with a quick, "you have the tools to protect them, you know that." I felt I was about to get more advice to just disappear into the world and try to move on with things, but then I told him about my why, or my more personal why.

"Oh, I see," he looked down at the floor, deep in thought. "Your why is to save the woman that saved you. Now that I can completely understand, but again, you aren't asking the right question. You don't want to know where Jean is so you can kill him. You want to know how you can help Mrs. Marie Norton escape, and Larissa, there are many ways to help her."

"But we want to kill him too," Clay growled, causing a jerk by Master Thomas.

"Son, I completely understand the sentiment... I do... really, but setting a goal that extreme will only end in either disappointment or death, when there are so many other ways to achieve what you want. Rescuing Mrs. Norton is possible. Protecting yourself from Jean and his coven forever is absolutely possible. All of which can happen without taking such an extreme risk."

"What about protecting others from his reign of terror? What about being an example and standing up for what is right? What about restoring witches to what they were, undoing the curse of the crescent moon and stopping all of his future curses?"

"What do you know of that curse?" he asked, stunned.

"A great deal," I replied.

Master Thomas looked nervously at Clay, and I picked up on his meaning. This was going to be a witch's only conference. "Clay, can you leave us?" Clay left without protest. Master Thomas then gave Nathan the same look, but I dismissed the concern. "He is okay. He was there when I was told about it."

"So, your mother told you about it." Master Thomas assumed, but I shook my head to correct that bad assumption.

"Mrs. Mallory. Ben Mallory's wife. He was a friend of mine back then. She told me all about the curses Jean placed and how my father had countered some of them and was trying to counter the curse of the crescent moon when Jean had Reginald and the others attack us." Chances are that my father was going to counter it with a spell that night. When we got home, I looked it up via Mike's phone. The day of my death was a waning crescent moon. "Why hasn't the coven removed it yet?"

"That's not an easy question to answer, Larissa."

"Try me," I shot back, wanting a direct answer.

"Look, this is difficult stuff. It is well beyond the reach of most witches, and those that can..."

"Are scared?" I abruptly asked, interrupting him. The look on his face was one of shock, and I realized I had never treated Master Thomas so disrespectfully before. My frustration was boiling over, and I let it out on the one ally I had. Not the smartest move for me, and my future. Though at the moment, I don't believe I was thinking more than a few seconds ahead.

"To be just as abrupt, yes."

Hearing him admit that defused the ticking time bomb, and a chorus of all the warnings I had heard over the last three days played in my head like a lecturing round, with a new realization that perhaps they were right.

"Look Larissa," he said and turned toward me, placing a hand on mine, which were crossed over my knee. "I get it. You want to help Marie? You want to kill Jean for what he has done to you, and for what he will most likely continue to do. If only we lived in a world so black and white. Things are more complicated than that."

"If you are going to tell me about some balance in the universe that needs him, I don't want to hear it." I said calmly, no vinegar, suppressing what I really felt.

"I am not saying that at all, but there are reactions for every action, so we have managed the situation. We counter the effects of his curses when they happen, to minimize the impact. Some of them have been good for the lore of this place, helping the city when you think about it. Each risk or problem they pose is reviewed and handled. The result may not always be the best, but more often than not, it is something that is acceptable." His face twisted, like he had bitten into a bitter fruit. "I don't even like saying that. Do I wish we could just wipe him out and every one of his followers? Absolutely. Would there be hell to pay if we did? Absolutely. Another vampire coven or others would come looking for revenge, not because it was Jean, but because it was one of their own. Just as we would if they killed one of ours. Remember that hidden war I mentioned? This is part of it, and it is very real."

My head dipped, and I pulled my hands from his so I could cover my eyes. I didn't want him to see the tears that were now rolling down my face. This wasn't a single tear hanging in the corner of my eye that I could sniff back. This was a flood, all caused by the witch I looked up to most, telling me there really wasn't anything we could, or worse yet, should do, about Jean St. Claire and his coven here. Dooming Marie Norton to an eternity of pain and torture, and me to a life of always being on the run.

"Look, I'm not saying we can't do anything. There are ways. They will take time, and it won't be as simple as just rushing in and attacking, or even sneaking in. We have to be more diplomatic about it. But first, I need to show you something. There is much you need to learn before you are ready. Leonard and I were just scratching the surface." Master Thomas stood up and walked out into the hall, where he looked at the old grandfather clock that still worked. It was the one thing in this place I didn't have to *help* to make things livable. "You have a couple of hours yet. I want you, Nathan, and anyone else you want to bring with you to get dressed. Tonight is the winter solstice ball, and you are all going to be my guests. I assume you remember the attire."

Remember the attire? I didn't remember the ball. "The winter solstice ball? I'm afraid I don't remember that. I remember the Holiday Gala, but not a Winter Solstice Ball."

"It's one and the same. Not even our coven can escape the impacts of political correctness, and besides, being who we are, Winter Solstice sounds more magical. You can handle the attire, right?"

"Um, yea," I answered, and before Nathan knew what hit him, he was in a tuxedo with a red bow tie and red cummerbund. There was no way I was wearing a red velvet dress to this like I used to, but thanks to Mrs. Saxon's party, and having my memories back, I had some ideas of what to wear. Now the only question was, who else was coming with me?

"Good. I will pick you guys up at eight." A hint of Master Thomas's normally jovial personality made an appearance. With a smile and a point as he headed out the door, he informed me, "I have such things to show you, Miss Dubois. Such sights to show you."

14

After much discussion, Jack and I helped everyone with the proper attire. If either of us knew a spell to enchant the rooms of my home to behave like those in the coven, it would have been a lot easier. It took a while for Laura and Amy to decide on something. Well, Amy didn't really decide. I kind of talked her into a red velvet dress, much like she wore to the Christmas Tree decorating party. She didn't put up much of a fight after I put the string of pearls around her neck. Magic did not create these. They were one hundred percent real, and I had heard the story of how my father got ahold of them for my mother many, many times. A poker game at the coven with another witch from Singapore. Seemed he wasn't particularly good and barely left the game with the clothes on his back. I guess he didn't know that poker was the national pastime down here.

My journey to retrieve the pearls should have been easier than what my father went through to acquire them. They were in the jewelry box in my mother's room, right where I watched her put them back after the last time she took them off. Ironically, that was the last Holiday Gala we went to. She always told me one day they would be mine. All I needed to do was walk in, lift the top off the small oak box, and remove them. Of course, the door was an enormous obstacle, and after many attempts, Laura agreed to retrieve them.

The biggest challenge of the night was getting the guys ready. I had thought this would be simple: black tux, bowtie, and cummerbund. Whether it was the style, color of the bowtie, the discussion around whether to even wear a bowtie because they saw someone once in a movie like that, to if they needed a vest, everyone had an opinion and wanted to try out the look. It was exhausting. Jack and I must have changed each of them more than a few dozen times, trying varying options until we grew tired of it and Laura threatened to leave them all home. I was at the point where that didn't sound like a half bad idea.

Once everyone settled on what to wear, I still needed to help a few with how they looked. We all agreed it was safe for Mike, Laura, and Clay to come. The recent feeding had taken care of any primal urges they may feel in such mixed company, and to be honest, I trusted them, which I did, whole-heartedly. If I didn't, I wouldn't have left Amy with them while we went out looking for information. Mike wasn't all that happy about this, at least until he saw what I did for Laura. He almost fell to his knees at first sight of her. She wept at her own reflection in the mirror.

When it was Clay's turn, he was more than eager. "Are you ready?" I asked.

"Go for it," he replied while standing in front of a mirror, waiting.

I raised my hand and traced down his body. The world around him glittered with silver sparks that burned out before they hit the floor. His hand reached up and rubbed his own face at first. Almost probing to make sure what he saw was real. Then a huge grin appeared. "My other face is still foreign to me. This is how I still see myself." He latched on with the biggest hug I had ever received. "Thank you," he whispered into my ear.

By eight, we were out on the porch waiting for Master Thomas, who was, of course, fashionably late. Why wouldn't he be?

"I hope he has a big car," Rob joked, just as a big disk appeared and spun in front of us. It opened with a flash and Master Thomas stepped out.

"Everyone ready?" he said, looking us over.

"We are," I responded on behalf of everyone.

"Oh good. I was hoping you would come," Master Thomas said and shook both Mike's and Clay's hands, and then gave Laura a quick gentlemanly kiss on the cheek. If only Gwen was here to see that. She would die. She would die just knowing we were about to head to the Solstice Ball with him.

He walked back toward the disk, but stopped next to me and leaned in, and I prepared myself for my kiss on the cheek. Now I really wished Gwen was here. Too bad no one had a camera. He whispered into my ear, "Nice work. I'm impressed." There was no kiss on the cheek after he said it. Much to my disappointment. Laura stuck her tongue out at me and I could only smile.

"Shall we," he announced and motioned for the disk that was still open.

I looped my arm through Nathan's. Laura did the same with Mike. Rob tried to get Amy to take his arm, but she looked up at him with a defiant look shook her head before marching right up and taking my hand. There were snickers and ribbing behind us as the three of us stepped forward and followed Master Thomas through the portal.

There was no entering at a safe spot and walking to our destination here. This portal took us right to the front door of the Iberville Ballroom in the Hotel Monteleone. The very same place they held this event when I was a child, and honestly, it didn't look much different. A magical shower of lights, music, and decorations that screamed the holidays. They can call this whatever they want. To me, it's still the Holiday Gala.

I bent down and whispered to Amy, "Look at the trees." She already was with the wide-eyed wonderment any child might have if they walked into a room lined in Christmas trees. Each decorated in a different theme. I knelt down as low as my tight black dress allowed. This may have looked good on me in the mirror, but I hadn't really thought about how moving or even dancing would work. It was a good thing I could alter it on the fly, and not a soul in here would care. They were all just like me, well, me and Jack. "Amy, each tree is decorated by a different family in the coven. When I was your age, we had one we would decorate every year."

"You did?"

"Yep, we sure did. My mother and I would spend a few days on it before we sent it here."

"What did it look like?"

"Well," I said while I looked around the room for any that might have an abundance of red ribbons spiraled around it with loads of colorful balls on it. These all had modern LEDs and lights that chased or twinkled, and none had ribbons spiraled around it. "I don't see any that look like it, but it had lots of ribbons around it and large, colorful balls." Then I remembered. "I think we have a picture of one in the photo albums at home. I could show you later if you want."

The huge smile on her face was a yes. Sitting there with Amy looking through some of those old albums might not be a bad way to unwind later, and then a true feeling of nostalgia hit me when I remembered doing the same with my mother. I stood up and quickly turned from Nathan. My hands worked fast to wipe away the tears that had started. I didn't have any concerns about my makeup running, but I didn't want to be seen.

"What's wrong?" he asked, looking over my shoulder. He gently placed his hand on the small of my back.

"Nothing," I replied tersely.

"Something is," he pressed. His mouth was now closer to my ear. The warmth of his breath on my neck, stirring a desire for more touch from him.

I spun around, maybe too quick for present company, and wrapped both arms around his neck. "Nothing is. It's perfect." I kissed his cheek, and then kissed him on the lips.

The little girl giggled and then ooo-ed.

"Get a room, lovebirds," remarked Rob as he and Martin walked past on their way to the food table.

Mike laughed as he escorted Laura to the dance floor, where they appeared to fit right in. Oh, how those other couples would react if they knew there were two vampires dancing with them. That was proof we could live together in harmony. Clay and Jack were talking with Master Thomas behind us, right until he dismissed himself and grabbed Nathan and me.

"Come with me. I have someone I want you to meet."

We followed, with Amy in tow. I wasn't sure what this was all about, so as we passed the dance floor, I motioned for Mike to take Amy. She readily went to him and Laura, and was all smiles when the three started dancing.

Jack joined the feast with Martin and Rob. I sure hoped he wasn't going to try to keep up with those two. If he did, he would pay for it later. Those two can put it away with their animalistic metabolism.

We approached a group of people standing, not sitting, around the tables that surrounded the dance floor. Many people greeted Master Thomas as he passed them. Some with a dignified nod of the head. Others with a friendly handshake and greeting of, "Evening Master Thomas," or "Good Evening, Ben." They didn't regard us with anything more than a curious glance as we passed following the esteemed council member. That was until he pushed through the crowd to one table where an elderly woman was sitting, with her back to us. She was watching the jazz band perform up on stage. The selections for the night seemed to be a staple of old classics from the thirties and forties. Master Thomas walked around her chair and stopped in front of her. When Nathan and I joined him, the woman stood up and grabbed me by the shoulders.

"Oh, my word!," she exclaimed. "It can't be. It can't be." She looked at Master Thomas with question marks in her eyes.

"It is," he said.

"It's impossible" The brown eyes of the woman who still had hints of freckles on her skin looked back at me. It was then that I noticed the familiar smile. Her raven hair had become a mane of white, but there was no denying it. It was her. "Larissa? Is this really Larissa Dubois? In the flesh?"

A feeling welling up inside kept me from being able to form words to answer her.

"This isn't a trick, is it?" She asked Master Thomas. "It's not nice to play tricks on an old woman."

"Gerty, it's me," I finally managed to say.

She covered her mouth and fell back to her chair in shock.

I knelt down quickly and grabbed both of her hands. "It's really me."

"But how?"

I tilted my head to the side and cautiously said, "Think about it."

It didn't take long. The look of shock mixed with fear told me she had done the math correctly.

"Relax, I'm fine."

I felt her hands try to jerk out of mine, but it was only a quick movement, then she gripped mine tighter. "Are you really?"

"I am," I said, smiling behind the tears of joy that were running down my face from sitting here face to face with my old friend Gertrude Bergeron.

"I told my grandson he must have heard wrong when he said someone with your name came around asking about me," she said. Her voice was still quivering from the shock, but she was calming down. There was no shake in her hands. They were clamps of granite that had a firm hold on my own.

"That was us. I came to find you to see if you could help me."

"You scared the crap out of him. That is what you did." She gripped me again, harder. Her fingers rubbing my hands. "Are you sure you are fine?"

"Don't I look fine?" I asked, trying to reassure her. I believed I looked radiant if I said so myself.

"But you are," she leaned down close, "a vampire."

"I am, but I am fine. Don't I seem fine?"

When she sat back, she laughed, amused at something. What, I wasn't sure, but it was good to see her laughing, and not scared. She pulled a hand away from my grip and covered her mouth as she laughed. It muffled the joyous sound. She laughed hard for several seconds before she pulled herself together enough to talk. "I'm sorry. It just hit me. I am here wondering if you are okay, and worried about what you have become, and yet I am the one who is so old that I am practically falling about, and you, you look just like I remembered you when you were sixteen. Now I wonder who really is the cursed creature."

Now I saw the humor in all this, and I couldn't resist a little chuckle myself. Even Nathan saw it and laughed a little, along with Master Thomas. Gerty reached over and pulled out the seat next to her and spun it around, and even knowing what I was, she didn't hesitate to pat the cushion and offer, "Have a seat, let's catch up."

For the next hour, we did just that. We talked about my life, which, while it was as equally as long as hers, it seemed so much shorter. It was almost as if time stood still or slowed down. In the time since I last saw her, she had married Tom Marsh, a name I somewhat remembered, but I couldn't place him from before. They had two children and five grandchildren. I met her grandson the other day. In the same length of time, I had done little besides just passing the time. The thought made me dizzy to ponder.

What she was most interested in about my life, besides the natural curiosity about being a vampire, was Nathan. She told me she was rather impressed that I could pull such a hottie. A phrase that seemed strange coming from someone who looked to be old enough to be my grandmother, even older than Mrs. Tenderschott.

Everything was light and bubbly until I finally touched on the topic I had avoided during our catching up. The why I was here elicited the same reaction from her as it had everyone I spoke to, but she didn't flat out refuse to help me. She was about to explain how she was going to when Amy rushed over and asked me to dance with her. I asked Amy if I could get the next dance, but Gerty said, "Larissa, I will be here. Go dance with the girl. She really wants to. There is a time for dance, and there is a time for serious discussions. Tonight, is about dancing. Go." Her hand reached over and pushed my shoulder to urge me up. For someone of her age, she had a firm touch, and I felt something else forcing me up and out of the chair. She would not take no for an answer, and that was fine.

Amy grabbed my hand and yanked me to the dance floor with her. The song was a jumping jive, and so was our dance. Amy hopped all around, holding on to both of my hands, and I did the same. The girl was a ball of energy that had out lasted my poor boyfriend, who now was watching from a chair on the side sipping on a soft drink with Rob and Martin. I watched as Master Thomas and Gertrude joined them at the table. My attention stayed locked on them when I saw Gertrude engage Nathan in a conversation. The music was just loud enough to block my attempts to hear what they said, but that didn't make me at all uneasy. Behind them was Jack, Rob, Martin, Clay, and Master Thomas in some sort of lively and very friendly conversation, and right beside Amy and me, Laura and Mike were cutting a rug with the best of them, showing me a side of them I had never seen before. Seeing all that warmed me. The heaviness of our cause was gone for one night. The worry, concern, and feeing of absolute failure were gone. We were all enjoying ourselves. And, as I looked down at Amy, hopping around like a possessed rabbit, was the happiest I have ever seen her. The warmth lasted but a second before I felt ashamed. How could I enjoy a moment like this, while Marie Norton was suffering?

I did my best to hide that from the others and danced right along with Amy. Even I struggled to keep up with her pace. When the music slowed, Nathan joined us out on the floor. He scooped up Amy in his arms before she even knew he was there, and the three of us were one, dancing under the sparkling chandeliers above.

"Why don't we take her?" Laura offered, reaching for Amy. "Amy, let's let Nathan and Larissa have one dance alone." She didn't fight and went right to Laura, who looked more than happy to hold her while they danced with Mike.

Jack had taken to the dance floor with Gertrude for this song. I recognized it. It was one Thomas and Marie Norton had danced to on more than one occasion in our living room. There was no live band then, but the original record of Glen Miller's band playing Moonlight Sonata. I felt weepiness coming on and pulled Nathan even closer for this dance. I needed to feel his warmth. I needed him to help me through this moment, help bring me some of the happiness they were all feeling, and it was partially working too, right until the band abruptly stopped, as did all the dancing.

The attention of everyone shifted to the main entrance that was behind me, and the normal vibrations of the world tightened, almost squeezing together. Nathan's arms did the same, and I felt him shudder. When I turned, I noticed Master Thomas was up on his feet, holding up a hand toward the door. Then I saw what the interruption was. Standing there in the entrance, in a tuxedo with a top hat and white cane, was him. Jean St. Claire, flanked by five formally dressed vampires. Pale skin and dark hair slicked back, like the boy band from hell. A chill ran down my spine at the sight. I had seen Jean before, in my head, but this was real. He was here in the same room with me. Impulses to run and attack fought with each other, causing me to freeze.

"Jean, we have no quarrel tonight," exclaimed Master Thomas. "Now leave peacefully."

"Benjamin, Benjamin, Benjamin. I am not here to quarrel, but I will say my feelings are a little hurt. It seems my invitation to this soiree must have been lost in the mail yet again. No matter, I heard about it and cleared my calendar so I could attend."

My body had decided how it was going to respond to Jean and tensed up. Nathan tightened in response, and whispered in my ear, "Don't." I could have slipped his grip easily, but he was right. This was not the time. As far as I knew, he didn't even know I was here. His entrance was an eerie moment of déjà vu. He and several members of his coven had crashed the last one of these I attended as well, in a similar fashion.

"Jean, do we really need to do this dance again? You know you are not invited. Now please leave." Master Thomas' attempt at de-escalation had failed. Jean walked forward, with his escorts following him step for step.

"But this is such a joyous occasion." He approached the buffet table and picked up several pieces of food with his gloved hand, regarding them in disgust before letting them fall to the floor. "Perhaps we shall stay and enjoy the atmosphere, the music. Start the band back up."

Far to my side, over by the tables, I saw a hint of movement, and before the seething Clay could take a step forward, I had him blocked, and forced back in his seat. This did not go unnoticed by anyone in the room. Witches or Vampires. Jean walked halfway across the room toward Clay, studying him the whole time, while I held Clay down to the chair with everything I had. He was strong and threatened to break free. I felt Jack pitch in, relieving some of the strain. Then I felt someone else step in. Master Thomas locked him down. Each of us using one of the most basic of skills to tie his butt down to the chair.

"It's you," Jean said, and then cackled. "The boy." An evil and devious smile crept across his face when his thoughts made the next logical leap. His icy stare scanned the tables and then the dance floor. When it found me, we locked on to each other, and he pointed with his white cane. "Larissa, there you are, my child. So good of you to come home to me." He tilted his head back and forth, studying me. "And you look so alive."

As he walked toward us, Nathan's grip on my arms turned into a death grip, and if I were human, it would undoubtedly leave finger sized bruises on my arm. He used his cane to politely ask those in his way to move as he strode across the dance floor. What his intention was, I wasn't sure. But each step closer he came, moved me closer to my boiling point. "You may have forgotten my invitation, but I see you knew what was on the top of my Christmas list."

Mike handed Amy to Laura, and he balled up his fist. I shook my head and prayed to God he listened to me. He stayed still, even when Jean regarded him with a "Tsk. Tsk," as he passed. Once he reached me, he was giddy, almost salivating. His eyes scanning me up and down, only pausing for a few seconds at the blood charm around my neck before continuing. "Larissa," he sneered. "Come with us now. We have such plans to discuss."

"She isn't going anywhere, Jean," barked Master Thomas.

"You can't really stop me. You know that," he replied without diverting his focus from me. "Plus, you need to ask yourself, is she really worth making a bloody mess of your party? We don't want that, now do we?"

"There will be none of that, Jean. Not tonight," said another man from off to my right. Other witches were now stepping forward. Jean rolled his neck and let out a groan.

"You really don't think you can stop me." He reached forward toward me, a single finger pointed inches from my chin, but I held steady. "Larissa, save them the trouble and come with me. It's how tonight is going to end, anyway; the only question is how."

Mike reached for Jean, and one of his entourage grabbed Mike from behind. Mike flipped him over and sent him crashing into the wall. Jean took notice and spun around. A single swipe of his cane threw Mike crashing into the tables and sent Laura sliding across the floor. Amy hit the ground and screamed. She sat there and cried out. Jean looked down at her, and then back up at me.

I didn't give him a chance to look back at her again. She was too pure for his gaze. I shrugged Nathan's grip away and took one step forward and brought my hands forward right into Jean's chest. As they hit him, I unleashed the largest fireball I could muster, not worrying too much about control at this moment. It came out as a column of blue fire about a foot in diameter blasting Jean all the way to the door he entered through. I didn't stop there. I kept it going, sending him tumbling outside out to the street, and then ratcheted up the intensity until it was a single continuous bolt of lightning. Overhead, clouds gathered, and thunder rumbled in what was originally a clear night. In my mind, I quickly drew the symbol of the wand, a simple line, to draw down the power of the moon. The vibrations of the world tightened around me and became one. Jean continued to tumble out to the street, and just for good measure I cast a Besom at him. At that moment, the world around him turned purple, and I saw flashes here and there. Both close and in the distance. Then that dissipated from view, leaving Jean smoldering on the ground, being helped to his feet by his followers.

"Try me!" I exclaimed in their direction, with blue orbs glowing in each hand, ready for them. They didn't. They gathered Jean up and disappeared into the shadows. I thought about giving chase but thought better of it, not knowing what I would run into and knowing good and well I had bruised his pride tonight. Something I was sure he wouldn't forget the next time we met.

I ran back in to check on Amy. Nathan was already with her. She was crying, but unhurt. I pulled her into my arms, and she buried her face into my chest. Master Thomas knelt down and asked, "Is she okay?"

"Just scared," I said, caressing her head to soothe her. "You still think I'm not ready?"

"Yes, but let me explain."

15

"He's nothing but a bully."

"Larissa, he is quite a bit more than that," argued Master Thomas. "Don't let what you did tonight go to your head."

"Probably just caught him off guard," added Gertrude. "Not sure why, though. Your parents were powerful. He, of all people, knows that."

"Her lack of training. All the years she spent in hiding with no true formal training," added Jack from behind the three of us. I cast him a disapproving look.

"Probably so. That would be an easy tactical misjudgment to make, but he won't make it again. Understood?" asked Master Thomas.

I wasn't exactly in agreement. Yes, he probably misjudged me for one of many reasons, and maybe Jack had a point, but this wasn't necessarily a bad thing. I thought he was now afraid of me, and fear could be a formidable ally. Something Mr. Helms had told me once. My being a vampire could make some afraid of me giving me a psychological edge. I didn't have the psychological edge in this discussion though, and there was nothing to gain by arguing with someone I viewed as a mentor, so I agreed like any good student with a nod, which was better than the sarcastic "Yes, Master" that played in my head.

Amy tugged on my long dress, and I looked down to find an exhausted little girl. It had been a long night, and we were still walking through New Orleans following Master Thomas, who wanted to show us something. I reached down and picked her up. She immediately laid her head on my shoulder, and I knew if we kept walking through this quiet part of the city, she would fall asleep there in my arms. I was right. We walked another dozen blocks more, and she was out by block five. Her long deep breaths helped soothe what had raged inside me to nothing more than an orange ember now.

"Here," Master Thomas said, jogging out to the trolley lane of Canal Street. He motioned for me to join him. I handed Amy off to Nathan without waking her and walked curiously out to that spot.

"Jack, why don't you go ahead and go?" encouraged Gertrude. "You need to know this, too."

"Of course," responded Master Thomas. "Come on out here, Jack."

When we both arrived at the spot in the middle of the trolley tracks, Master Thomas stomped on specific spots on the pavement he wanted us to stand on. We followed his direction, not really knowing what we were here for. As far as I knew, this was a test, and a streetcar was going to come right at us, and he wanted to see how we handled it.

"What do you see when you look up at the sky straight ahead?" he asked.

From where we stood, we had a clear view for as far as we could see. No buildings were directly ahead of us to block the horizon. It was a beautiful, cloudless night. Stars twinkled in the dark void above us with just a simple glow of the city lights right along the ground. "The sky. The stars," I said.

"You're not looking right. That vibration you feel, Larissa. Focus on that. What do you see?"

I closed my eyes and focused on that sensation that was always there. It felt a little chaotic. Ripples traveling up and down it from all directions. Some all at once, and others like volleys or shots fired back and forth. I concentrated further on the vibrations and felt I could see the source of each vibration that traveled back and forth. They weren't too far away from us, maybe a few blocks away.

"See anything yet?"

"No," I replied.

I was about to explain what I felt though, when Master Thomas whispered in my ear, "your eyes are closed, open them." I did and almost fell backwards. The sky was a brilliant shade of purple, black, and yellow. Flashes of green and white reflected in the buildings up and down Canal Street. Each flash going from one side of the street to the other, landing with a thud that I wasn't able to hear until now, but I could feel them. They coincided with the vibrations.

"What is that?" I whispered.

"Let me go handle things, and I will explain when I get back." Master Thomas took off in their direction. I wanted to follow, but I also didn't. The thought of running into the unknown, this unknown, had me hesitant.

"Jack, do you see this?" I asked without turning around to face him.

"No, I see nothing," he reported back, frustrated.

"The flashes? The purple?"

"No. Just the night sky," he said, sounding even more frustrated now.

"You haven't ascended yet, have you?" asked Gertrude.

"No ma'am."

"Oh dear," Gertrude said, sounding concerned. "We assumed you had." Now I knew why she was concerned. The warning Mrs. Tenderschott had given me about talking to anyone about what it was like. Now we had Jack wondering, and if I explained to him what I was hearing, it might impact his own. "Umm, I am sorry Jack. This is something you can only see after that happens, and..." she hesitated, "I guess I could explain some aspect of what is happening without breaking any rules. Plus, I am an old woman. What are they going to do to me anyway?"

Master Thomas wasn't far from the sources of the flashes when he let out one of his own, a bright yellow whip that struck from one side of the street to the other, knocking down both sources of the flashes. That was when I saw the sources, people. One directed two more flashes at Master Thomas before taking off into the darkness. The other tried, but Master Thomas let out another whip and grabbed that individual before he could get away. Like a sheriff who had apprehended his fugitive, he walked him back to us, wrapped in the yellow energy.

"Jack, please tell you see that?"

"If he doesn't, he is blind," responded Martin from the side of the road. I looked over at my group of friends and each of them were intently watching the show that was returning to us.

"Dale Halls you know better than to fight out here in the streets," Master Thomas commented as he walked past us with a young man, no older than his mid-twenties, with straggly red hair wearing jeans and an Iron Maiden t-shirt. "Stand here."

"Oh, come on," the young man protested with his deep creole drawl.

"You know the rules," responded Master Thomas.

"But I wasn't breaking any. I am on our side," he countered.

"No matter. What you did is forbidden. Now, to the coven with you." Master Thomas summoned a portal and pushed him through in a flash. When it closed, he turned to regard each of us that was standing there slack jawed at what we had just seen, me most of all because I had seen more than the others. "I am guessing you are all wondering what that was. Well, let me explain. This is something Larissa and I have talked about a few times. There is much more to this world than any of you will understand. Wars wage under the cloak of darkness or dimensions between various factions. Witches and vampires, which you know about. Vampires and werewolves, which you probably know about, too. But there are even battles inside each of those groups. Factions with different belief systems. In our world," he looked at me and Jack, "there are those that will abide by the rules of the council, and those that won't. Those that understand they are to live within the world of man, and those that feel they can rule the world of man. What you saw tonight was a small skirmish between two witches on opposite ends of that disagreement. Dale is a mage, and he knows it is against the council's wishes to engage in conflict without explicit charge to do so. I believe the other was Marcus DeLeon, a sorcerer." He walked back to where he told me to stand, which I hadn't left. "This is the war I told you about. Not everything is at peace with our own. Those vibrations you feel, that is the supernatural world reaching out to you. The world that in time you will see just as clearly as you see the natural world. Like I said, there is still much for you to learn. This goes along with the mastery we discussed. Understand now?"

I threw Master Thomas across the road as one of those vibrations approached. I imagined a rope, and just like I used to do in my room to grab the handle on my closet door, I looped it around the man who had rushed at Master Thomas from behind and yanked him off his feet. "I think so," I replied.

Master Thomas stood up, stunned, and did not brush the mud from the gutter off of his nice black tuxedo. I stood there over the one that got away and felt pretty proud of myself. If I were any prouder, I might prop a foot up on him and pose like a big game hunter, but my father once told me pride is a weakness, and that weakness plopped me on my ass. I never even saw the flash, but I sure as hell felt it, and just that quick he was gone.

"Yep, you sure do," remarked Master Thomas while he helped me up to my feet. "Marcus obviously just wanted to get away and had no interest in killing you. If he did, you wouldn't still be here. That was just a little tap."

A little tap. That little tap felt like a building fell on me. I hurt everywhere, and my ears were buzzing. By the time Nathan made it to my side, the pain was gone, but that pride that got me in this mess was more than a little bruised.

"As I was saying," continued Master Thomas. "There are factions. I am going to teach you more about that part of the world of witches. It is part of your bigger goal, remember?"

I clearly remembered my agreement to restore witches to who and what they used to be. A goal that at that moment felt more daunting than it had ever felt before. I nodded.

"Jack, I am going to teach you too, but a lot of this won't make sense until you ascend."

"Thank you, sir."

Gertrude walked forward and brushed some dirt from my forehead, and then straightened my hair out. "You're a mess," she said with a laugh. "Messing with someone like Marcus can do that. Benjamin and I can teach you about the world of witches, which you would already know if you weren't taken from us, but there is someone you need to talk to, Theodora Raudeau."

"Who?" I asked abruptly.

"Well, if you give me a minute, I could explain. You were always quick about jumping to conclusions. I see you haven't grown out of that trait." I found it odd that I was now being lectured by an old friend who was actually younger than me. "Theodora is an old vampire. She is probably older than Jean, and she doesn't share the same beliefs as he and his followers. In fact, she doesn't share the beliefs of anyone except those that believe in decency. She likes to keep to herself and stay out of people's way, but she can tell you about the world of vampires and all the factions that exist there."

16

"I'm coming, and that's that," demanded Nathan. His whole body leaned forward and when he concluded, I heard a light thud from down where his feet were.

"Was that a stomp?" I asked.

"No, it was not, and I am coming. End of argument."

"It sounded like a stomp to me, Nate," answered Mike. His answer earned him a sneer from Nathan.

I reached out and grabbed his hands, holding back a snicker. "Look, this is probably the least dangerous trip we have made the whole time we have been here. It's just going to be vampires and two witches."

"Two vampires...", Nathan mounted a protest, but I let go of one of his hands and hushed him with a delicate finger over his lips.

"Actually, there will be six. The four of us and the two of them, but see, I don't know them, and I am not sure how they will be around a human. So, it is best if you stay here with Amy. Got it?"

This was a question of the rhetorical variety, but the grip I felt on my hand gave me the unnecessary answer. I leaned into him. Pressing my body against his as I inched my lips up to meet his. His pulse quickened, and his grip loosened. I wasn't using compulsion or any magic for this reaction. This was our own brand of magic. The type any woman who wanted to get her way had used since the start of time, and it usually worked if performed correctly.

My lips brushed his, lightly. Then I said softly, "We will be fine. Mike and Clay have our back." Then I pressed my lips into his firmly, gently parting his with my own, and then exploring slightly. His hand released mine and found the small of my back. The other was around the back of my neck.

I don't know how long we were there before Mike said, "We gotta go. I am sure they are already waiting." I had gotten lost in the moment and found it hard to pull away. Maybe this had backfired. I pulled back away from Nathan and instantly felt the hole where he had been. He was still there, but not like we were. That presence, the one-ness, it was gone, but only for a second.

He pulled me back in for one last kiss, and then said, "Be careful." His arms let go of me, and I walked backward to the front door, feeling the need to not take my eyes off of him. Luckily, my chances of bumping into anything in my old house were low. Of course, there was the door that I backed right into before I reached behind my back, embarrassed, and grabbed the brass door handle and opened the door.

"I can't believe that worked," remarked Mike.

"It will work until the blood returns to his brain," said Laura and she walked right toward the portal Master Thomas was standing next to just down the front steps. He knew where Theodora was, and since I hadn't ever been there, I lacked the presence of its place to open a portal to it.

"Have you ever done that to me?" asked Mike.

There was no response.

We stepped out on an old limestone narrow driveway that ran between two columns of large magnolias. It looked eerily similar to my own. Even what we could see of the house from the driveway looked like my own. A white house with a front porch. That was where the similarities ended, though. As our party walked closer, it became clear. This was no simple farmhouse, even though I wouldn't really call my family's house a simple farmhouse. This was a mansion, with wings branching off the center, and a wrap-around porch. Behind it, clearly in view, were expansive sugar cane fields as far as the eye could see. The fields were being tended to by teams of workers using modern equipment.

Master Thomas knocked on the large leaded glass front door. Through the panes, we could see all the way through the main entry to the sunlight coming in the door at the other end. Soon, a shadow interrupted the light and approached the door. It opened, and a gentleman wearing khaki plantation pants and a white button-up shirt stepped forward.

"Master Thomas, it is so good to see you again. It has been too long."

I looked the man over but it was not what my eyes saw that told me this wasn't Theodora or John Milton, someone Master Thomas described as her house guest for the last few centuries. This person had a pulse.

"Clarence, I agree it has been too long." Master Thomas grasped the man's hand and shook it heartily.

"Madame Bergeron, now this is an occasion." He leaned down and hugged Gertrude.

"Good morning Clarence. I take it you have been well."

"Busy as hell, but doing well. You know she bought out the farm next door. Extending us another fifty acres." His eyes finally broke from his two old friends and caught us, the new visitors, standing there out, under the partially overcast sky. "Umm, yes. Come on in. Miss Raudeau is in her study."

He moved from the door and allowed each of us to enter the spacious entry. Now, instead of resembling my home, it resembled the coven. Staircases lined both walls, going up three floors in the cavernous entry. Everything was cherry wood, with a heavy layer of lacquer. Clarence stood with one hand on the door as we filed in. He regarded each of us with a curious look, which I found curious myself. It wasn't as if he hadn't ever seen a vampire before.

We followed Master Thomas through the entry and past the stairs. Our footsteps echoed in the enormous room like a herd of stampeding elephants. Both Master Thomas and Gertrude walked right up to a pair of French doors that were just beyond the stairs. Without hesitation, they opened them. We followed them into what I could only define as an enormous study. It was basically two, make that three rooms. There was what resembled a living room in the center, with a brown leather sofa, and love seat with several matching easy chairs sitting on top of a red area rug. Around it on the wall, all the walls, were shelves upon shelves of books. Then, at the end of the room, was a single desk where a woman sat. She was on the phone and pointed Master Thomas toward the sofa area. We followed his lead and had a seat, leaving the chair at the center of this area and the one next to it for our host and her guest. This had to be Theodora Raudeau. If her pale complexion under the perfectly flowing blond hair wasn't a huge tipoff, the lack of any pulse was.

We sat there, looking around at one another and our surroundings as she completed her call. Even with my hearing, I couldn't hear much more than a few words here or there. They were terms like bushel, gross, and truckload. It was obviously a business call, and while I wasn't trying to snoop, I was curious about how the business ran here. Was she involved in the day to day, or just a background player to hide her unique identity? It was quite clear she was involved in the day to day, and hearing her yell for Clarence when she put the phone down helped me identify him as some sort of foreman or boss.

"Yes ma'am," Clarence rushed through the door with a spring in his step.

"The Southern Sugar load? When is that set to leave?" she asked, while studying a large fanfold printout on her desk.

"First thing in the morning. It's on schedule, if that is the question."

Theodora Raudeau stood up from the desk, dropping part of the printout allowing the paper to accordion down to her desk. "Nah, it's not that. I know it is. That's a full truck, right?"

"Yes ma'am."

"I just got off the phone with them. Another farm stiffed them, and they are going to run short, and were wondering if we could increase the order."

"We could, but not until Tuesday at the earliest. We just don't have a truck available."

She dropped the rest of the printout before she responded, "That will have to do. I will call them soon. Get it started, a full truckload order to go out Tuesday." She stood up from behind her desk, and I was happy I had left Nathan at home. Laura elbowed Mike.

"Yes, ma'am." Clarence rushed out of the room, but not without giving us another curious glance as he passed by.

Theodora Raudeau, all five foot ten of her, walked out and around her desk and strutted towards us. Her form fitting navy blue business suit with a skirt attempted to give off a conservative appearance, but her curves, high hem line, and unbuttoned white shirt that was under her suit jacket exuded the opposite. She was striking. I was more than a little jealous. Being turned at sixteen, and not somewhere in my late twenties, robbed me of the chance to fill out and mature as she had. If that was even possible. She sat in one of the two chairs we left open for her, and slowly crossed her long, slender, toned legs.

"So sorry about that. Business," she said with a voice that could melt butter. "How long has it been, Benjamin?" she leaned over and tapped Master Thomas on the knee.

"Oh, I don't know. Maybe two or three years. Not all that long in your world, I imagine."

"True. True. And Gerti, it's great to see you again. I told you not to be a stranger."

"I just don't get out this way much," Gertrude responded, but Theodora already had her sights set on me. Even her black eyes looked alluring tucked above her perfect cheek bones. She didn't even try to use any makeup to accentuate or provide any signs of life, just her natural beauty.

"And you. Do you remember me?"

Her question surprised me, and I looked over at Clay, who was sitting next to me on the sofa thinking maybe his family had some business with her.

"You don't remember me, do you, Larissa?"

"I'm sorry I don't," I apologized. I didn't, and I was fairly sure I would have. She had an unforgettable presence. Not to mention, if she was as old as Master Thomas said she was, she would have been a vampire then, and other than Jean and his crew that attacked us, I had never seen a vampire before. I was sure of that.

"You were probably way too young. You were only four or maybe five the last time we met. I remember you hanging on to your mother's skirt the whole time while your father and I talked about combining our deliveries to common customers. I imagine my appearance frightened you, but look at you now. Such a beauty." She diverted her attention to the two opened French doors. "Ah, John. Just in time."

In walked her house guest, John Milton. He was basically a human skeleton dressed in a black suit. It appeared time had all but run out, but his black eyes told me it had stopped for him. Each step was smooth and confident, and he easily carried a silver tray with several drinks on it. His aged frame didn't give him any hesitation as he leaned with the tray over Master Thomas and Gertrude. "Sweet tea?" he offered.

"It's fresh brewed," Theodora added pridefully.

"Why, thank you." Master Thomas removed two glasses from the tray, handing one to Gertrude. The two glasses he selected differed from the others.

John pulled the tray back, and then leaned over Mike and Laura with the tray and said, "Refreshments." I thought I had picked up on its aroma when he entered, but there was no doubt they had, and both quickly took their glass.

"That is freshly brewed too," giggled Theodora.

John next moved to Clay and me, and we followed suit. Clay was salivating over the red liquid in his glass. Mike sat back on the sofa while lightly swishing his around the edge of the glass before taking a sniff like a wine connoisseur. Of course, this wasn't wine. Laura just sat there, staring at the contents of her glass. She knew what it was. I did too, but there was something obtuse about seeing it in a glass like a normal drink. Having it served to us on a silver platter put the whole moment over the top.

John gave one of the last two glasses to Theodora and then took his and had a seat in the last remaining chair.

"Drink up. It came from my private donation pool." Theodora downed her drink in a single gulp. Clay did as well. I wasn't sure why, but I sipped at mine, like Master Thomas and Gertrude did their tea. Mike was still playing with his, and Laura couldn't take her eyes off of it.

"I could get used to this," Mike remarked as he took his first swig.

"A good life has several benefits," remarked Theodora. "Now Benjamin, you said something about needing my help. Am I to assume it is related to the guests you brought with you?"

"Yes, Theodora. It's for Larissa. She needs help with Jean."

"Don't we all?" snipped Theodora. John chuckled from his chair next to her.

"He is still chasing her," said Master Thomas, and that seemed to get Theodora's and John Milton's attention. She leaned forward, not in my direction, but in Master Thomas'.

"But why? After ninety years?" she wondered aloud.

"Yes," he replied, and then motioned toward me. "Larissa, would you care to explain why?"

Theodora sat back in her chair. Her right hand propped her head up as she looked almost down her nose in my direction. "Why does Jean still want you?"

"I am a witch–,"

"Were a witch," John interrupted. Theodora admonished him for doing so with a simple wave of her hand.

"I'm a witch, and a vampire." To help make the point, I sent my glass, still with blood in it to the silver tray across the room from me. Four very black eyes followed it with immense curiosity.

"She's not just any witch. She's her mother's daughter. Larissa appears to have kept her family's traits," explained Master Thomas.

"My God," exclaimed Theodora. "How can it be?"

"We don't know, but it happened. Now you can imagine why Jean would want her,"

I felt John's glare on me instantly. Well, not on me, but on something I was wearing. "Oh dear," he remarked, and pointed. "Theodora, look."

"What is it?" she turned to John, annoyed, but she only made it half the way to him before she saw what he was pointing at. "That is, isn't it?"

"That is our theory," Master Thomas replied. "He either wants her blood charm or her. Either way, he sees her as a link to what he tried to get from her father back then. If he could gain her ability, well, you can imagine what that would mean."

"An immortal witch," Theodora gasped. Her eyes shook as they stayed locked on my blood charm. "He is barely controllable now. If he were able to... It wouldn't just be the witches that would be endangered. It would be everyone."

"Why not just destroy it?" suggested John.

"Hey now!" yelled Mike. He tried to pop up off the sofa he was sitting on. Laura blocked him, but he remained coiled up, ready to strike.

"Her charm, not her," clarified John.

"Oh." Mike settled back down.

"I thought about that, but I couldn't ask Larissa to give up her opportunity to undo what she did if she ever turns anyone. Remorse can be a strong emotion. And it's not mine to take or even ask for," replied Master Thomas. His show of respect for what the charm symbolized earned a nod of respect from Theodora and John. "Plus, we still aren't completely sure he needs her charm. It contains the last drop of her blood before the venom took hold. He may just need the blood that is in her veins now. There is much we don't know, but we are sure he wants what she is. That much is clear."

"He tried with my father, but wasn't ever able to make it work," I said.

"I know. I remember that," Theodora said.

"We need to kill him. That is the only way." I was looking right at her, pleading.

"That is a way, but not the way," she responded, deep in thought. "In fact, it is completely out of the question. If you killed him, it would be viewed as an attack by witches, and the peace between our people has been tenuous for centuries as it is. Some are just looking for a spark to ignite the war they have been looking for." She paused and studied my reaction. Until then, I didn't realize I was all but out of my seat, leaning close to the edge toward her. As if my physical presence would urge her to agree with me. "She doesn't know, does she?"

"I have told her much of our history and ways. I felt it best if one of her own tells her about your ways," explained Master Thomas.

"So, you brought her to me?"

"I did."

"Well then," she stood up and walked around her chair. "I have a lot to explain." She put both hands on the back of her chair and regarded the rest of us. "You can't just go around killing vampires. There are rules. Especially you." She let go of the chair long enough to point a finger in my direction. "That would be seen as an act by witches against not just a Vampire Coven but against all vampires. There are rules you need to follow, and even then, you can't just kill him." She let go her chair for the second time and walked around, grabbing what remained of John Milton's drink, and downed it before she sat. "Just like in the world of witches, there are covens. Then there are factions of covens. Ones that have shared beliefs. They stay together, where those like Jean do whatever they want up to a limit. There are certain lines that if he were to cross, the more vocal and prominent coven leaders and faction members would step in to correct him, but he hasn't crossed that yet."

"What? Killing my family? Hunting me down for almost a century? Not to mention the curses he has this town under, like the curse of the crescent moon. None of that is crossing the line?" I asked in a state of complete disbelief. What line was there he hadn't crossed yet?

"To be blunt. No. Not even that. This isn't like the world of witches. We don't have a council that governs us. We govern ourselves to a point, and even then, there aren't defined rules, or even a defined leadership like the council, but as you can imagine, he who can mass the most support among the prominent players in our world, leads. And Jean has done an excellent job of that through the years. Taking things to a point and stopping just short enough to appease any concerns while making sure he shows he helps maintain order, which earns him certain levels of respect and gratitude." She paused, and her normally cheerful and attractive features turned grim. "As vile as you may view the death of your parents, it is who we are." She sat back and looked around at all of us. "Some just show more restraint than others. It is something you need to learn to accept, Larissa. You are one of us."

"What the hell!" The instantaneous flash of my temper threatened to propel me from my chair.

"Now I am not saying it's right. It isn't, and it wasn't. That is one reason I have chosen to live outside of that world. There are others like me, and some factions, that do as well. But to Jean, and others, your father was interfering with Jean's business."

I was about to spurt out a line of expletives about Jean's business, but Mrs. Raudeau delicately put the cap back on my eruption with a single hand up in front of me, and a quick shake of her head.

"Now, this is where the biggest split exists between the factions. There are those that believe it is fine to exert influence over humans, whether through fear or other means. They view ourselves as superior creatures, and humans as almost subservient, though no one has gone quite that far in a long time. All the trivial things Jean does like having packs of his vampires roam the streets to strike fear in the community, attacking the families of prominent witches that might attempt to stop him, and even things like the curse you mentioned, are all means to that end. He may get away with everything short of enslaving humans, and ascending to some kind of demigod or leader over them. Until he does that, no one, and I mean no one, will permit anyone to touch him. Myself, I don't believe in this, which is why I choose to live my own life, away from all that. Others have too."

She got up and walked over and kneeled down in front of me. "I am sorry," she apologized, while brushing the hair out of my face. "I know this isn't the answer you wanted on so many levels. There isn't anything we can do about Jean until he crosses that line. This is bigger than any one person."

Another flash sent my temper right to rage. "If you are going to tell me I should just disappear, you can stuff it..."

Master Thomas interrupted me before I could tell her where she could stick her advice. "Wait, Larissa. There is another angle. One Gertrude and I thought about. It's something you are missing here, Theodora."

"I don't see how."

"What if Jean could obtain Larissa's gifts? What would he be? How would the others view him?"

"A threat to all," answered John Milton. Hearing the normally silent man speak stunned the room, but he was right. I knew it. Master Thomas knew it. That was why we were here. Now we needed Theodora to see it, but even if she did, would it help? I knew Master Thomas set this meeting up, and I doubted he did it without a purpose and the outcome in mind. He reminded me of one of those people who was always two steps ahead of everyone.

"You wouldn't be able to keep him in check then, and he would know it."

"You're right, but we don't have any guarantee he would use it."

"Come on Theodora. Search your feelings on that. You know as well as I do what Jean would become."

"There's got to be something we can do," I begged, looking right into Theodora's big black eyes. "Forget that he is hunting me. He has Marie Norton. The woman that raised me as her own. He is torturing her."

Theodora nodded. "I know. I have heard, and Larissa, I am sorry, but that is all acceptable in our world. What she and Thomas did is considered treason to their own coven."

My anger was already at the top, but when she uttered that word—treason–it all came close to boiling over, and then I wasn't sure what would happen. All I knew was the world shook in my eyes, and I heard the wooden frame in the arm of the sofa I was sitting on crack in my grip. But again, just like before, a touch from this woman soothed it. Put the cap right back on it, and tamped it down, bringing the world in focus.

With a single hand under my chin propping my head up, she said the words that turned that anger to tears, "It hurts me too. I knew them both well and considered them friends." She hugged me. Not just a friendly one arm hug, but a strong shared grief hug.

"John, Theodora, there has to be someone we can talk to."

I was still firmly planted in Theodora's arms when I felt the wetness of her own tears against my cheek.

"Master Thomas, I see where you are going here," John said. Theodora was still holding me, and neither of us showed any signs of letting one another go. "If we were to explain to the other factions what Jean is after, maybe they will see this for what it is. A threat against all of us. Our peace."

17

"So now what?"

"We wait." I wrapped my arms around Nathan. He felt tense. I was with him. I didn't like waiting, but that was what we needed to do. Theodora and John promised to get back to us in a day or so after they consulted the others, but that just meant another day living under Jean's constant threat and another day of torture for Marie Norton. Even another second was too much for me to bear.

Earlier, before the sun went down, I looked up at the shadow of the moon that hung there in the dusk sky. I thought of Marie, and all the nights the three of us spent looking up at that same moon, and I prayed. I honestly couldn't remember the last time I had prayed, and even wondered if I was doing it right. They weren't deeply religious for obvious reasons, and well, neither were my parents. That's not to say we didn't talk about God, or didn't attend church on major holidays, but it wasn't a central focus in our life. We had a Bible, and I read through it once when I lived with the Nortons, but that was more out of curiosity than devotion. What I remembered from the few times I attended church when I was younger was it didn't matter where you were, or how you did it, God still listened. I hoped He did. Marie needed Him. What she was shouldn't matter. How she had protected and taken care of me proved she was worthy of His help.

"Can we read this one?"

Amy yanked on my pants leg with a book in her hand. I didn't even look at the book when I took it from her. I didn't care. I could read her a cookbook sitting there with her in my lap on the porch swing and it would be all right with me. It wasn't a cookbook. It wasn't even something that I would think Amy would enjoy, and to be honest, I didn't remember my parents having a copy of Chaucer's "The Canterbury Tales" in the library. Not that I would have picked it up if I had known about it. It was rather dry to read, but that didn't seem to bother Amy, whose head snuggled into my chest while I read, and Nathan sat in one of the old wicker rocking chairs. She was out by page five, but I read another page, just to feel her there. I didn't ask what she and the others did while we were in our vampire meeting with Theodora today, but whatever it was tired her out. Probably some running in the fields with Rob and Martin. Amy made a comment about one day wanting a dog.

I carried her upstairs to the bed and got her settled just as Nathan walked into the room we all shared. He glanced at me as I sat there on the edge of the bed, brushing the hair out of her face and adjusting the covers to make sure she was warm enough. It was a cooler than normal night, and the fires downstairs only did so much, but the look on Nathan's face could stave off the ice age. His hands retrieved clothes from the drawers while his gaze brightened my life. When he closed the drawer and walked to the door, he motioned for me to follow, and I did.

"I'm going to take a shower before turning in," he said.

"Okay," I replied, and he started down the hall, and I pulled the door partially closed behind me before I headed to the stairs. Nathan yanked his shirt off before he reached the bathroom and I stopped to marvel at how his broad shoulders looked in the moonlight coming in through the window at the end of the hall.

"Larissa?" He asked without turning around. I quickly turned and headed to the stairs, not wanting to be caught gawking. I had reached to the top of the stairs when Nathan finished his question. "Want to join me?"

My knees wobbled, and my hand grabbed the newel post. I rushed to close my mouth, which hung wide opened. Thoughts fluttered through my head. Some of the images they produced shouldn't be there. The water running down both of our bodies. His hands. Oh, his hands. Touching me. Caressing me. Exploring me. My own as they traced every muscular ripple of his frame, a combination of hard and firm, and soft and sensual all at the same time. I felt flushed. It wasn't possible. I knew it. Probably a psychosomatic reaction to the thoughts, but it felt real enough. Oh, how I wanted to say yes. That was what nature wanted me to say. Logic had to fight through all the lust filled emotions and force myself to say, "another time, perhaps."

"Okay," replied Nathan with a hint of disappointment and a lingering look before he closed the door. When I heard the water running, I wished for a second bathroom so I could run myself under a cold shower. Maybe that would wash the thoughts of him in the shower out of my mind. The temptation to spy on him, as I had done once before, was strong, but my own will power prevailed as I walked down the stairs, each step a little steadier than before. Each step came with the reminder that I said no for a reason. That this wasn't the right time. My body yelled back a few times for my mind to shut up, but by the time I was at the bottom of the stairs and back out on the porch soaking in the chilly night air, that argument was done, well, sort of.

Now I was arguing with myself about why this wasn't the right time. The only answers that came up had to do with why we were here, and my concerns for Marie and what was happening to her, and the safety of everyone here. That I needed to stay focused. I was way beyond beginning to hate that word. I was focused on every one of those tasks. Was there something else? I asked myself that question as I sat down. The answer didn't come back no. It came back unsure.

The moon was brilliant on this clear night and gave me a full view of its current phase, which was a stark reminder of another new detail that needed my attention. We were two days away from the next crescent moon, and still had a ton of questions, and I knew exactly who to ask. I went back in and heard the water still running upstairs. There was still a chance. I just needed to walk up the stairs instead of down the hall to the kitchen, but I didn't, and took my normal seat at the table. I didn't really need to be here for this. I could be anywhere to do this, but there seemed to be a symmetry to sitting there in the chair that I would appear in any way.

"Mom, I found Gertrude," I said before she even knew I was there.

"That's wonderful," she responded as she turned around and headed for the table.

I debated giving her the full details, but I figured there were a few she might enjoy. "We met her at the Solstice Gala, which is what they are calling the Holiday Ball now."

"You went to the ball?" she asked, leaning across the table, beaming.

"We all did. It's kind of a long story, but news of us approaching families got back to the coven here—I had no doubt that one of the families turned us in—and a council member came to the house." She backed away from the table, concerned, but I quickly waved my hands to dismiss that concern. "But it was okay. He is someone I know and trust. He's the one that has been helping me with my training, and he was who invited us all to the ball. It was wonderful, getting all dressed up and dancing... and no, I didn't wear a red velvet dress."

"You were always adorable in those," she said, grinning from ear to ear.

"I know, mom, but I'm not a little girl anymore. I wore this." I waved my hand and an image I had in my mind of Nathan, myself, and Amy all dressed up at the ball appeared. I rushed to answer the question that I knew she was going to ask. "And no. We don't have a child. That is Amy, a young shapeshifter who recently arrived at the coven, who we both love to death." The picture faded.

"You guys look happy together. Natural," my mother had become as weepy eyed as I did when I thought about it. She wiped the moisture from her eyes and cleared her voice before asking, "Gertrude? Was she able to help?"

"Yes, but not how I was originally hoping she would. She doesn't know where Jean is, and I have to wonder if she would have told me if she did."

"Oh?"

"She and Master Thomas both believe if I went after Jean there would be... well, repercussions against the world of witches, and they are probably right."

"I'm sorry Larissa. They're probably right. I am sure there is something we can think of." My mother reached across the table and patted my hand consolingly.

"We already did. Do you know the name Theodora Raudeau?"

"I do, quite well," my mother said, sounding surprised and flustered. "I should have thought about her first. She is..."

"Not like the others?" I interrupted. "I know. Master Thomas and Gertrude took us to meet her. She explained a lot to me about my other half, including the factions of covens. If we can convince enough of them that Jean is a threat or has crossed some ethical line they have, they may help us. It appears the line is blurry, so I am not that hopeful about that, but I believe the threat is a slam dunk. Theodora is going to speak with them on our behalf, and we should hear something in a couple of days."

"That sounds like wonderful news."

"It is, or it could be. We don't know what they will decide, but at least we know what to do."

The prospects of Theodora coming up with a flat no, or an agreement that Jean was a problem, but no one will help was a black cloud that hung over my hopes. I asked Theodora for a guess at what the outcome would be. She couldn't tell me. The factions can be rather fickle. For some, it may depend on how moving on Jean would benefit them. Theodora asked me to trust her and her experience with them. What choice did I have?

"Mom, there is another reason I am here. It's about a curse Dad was working on removing. The curse of the crescent moon. Have you heard of it?"

My mother's mood changed. The smile and grin she had before became somber and frightened as she leaned back away from the table and against the back of her chair. "I do, and Larissa, you need to get whatever thoughts you have about that curse right out of your mind. Those thoughts will only lead to trouble."

"Mom, I know. They told me that is why Jean came after Dad."

"It's not just that, Larissa. He was obsessed with every curse or hex Jean had some old witch doctor place on the city. Most of them took months to work through. He spent years on that one, and he still wasn't able to get rid of it."

"It's still in place today, and the next crescent moon is in two days," I informed her. "Do you know if he was close to solving it?"

My mother looked around, almost trying to avoid eye contact. Her movements were sharp and abrupt.

"Mom, was he close?" I asked again.

She threw her hands up, and both landed on her thighs with a huff. "I guess. Maybe. I don't know. According to him, he was always close. Larissa, please tell me you aren't going to try. Casting a spell on a person or two is not the same as casting a spell on an entire city. You aren't ready for that. I am not even sure he was."

Normally, that phrase carried quite a sting to my ego, but hearing it come from my mother was different. I felt the weight of the caution it carried. Probably because she would be the only person who could truly gauge what I was ready for. She was my original teacher. "But he did," I reminded her. From what I had heard from Ben Mallory's widow, it was a constant chess match between Jean and my father.

"He did, but it isn't easy. Many tried, but couldn't, and don't forget you just told me that the crescent moon curse is still in place. It's been almost a hundred years. Don't you find it odd that in that time no one has removed it?"

"They are scared to," I replied.

"Scared?"

"After what Jean did to us, no one will stand up to him. That is what I am hearing. That is why every time I ask anyone for help, I am told to just run and hide. That is why when Mrs. Mallory and I were talking about it, she told me no one had attempted. Gertrude told me the same. There are those that might be capable on the council." This was a point I had to assume, considering the self-created education gap between the council and others that Master Thomas told me about. "Mom, they are all just frightened. Jean has this entire city in a stranglehold, just like he does me, just like he does Mrs. Norton. The only way to stop him is to stand up to him." My voice grew in strength as I reached this next point. It was something I had thought about on the way back from our visit with Theodora. The speech itself, I'd rehearsed several times in my head before I settled on exactly how to deliver it with the most impact. "Mom, he is who and what he is because people let him. If the vampire factions come back with a no and won't help us with him, showing him we aren't afraid to stand up to him is the only way. If we can't kill him, we have to put him back in his place and show him we are watching."

I waited several seconds as I watched my mother chew on her bottom lip as she thought this over. Timing is one of those human attributes that Jennifer taught us in her classes about how to be more human. A phrase, or point delivered at just the right emotional state, would solidify a point in their mind. The art was finding that perfect time, and that was what I was doing now. I was watching my mother mull this point over to find the perfect moment to nail it. She paused in the chewing of her lip and looked up. And there it was.

"It's the only way, mom. If we don't now, then when? It's been almost a hundred years and the witch community is only getting weaker. Remember what you told me to do during my ascension?"

She nodded, and mouthed, "Okay." Then she wiped tears from her eyes, and I saw her face crinkle like it did when I told her who and what I was. She was about to cry.

"Mom, I know this is dangerous, but don't be afraid. One, he can't kill me," I gave her a smirk to remind her of that, "and I won't be trying this alone. I will have help from members of the council." I knew I would have the help of at least one member. I had hoped he could sway more.

"Okay," she said, pulling back a sniffle. "Your father left journals of his work on each of the curses, including that one. They are in the house. I can't go with you to show you where they are because I am bound to this room to communicate with you. But I can tell you where to find them."

At this moment, I wished Lisa had followed the others. She, with her dark magic, would love this place, and if anyone would know how to allow my mother more access to the world of the living, she would. The thought of checking the books of spells in the library crossed my mind, but I remembered the point that Mr. Demius had once made. Different witch, different magic. The dark magic doesn't flow through everyone. I felt there may be some in me, but how much and could I do it? I didn't feel comfortable attempting it unsupervised for the first time on the off chance it would ruin my ability to visit my mother. The feeling of being cautious was disturbing. It went against my more aggressive just-do-it nature. Was I growing, or was this the higher level of awareness Master Thomas talked about that the ascension would be the first step in acquiring?

"Where is it?"

"It's not an it. It's a place. It's an entire library. Go into our main library and look for 'On Origin of Species' by Charles Darwin. If I remember correctly, it's in the second set of shelves on the long wall, on the third shelf. Tilt that book and step back."

"Thanks mom." I got up, but she reached across the table and grabbed my hand. Hers shook.

"Larissa, please come see me before you do anything. Promise me that?"

"Yes. I promise."

"I love you with all my heart. You have a lot of your father in you. Which is both a good and bad thing. Be careful."

I rose from the chair and walked around the table and hugged my mother. "I love you too, and I will be careful."

With that I returned to the world, and a dark kitchen. Most of the rest of the house was dark as well. Rob and Martin had just returned from a patrol and heading up stairs. Clay, Laura, and Mike were in the parlor watching television, and I went to the library. I had a date with Mr. Darwin.

18

I found Mr. Darwin right where my mother said he was, and behind him, I found so much more. I tilted the book back, and felt something catch, then I stepped back. It was a good thing too. The entire bookcase rotated out into the room like a large door, and behind it was a room, just as big as our main library itself. Shelves upon shelves of journals sitting upright and face out with dates and names on them lined the walls. The real mystery was *what* was this room. I knew for a fact; the back wall of the library was the back wall of the house. It had always been that way, and through the window I had seen my father and many of the farm hands as they walked around the house. Of course, that was when I was thinking of the simple world. My time at the coven had opened my mind up to so much more, and that gave me the answer. This was a space that only existed for us, a magical room, accessible only through this door.

I walked into the room, which was decorated with the same wooden floors and plaster walls as our house was. Even the shelves were the same as the ones we had in the library. The difference between the two rooms was the desk that sat in the middle of the room, with a big wooden chair on rollers and a reading lamp. A pen sat on the right side of the desk, waiting for my father to pick it up and make more notes.

Simple white cards tagged the front of each journal with a handwritten label of the event and date. They were arranged on the shelf with the card facing out for easy recognition, and in chronological order. The ones on the shelves by the door started in 1917. These were journals my father started when he was really young. My gaze followed the journals around the room, behind the desk, and around the other wall where half of the shelves were empty, with plenty of room for more. I walked around, looking at each journal more closely. When I rounded the desk, I noticed a stack of what I had to assume were empty journals sitting there, waiting for a purpose. That was when it kind of hit me. I was standing in the middle of my family's life's work.

I pulled down the first journal.

Blight–1917

Problem:

All the cotton crops on the north shore of the Mississippi delta died within a three-week period. I believe that Jean St. Claire and Madame Laveaux stood in the river of New Orleans in either Hester or Covenant to cast this and allowed the current to carry it downstream. Initial study by myself and several other members of the coven found no evidence of blight north of Hester, so I believe this is the starting point, and finding such a point is of the utmost importance. If we are off when we attempt to reverse it, any point still left with the blight will propagate downstream. Time is of the essence, and I am not afforded the time to perform experimentation. The plants are dead, but the roots are not. This season is lost, but if we can reverse it in the next two weeks, we can still salvage the next season. The next full moon is in eight days. That is when we need to act.

Action Report:

On the night of the full moon, myself and Robert Tolison entered the water of the Mississippi River just north of Hester. We picked this place for complete coverage. We sprinkled the mixture into the water at midnight on the full moon. The water shimmered under the moon as the mixture spread downstream. I repeated the phrase, "Luna, grant us your protection for our crops. Clear the evil souring of the ground and restore its fertility."

Gold Flakes (clearing agent)–1 teaspoon

Powdered Rosewood (for growth and protection)–premixed with water to make 2 ozs of a paste

Ground Cotton Seed (what we want to grow and be protected)–10 pounds.

I returned to the river the following night and still observed the shimmering. The sky was cloudy and there was no source of light.

Follow-up:

Six weeks later, and new cotton blooms began appearing across multiple plantations.

Alternatives:

The next twenty-four handwritten pages were alternatives my father thought of attempting if this occurred again. Some he hypothesized would last longer, such as Red Alder instead of Rosewood as both the clearing agent and protecting agent. Each had a slight variation in the spell that accompanied it as well. In one such alternative, he mentioned using something I hadn't ever heard of anywhere except in literature's references to witches, a wand. He called it a focusing agent. Overall, the journal appeared rather scientific. For some alternatives, he even purchased his own plants, cast his own blight curse on them, and then tried the variations, recording the results for both effectiveness and the time it took for the first observation of success.

I had to take a seat at the desk while I flipped through it looking at all the handwritten notes, with a new appreciation of who the man I knew as my father was, and a new appreciation of what being a witch meant. Nothing Mrs. Saxon, Mrs. Tenderschott, or Mr. Demius had taught me covered this. This approach to witchcraft, this responsibility to understanding and treating our craft as, well, a science, a business, a lifelong pursuit of knowledge, was perfection. Master Thomas was right. There was so much more to this world than I had even realized, and because my father did this, I felt that same responsibility to continue it. The responsibility to continue his work and to teach it to others.

How long I was actually in there was anyone's guess. By my measurement, it was twenty-seven journals long. My father handwrote all the journals. Reading them put me in touch with him in a way. All extensively detailed beyond anything I had ever seen. I couldn't wait to show them to Master Thomas. These were too valuable to keep hidden away. Just reading the ones I had, I felt my head was going to explode. It was a master class in spells and potions, or mixtures as he called them, and yes, there were the symbols. They were scattered all throughout the journals in usages I would have never considered. What was even more fascinating was his method. My father was no stranger to failure. More than one spell or potion failed, which that in itself led to discovery. It took his failure against the red tide of 1924, another one of Jean's gifts, for my father to find the restorative ability of Aromatic Cedar, which appeared to become a favorite of his from then on. His notes documented his failures, which caused him to give up on his old favorite rosewood. He tried many alternatives. All failed, except one. One that a native American healer told my father about, at least that was what he documented. In forests that were destroyed by wildfire, Aromatic Cedar was the first to regrow in the desolate landscape.

I closed the twenty-eighth journal and put it back on the shelf where it had sat for years. My father had a system, and I wasn't about to disturb it. The darkness of night had finally given up its battle with daybreak, and light was spreading fast. I knew I had to be fast myself to beat the light upstairs and snag just a few magic moments with Amy and Nathan. My hand was on Mr. Darwin's greatest work when my plans shattered before me.

"Larissa, we have a problem." I turned around and found Jack standing in the library's doorway. Behind him was our problem. A five foot two, ill tempered, sour expression wearing, dressed in a long gown, council supreme.

"Miss Dubois, you have a lot of explaining to do." She marched forward. Jack looked at me over her shoulder as she approached. He was scared to death. "You left the coven, which you promised not to do. You brought the others with you, putting them all in danger, and you... you..." she stuttered. Her attention diverted. It was no longer on me, but on what was behind me. "Is that...," she started.

"Yes. That's my father's office and his journals."

Mrs. Wintercrest stepped through the door and into the office. Her finger tracing along the middle shelf of the first bookcase. I could see her eyes scanning all the journals it held. She appeared to have the same wonderment I did when I first saw them. "There were rumors he had such a place, but we never found it and lost hope."

"I believe it is every journal he ever made. Some are focused on curses created by Jean. Others are his experimentation in spells and potions."

"Yes, I see," she said, mildly distracted by her own amazement.

"They are quite detailed," I said, proud of my family's work.

"Are they?" she asked, again distracted and still sounding as condescending as always. I felt she was coming out of the fog created by this discovery and was about to reveal why she was here in the first place. Our appearance at the Solstice Ball would be my guess. This is her coven, and anybody who was anyone was there. I just didn't remember seeing her.

"Yes." I rushed three bookcases ahead of her and pulled one of his general spell journals from 1927. It was his sixth volume on spells. "See ma'am. Look at these notes."

I laid it down on the desk where she joined me and stood there looking at page after page of notes. Flipping them, with remarks such as, "oh my," and "unbelievable." Her finger traced several passages.

"Miss Dubois. This is astonishing, and a treasure to behold. I wasn't aware any in recent years had worked such detailed studies."

"There is more. They continue all around the room." I pointed at the other cases, avoiding the ones that were empty.

"I can see that. This will take years for our scholars to study."

I wasn't exactly sure I wanted to share them with her and the coven. Not with how they had regarded and treated me so far, but I couldn't let my selfishness rob me of a perfect peace offering. "I would be more than happy for them to study them here." To me, my suggestion sounded like an amenable idea. To her, it must have been as bitter as vinegar.

"Miss Dubois, you act like you have a choice. Your father was an esteemed member of our coven. These are practically coven property," she announced rather astutely.

It was a point I felt like arguing, but at what price? She was here, and obviously unhappy we were here. A crowd had now gathered in the doorway. No doubt the sound of our conversation attracted those coming downstairs for breakfast. Jack remained in the doorway. Nathan was behind him now, with Amy. Clay, Laura, and Mike kept their distance. Rob and Martin were the only ones that had ventured into the library, but still kept their distance.

"We will tend to this, as for you and your friends. I order you to return to the coven immediately. I don't know what you plan on doing here, but whatever it is must end."

"Mrs. Saxon won't let us back," said Martin.

"Excuse me," shot Mrs. Wintercrest with a load of disdain.

"She told us we weren't allowed back if we left," explained Martin.

"Mr. Nash, who is this vile creature that speaks to me?"

Martin squeezed his fist. I half wanted him to phase right there and teach her a lesson, but again, what would that accomplish? She was my supreme, and as my mother told me, I needed to respect her. Not to mention, if the council was to ever trust me, we all needed to be on our best behavior. So I bit my tongue while Jack waited to see if I was going to pounce. When I hadn't, he finally answered his supreme's question.

"Martin, my supreme. He is a werewolf."

"A werewolf," she scoffed, and then stopped, and stared a hole right through the member of our party that she had just noticed. "Master Saxon. You, of all people, here. You need to take Mr. Nash and the others back home immediately. That is an order to both of you. Understood?"

Nathan put Amy down on the floor, and she quickly gravitated to Laura behind him. He stepped around Jack and walked into the center of the room. There was no stress in his body. He was relaxed and resolute as he approached her. "It's true Mrs. Wintercrest. My mother kicked us out."

"Poppycock. You are her son; she will let you back in. She will let you all back if I order her to." She looked around the room at all the others. "Even the rest of you. Now get your things. This discussion is over." Mrs. Wintercrest spun around to me. Her eyes pinched to just little slits. "You will stay, and I will deal with you here, Miss Dubois. We've had just about enough trouble from you. It's time you learn your place."

"Her place is right here," said a new voice to the discussion. There was no quick turn in its direction. Instead, there was a slow and reluctant one.

"This is her home. So, it is more her place than yours, and she can have anyone as a guest as she wants." Master Thomas squeezed through the crowd in the doorway and made his way into the library. He was dressed in his normal suit and bow tie, just like always, and I would have to think hard to picture a time I hadn't seen a smile across his face. This is probably the first. "Larissa is well beyond the age of property ownership, and the last time I checked, she is the last living heir of her family which under our rules, means everything passes to her, unless there has been a change I'm not aware of. Has there been, Mrs. Wintercrest?"

"Well... no," she stuttered.

"And actually, no one here is Larissa's guests. They are mine. I am hosting them here at her family farm. Is that a problem?"

You could have cut the tension in the room with a knife and served it up. Master Thomas stood there waiting for his answer. He appeared to be a man who would wait until the end of time for it, just to make his point. It was either his personality that eroded away at the arrogance of Mrs. Wintercrest or the wounds he gave her the last time we had all been together; she seemed unsure as she stumbled out of the hidden door of my father's office and back into the library.

"Don't think I am not aware of what you are really here for. I heard about the queries you were making."

I was about to answer when our *host* jumped in. "There is no hiding anything. Larissa has a problem that originates here, and she is here, so I can help her. Isn't that one purpose of the council?"

"It is," agreed Mrs. Wintercrest, "but I know what her problem is, and you can't help her." She wagged a bony finger in his direction.

Master Thomas was unfazed and even smirked at her display. "There are many ways to help Miss Dubois. Remember, she is not just a witch. I am helping her make connections. That is my part, and while she is here, I am continuing her training. I see nothing wrong with either of those. Do you have any objections, my supreme?"

She frowned at his condescending tone, but I knew what he had done. Master Thomas had laid an argument at her feet that was wholly correct, and not one she could deny. In fact, based on what Gwen had told me about the council, if she had denied such a request, it would go against the very nature of the council. He had backed her into a corner, right where he wanted her. I wasn't the only one who realized it, either. There was an uncomfortable stirring in the room while we waited for her reply.

"Don't take me a fool," she warned, now focused directly on Master Thomas.

"I wouldn't dare," Master Thomas replied with a half bow in her direction.

She frowned at the gesture and walked toward the door. Jack and the others cleared a path for her before she had even reached them. "I will send someone for the journals. They are precious."

"They can study them here, unless we have a new rule that allows the seizure of private property," replied Master Thomas. Mrs. Wintercrest paused at the reply and bowed her head before continuing out and down the hall. Everyone remained silent and looking around uncomfortably, like the cat that ate the bird, until we heard the front door close. There was a communal exhale in the room. Even I joined in on that one.

"Who wants breakfast?" asked Rob.

Amy was the first to scream "me". Rob picked her up and carried her into the kitchen.

"I wouldn't mind a bite, but first there is something more appetizing." Master Thomas was already moving toward the open, hidden door. He entered with the same wonderment that Mrs. Wintercrest had. Jack and Nathan stayed outside the door, almost afraid to cross that line and enter the room. "I have never seen such a collection of journals before. At least not any done this recently. There are several in the archives, but those are hundreds of years old."

I gave him the tour. "Some are about specific curses, but some are just about spells and potions he experimented with." I pointed to each type as I passed by them. Master Thomas stopped at the one on general spells. His hand stopped just short of grabbing it before he looked at me for permission. I nodded. He opened it and leaned back against the old desk in the center of the room. He went through page after page slowly, consuming every word. His face lit up like a child's on Christmas morning.

"Astonishing."

If he thought that was something, I had something else he might find more exciting and relevant. I walked to the last bookcase that had journals in it and grabbed the last one. I held it out for him to see the label. His eyes widened as he read it.

The Curse of the Crescent Moon–1935

He reached for it cautiously and unsure, and looked at me again, as if asking permission. I placed it in his hand to give him that permission, and he held it there, studying the cover for several seconds before taking a step I hadn't yet, and opened it. Once he opened it, his eyes were in a race to consume every word on every page. Master Thomas was a child on Christmas morning.

"Where does it go?" he closed the journal and asked.

I pointed to its place on the bookcase, and Master Thomas carefully put it back in its spot. His hand lingered on the cover for a few minutes before stepping back. "Your father was remarkable," he commented to no one in particular as he walked past each bookcase of journals. "Truly remarkable," he said finally, regarding me. "And it is more than just the fact he kept the journals, but the contents. The work. It's extraordinary, and I'm afraid it's beyond you."

That stung, coming from him, even if it wasn't the first time he had pointed it out. "I can..." I was about to remind him I can learn when he interrupted me.

"I know, and you need to. For this. For you. For our future." The normal confident and borderline arrogance that always surrounded Master Thomas was slightly diminished. He seemed humbled to me, and that concerned me as he looked back at the journals listlessly. "I can help you some, but I have to tell you. Some of what I read is beyond me, so we will learn together, but first I need to talk to you all. Let's gather the others."

"Master Thomas," I said as he headed toward the kitchen door.

"Yes, Larissa." He stopped and turned toward me.

"There are two days before the next crescent moon."

Master Thomas went pale.

19

"She heard you were at the gala, and all about your interaction with Jean, and put two and two together and rationalized that you were staying here. A few questions around the coven, and she probably heard you were asking about him and again put things together to make the leap. Considering your story, it isn't a hard leap to make, but that is no matter at the moment. She is not our concern, nor is it why I am here. I didn't even know Mrs. Wintercrest was here when I walked in through the door. Theodora called. She has an answer."

There were several enthusiastic reactions around the table.

"Hold on a moment," warned Master Thomas. "It isn't all positive, but it isn't all negative either." He adjusted himself in the chair he sat on and scooted it closer to the table, producing a squeak from the chair leg. "They have agreed to talk to you. To hear you out, but under no circumstances will they allow you to kill Jean, even if you are a vampire. There is a concern that his followers might use it to galvanize the position more against the witches."

I sighed; this one was involuntary. I didn't even have to think about it. Nathan got up from his seat at the kitchen table and walked behind me. His hands rubbed my shoulders and the back of my neck. I could feel the support through his touch. He was trying to tell me to relax. I reached up and padded his hand to reply that I would.

"I was worried this might happen, Larissa." He continued. "I'm sorry. It was a real possibility. Think about it this way. If Russia attacks the United Kingdom, the United States will get involved, right?"

"Probably," I said, not understanding the relevance of international politics to my predicament.

"Same thing here. Action and reaction. Not that many would dig into the motivation behind the attack, just or not."

"So Master Thomas, what do we do?" asked Nathan.

"Talk. Listen. That is all we can do at this point. Theodora is arranging a meeting for you tonight. You will need to explain your side, which she already has, but they need to hear it from you, your voice. Then listen to any proposal or thoughts they have." Master Thomas leaned back in his chair away from the table and let out a sigh himself. With it, again, the exuberance that defined him vented away. "Larissa, I am sorry to say you will have to accept what they propose. We don't really have any other options here. Let's see what they say, and we go from there, okay?"

I nodded. What choice did I have? He stated it as plainly as it could be. This was not a negotiation. Present my argument and accept the verdict. That was the only option, and even though we all heard it, it didn't stop Jack from asking, "What if they say no?"

"Then it is a no," answered Master Thomas, who looked around the room at every person at the table. All seemed to accept the answer. Whether they liked it was not up for debate. There were several grumbles and moans of defeat. One such sound came from me.

"I could kill Jean," Clay said from the corner of the kitchen that he had plastered himself when the meeting started. "I'm not a witch. I am pure vampire."

"Actually, you can't," replied Master Thomas. "He is the leader of a coven. You can't touch him, not without the agreement of the others. It's kind of an unwritten thing, but as I understand it, you can take revenge on the one that turned you, as long as they aren't the leader of a coven. You better have ironclad evidence they are the one. There are rules, and we need rules to avoid anarchy."

"There has to be something. This guy is a menace," stated Laura. She had Amy in her lap and was stroking her blonde hair.

"I don't disagree, but this is one of those times you, we," he corrected himself, "have to remember there is a bigger picture here. It is not just about the one." Master Thomas paused and looked up at the ceiling. His signature smile made a split-second appearance while he was lost in thought, but then it disappeared just as quick. "Whatever happens, I need you all to understand that." Master Thomas leaned forward and placed his hands down rather harshly, rattling the few dishes sitting on the table. "Whatever the outcome, you all will have mine, and the Council of Mages full support to help in any way possible." After he delivered the promise, one that appeared to have some weight behind and provided comfort to all those in the room. He pushed himself back from the table. "Larissa, would you mind if I spend some time with your father's journals?"

He didn't wait for the answer before he eagerly left the room. Leaving us all there in a stunned silence. Rob sat there with food left on the plate in front of him. That was how stunned we all were at the realization of the situation. They hadn't said no yet, but I realized, and probably everyone else, that Master Thomas was preparing us for that inevitability. After Master Thomas, I was the first to move. I needed to. I needed some air and headed for the porch. Nathan wasn't far behind, and neither was Amy, who had wiggled out of Laura's grasp. The sun was out a little more than what I would have normally ventured into, but I needed to be anywhere other than inside. A throwback to my childhood. If something upset me, out to the fields I went. The openness of everything always helped clear my head, much like the cove had back in the coven.

I ignored the sting of the sunlight as I walked off the porch. I wasn't alone. Nathan quickly took one hand, and Amy took the other. They let me lead them out into our old lavender fields, where I picked the perfect spot among large tufts of the purple flowering plant, and collapsed down to the ground, ignoring the warnings my mother had given me over and over about it staining my clothes when I did that. Nathan and Amy did the same. She snuggled up against my right side, and Nathan moved up closer to my head and stroked my hair, gently. A heavenly breeze carried the scents of the surrounding flora over us. I closed my eyes and soaked in the moment.

"What if we just left?" Nathan suggested tenderly.

"He would find us," I replied just as tenderly, my eyes still closed.

"But what if he didn't?"

I could see where this was going. The circular logic of fantasy versus reality, and what if the moon were made of cheese? What if there were unicorns and we could ride off into the sunset on one of those? Maybe we could ask a dragon to come eat him. "He would. He already has. He will again."

"But what..."

I reached a hand up and pressed a single finger to his lips. "This is an argument I have played out in my head more times than I can count. He will eventually find me again. For the moment, can we just lie here and enjoy this?" There we were again, having a struggle I often did so much. Nathan was thinking of the future, which I often did, but I just wanted to enjoy the now, and this now meant everything to me, just like the next moment would, and the moment after. I removed my finger, but Nathan caught my hand and kissed it before he gave it back to me. Then he leaned down and kissed me, and I felt it all over, pushing the stinging caused by the sun away from my body.

"Ooooo," cooed Amy.

"Oh, you hush," I said, while giving her a little squeeze. Then I let her relax back on the bed of purple flowers, before I rolled over and started tickling her. Her giggles were infectious and was the medicine I needed to cure what I felt. I may have gotten a bit of an overdose. My mind made a few more passes over the what-if questions Nathan asked.

Master Thomas called my name, pulling my from my bliss. How long we'd lain there? I wasn't sure. The sun didn't rise high in the sky at midday during the winter like it did in the summer, making it hard to judge time based on its location or the length of the shadows. With the sun hard to our south this time of year, long shadows existed everywhere you looked, no matter the time of day. The three of us strolled back up to the porch, where he waited for us.

"Larissa, can I speak to you for a second in your father's library?"

He didn't wait for me to answer before he turned and walked back inside and down the hall. I gave Nathan Amy's hand before I departed him with a quick kiss and followed my teacher, thinking I was in trouble. When I reached our family library, I found the bookcase door open like it had been since I found it last night. Master Thomas was inside, standing at the desk with a journal open. "Master Thomas, is everything all right?" I asked, hoping this would not be another moment of unwelcome news.

"Yes. No," he stammered, "I'm not sure. I just finished reading your father's journal about the crescent moon curse and several others. I need to ask you. Are you sure you want to try to remove that curse?"

"I am." It hadn't been removed in almost a hundred years, and it appeared my family was the only ones who ever attempted to remove or counteract any of Jean's curses. It almost seemed like our responsibility, and I was all that remained.

"Are you sure?" he asked with a level of intensity in his eyes I had never seen before.

His expression gave me a moment of hesitation. Master Thomas had never appeared concerned before. Not even when Mrs. Wintercrest tried to skewer me with her inquest. Now, he was concerned if that was even a strong enough description. Dare I say it, he seemed worried. "I'm sure."

"All right, then you and I have a lot of work to do." He spun the journal around. "Look at these pages. Recognize anything?"

I looked at the pages, which were farther in than I had read earlier. A quick flip of the pages showed these were the last six pages in a journal that was probably some fifty pages long. It hit me with a cold spike through the heart. These were my father's last entries before... I plopped down in the chair and stared blankly at the pages. Memories of that moment they burst into the house played in my head. My fingers gripped at the arms of the chair.

"Larissa, do you recognize these?" asked Master Thomas. His finger ran under rows of strange shapes.

There was a cry building up deep inside. One I had to stifle before it emerged. "Some, but not really," I said, answering his original question. They were the symbols my mother had drilled into me, but at the same time they weren't. They were different, altered.

"Exactly," Master Thomas said, spinning the book back around toward him. "Your father was inventing his own magic."

Okay, if I wasn't impressed before, I was now, and that helped pull me back. I didn't even know that was possible to create your own brand of magic. Potions. That was the point to those, and why it was important to understand all the ingredients. A point Mrs. Tenderschott had made many times, and why I took copious notes in her class. I thought magic was finite, set in stone.

"These are not new symbols, but parts of many symbols combined to create something new. For example, look at this one here." He pointed at one clearly drawn by my father's own hand, probably by the pen that sat there on the desk. "The cross is the inner part of the sabbats, but he added the hook of the besom to the vertical part of the sabbats."

"How does that work?" I asked. What he described was clear in front of me, but what it meant and what it did was unclear.

"The sabbat is about the journey of life, and they use the besom for protection or to ward off evil spirits. If I had a guess, he was trying to return those evil spirits conjured up by Jean back to the grave as part of the circle of life," Master Thomas explained without ever looking up from the page.

"But how?" I asked. Questions filled my mind, and each one was a form of how does this even work? The symbols meant something. They did a task. What... I mean... how do you create new symbols and what out there recognizes what they mean?

"You see how it is drawn here? I believe he did the sabbat first..."

"I see that," I said, interrupting Master Thomas' retracing of the shape. "How does it even work? What out there knows what that combined symbol would do?"

"Oh," Master Thomas said, surprised by the question. Based on his reaction, I wondered if he even knew, if he didn't, we were in real trouble. Especially if this is where my father's work on the curse lead to. "Look at this first." He spun it around again and pointed to several lines of text.

I read the lines, and instantly recognized them as a spell, but it didn't sound like any I had ever heard before. Then I remembered what Mrs. Saxon had told me about the words only helping you to focus. I was going to tire of that word, focus. Normally, a spell had a keyword, a phrase, for what you were trying to do. This one didn't. It was just words. Again, the same question came into my mind. "I don't understand," I finally admitted. My mind was more confused than it had been in weeks, and that was saying something.

Master Thomas sat down in my father's chair. His elbows propped on the armrests and his hands supporting his chin as he rocked back to the limits of the chair's springs. "Let me see if I can explain it. Remember when we talked about mastery with Mr. Demius, about things coming second nature?"

I nodded. I remembered it and felt I was getting there. Most of what I did didn't take a major conscious effort. I just thought and it happened. Just like I showed him that night after the gala, when I grabbed that attacker. I completely ignored the fact that he threw me on my ass because I lost focus.

"This is some next level stuff. Mastery is about feeling the vibrations, the energies of the world, and knowing how to change those to do a specific action with. The symbols are reference points so you can learn how each of those energies feels.

As you learn them, you feel them, and can use them easier, almost second nature, like you do now. What your father did was not just learn the feelings so he could use them, but he understood why those particular energies did something, and why. What you see here, if I am understanding what he did correctly, and I may be only guessing at the moment," he shook his head as he looked up and thought. "I believe he took his understanding of the energies and how they felt to shape new energies. Ones that merged two or more of the traditional elements of the magic world to create something new, something stronger. What he wrote on the page is just a reference to remind him of what he did. If you or I tried to draw that symbol like we do the others, it won't mean anything. The traditional symbols only work for you because your mother taught you the feeling and energy that goes with them."

"So, what do we do?" I heard a long technical explanation of what my father did. There was nothing in there about what we would do or how we could use this to remove the curse.

"Without your father here to teach us these new abilities, there isn't anything WE can do, but there is someone that might be able to help us. I have sent for him. If he can't help us, we may need to start over, with our first attempt in two days. And I need to caution you. Your father made eleven attempts. Each unsuccessful."

Hearing a lot of 'can't' for us, and 'may' about this mythical person Master Thomas had reached out to, didn't exactly instill an exorbitant amount of confidence. "When will he be here?" I asked eagerly. I needed answers on two points.

"He is on his way now."

"What about the vampires Theodora has arranged a meeting with?"

"Tonight, late tonight. She said they don't really do much until the sun goes down, but for this they are making an exception to travel during the day. She will call me when they arrive." He pulled his cell phone from his pocket and placed it on top of the desk, then leaned back and sighed. What was left of his enthusiasm left with his breath. For the first time, I heard a tone of defeat from Master Thomas, and it moved my mood to match him. "Larissa, I have to tell you. I am not sure what we can do about the curse. I don't know anyone who is doing this kind of magic anymore. Remember what I said about us not being what we once were?" His left hand raised up from his lap and waved around the room. "This is exactly what I mean. It has been… I don't know when since this was last taught. Officially. I am sure some of those that live outside the covens practice magic in this way."

"Well, Master Thomas, I promise to continue it."

"Good, that makes me happy." He forced a smile upon his despondent expression.

His happiness wasn't my primary motivation, but I would not tell him that and take what he may consider a small win away. This was my father's work, and regardless of what promise I may have made Master Thomas and Mr. Demius, this was now about family. I just hoped I wouldn't disappoint my father. To say this discovery gave me a newfound feeling of responsibility would be completely accurate. It also energized me. It may be a foolish notion flowing through my head, but problems now seemed like bends in a road, not roadblocks. I just needed the perfect guide to work around those bends, and Master Thomas gave me doubts that he, or who he reached out to, was. Considering what the curse was, I knew someone who might be of help. "Master Thomas, there is something I need to tend to. Can you let me know when he arrives?"

"Of course," he said, sounding curious, and I left before he asked questions. I was on a mission.

20

"Just cover for me. Will you do that?" I begged Jack in a hushed voice in the kitchen.

"Why me? Why not Nathan?" He responded, and I quickly shushed him, and motioned for him to keep it down. I had a plan and didn't want to get busted by anyone before I put it in motion.

"Because if I tell Nathan, he will try to talk me out of it, and, well, you are a witch. Master Thomas is one of the best-known members of the council. I am sure you can think of a way to occupy his attention better than anyone else. Ask him questions. Let him teach you. Stuff like that. The man is a walking magic encyclopedia, and just imagine how much Gwen would hate it if she knew you were getting a private session with him." I gave Jack a light knock on the shoulder. "I need you to do this for me, just for a bit. Just an hour or so, please?"

The halfhearted shrug wasn't a yes, nor was it a no. "What if Nathan or the others ask for you?"

"Just tell them I am with Master Thomas and can't be disturbed."

I didn't wait for a response before I spun my hand around, thinking of where I wanted to be. When it opened and Jack got an unobstructed view of where I was going exclaimed, "Larissa, you can't."

"I can, and I am." I stepped through, feeling the sting of the runes Mrs. Saxon had put up to block me from coming back. They weren't strong enough to stop me, but more than enough to send me to my knees temporarily while the portal closed behind me. That crap hurt like a thousand bees stinging me at the same time. I wanted to stay down while it went away, but I knew I couldn't. I didn't have that long to waste. I stood up and knocked right on the door in front of me, hoping she hadn't headed to class. When the door opened, I rushed in, grabbing Lisa and cupping a hand over her mouth before she even saw me.

I kept my hand firmly over her mouth and put a finger up to mine.

She nodded, and I removed my hand.

"Larissa, what you are doing here?" she shouted in a whisper.

"I need your help. Will you come with me?"

"Are you crazy? Mrs. Saxon would freak out if she knew you were here."

"Are you coming or not?"

"No!" she exclaimed, again in a whisper. Her hands were animated with that answer, but there was something going on behind her eyes. I could see it. "Not unless you tell me what is going on."

"All right," I agreed and grabbed her by the hand and walked her to her bed.

There was a knock on the door. "Lisa, you ready?" Tera's voice asked from the other side.

I reached out with my hand toward the lock on the door and gave a twist. The lock responded with a click.

"I am still getting dressed. Head on down without me," responded Lisa.

"Oh, okay," Tera said, disappointed on the other side of the door.

I waited a few moments until I felt Tera had left and was out the door. Her pulse no longer thumped in my ears, even lightly, and I knew we were alone. "Here it is. Jean has a curse on New Orleans that causes the dead to rise and terrorize the city on every crescent moon."

Lisa's eyes lit up at the description, as I hoped they would.

"My father was trying to break it when he was killed. He left a ton of notes, but it is way over my head, and even seems too much for Master Thomas."

"Wait," she interrupted me. "Master Thomas is there?"

"Yep, he is there helping me with this and other things, which I can explain later, but this curse, it is right up your alley. I thought maybe if you looked, you might have some ideas. Plus, you will love the creepy factor of New Orleans. It's all about dark magic and the dead. They have parades for funerals." I gave her my biggest tourism director's smile to help sell what I was proposing.

"I don't know," she waffled. "It really pissed Mrs. Saxon off when you left. I could hear the screaming all the way up here when the others did."

"One more person will not make things any worse, and I really need your help here." I searched her face for agreement, but then added in a "Please." This was the second time in ten minutes that I begged someone for help.

"She won't allow me back, though. I heard what she told the others."

I shook off that objection. "I wouldn't worry about that. Mrs. Wintercrest told me this morning she would order her to."

Lisa went white at hearing that name. Fear set in her eyes. Hearing the name of your supreme can strike fear just out of respect. Add in what I went through with her, which everyone was well aware of. Her reaction was completely understandable.

"It's okay. She has only stopped by once. So, Lisa, what do you say? I really need your help."

Lisa looked at the books in her hand and then at the door, and back to the books. She was thinking about the cost of turning her back on all this, and while I could tell her what she will learn there with me and Master Thomas would be far beyond anything anyone here could teach her, I knew that wouldn't be enough. To her, this was home. It was comfort. People who loved her, her friends surrounded her. "Okay," she answered reluctantly.

I didn't give her a moment to change her mind. I swirled my hand, thinking of my kitchen, and watched as the portal opened and then fizzled out. The same thing happened when I tried again. That had never happened before, and I was feeling a bit confused and embarrassed, until... "Dammit, the runes." I jumped from the bed and raced to the door. "Lisa, you aren't going to like this, but we need to get out of the building. The runes she placed around are blocking me."

"Great!" she exclaimed, no longer whispering. "How do we do that?" She joined me at the door.

We cracked the door open and looked up and down the hallway. It was empty, thank God. "The backdoor. We need to get way out in the woods to be out of their range."

"How far?" she asked with an elevated level of urgency.

"I'll tell you when we are. My skin has been stinging since I came back. When that is gone, we are far enough." I stepped out into the hall and proceeded to the door that led to the stairs. Lisa followed me. I grabbed her hand before it reached the doorknob, and I backed us both up a few steps. With room to work, I drew the all-seeing eye and watched the wall disappear.

"Larissa, what the hell is that?"

"Something they won't teach you here, but you will learn all about it where we are going." I realized I should have thought about that earlier. It would have made the sale job easier. "The coast is clear. Let's go."

She jerked open the door, and we both sped down the stairs hand in hand. We hit the bottom and were racing for the backdoor when I heard two voices. First Steve calling my name from above, and then Gwen calling both of ours from behind. Steve wasn't much of a threat to my plan, so I ignored him, but Gwen cast two glowing gold streams trying to lasso both of us. We slipped through her first attempt with little trouble, and I wasn't going to wait for her second attempt. I glanced back and saw her standing there between the two staircases. Lisa was at the door. I probably didn't need to, but I sent her sliding on the floor, stopping short of the wall for good measure. We were out and across the pool deck before we knew it, but the sting was still with me.

When we hit the woods, I felt a sense of relief. It wouldn't be long now before we were back safely in my kitchen. Hearing the growling and deep chest breathing of the large gray wolf giving chase through the door was an unexpected complication.

"Oh, crap!" Lisa yelled between pants.

"Keep running," I said, and looked back to see Mr. Markinson clearing the pool deck. Inside, I was panicking. There was no doubt I could outrun him. There wasn't even a question. Lisa didn't have a chance. He would catch her in probably twenty steps. The still present sting told me we weren't far enough for me to open a portal. That didn't mean I was out of options. Towering options surrounded me, and with a few less than gentle tugs, I brought a group of trees down between him and us, hoping that would slow him up just enough. He leaped over the stack and didn't miss a stride.

"Run Lisa!" Not that my yelling at her was going to make her run any faster. If any sound would push her faster, the sound of his paws pounding the ground behind us should have. My pace quickened, but not faster than Lisa. I wanted to keep myself between her and Mr. Markinson. Over the next two steps, I evaluated my options. He was too close for anything that I felt comfortable with, and that comfort was all about him. If I wanted to, I could launch a full-on attack and stop him in his tracks, but I didn't want to hurt him. That was the last thing I wanted to do. He was a person, a friend.

"Stop!" I yelled, and slid to a stop. My feet dug trenches in the forest floor. The great gray wolf slid to a stop before me. The magnificent beast panted deep, echoing breaths.

"Lisa, keep going." She took off again, and as soon as Mr. Markinson spotted her, I moved in his way. "I don't want to hurt you," I said, facing him.

He snorted in response.

"I'm not trying to cause problems. I just need Lisa's help with a dark magic curse Jean set up. She knows this better than anyone around. This is really important, and will end his reign of terror over me, and over an entire city."

He stood there. His amber eyes peered into me while the gold flecks in his iris glinted in the early morning sun.

"I just need her help. I can bring her right back if it will make it better, but this is bigger than me, or her, or any of us really, and isn't this what we are supposed to be doing?"

The wolf leaned back on his haunches, and I prepared to take off running after him if he took off after Lisa, but he didn't. He phased back into the man I was familiar with, who looked at me with the same understanding amber eyes that the wolf did.

"Will you take care of her?"

"I promise, we will."

"Go," he said, and almost sounded like he was encouraging us to go instead of surrendering his chase. I didn't wait to see if he truly meant it before I headed off after Lisa. "I'll tell them you hit me."

That brought a reserved giggle as I ran after Lisa.

She had stopped just short of the cliffs at the cove where I caught up with her. The sensation was still there, but just barely. "A little further," I said and pointed toward the sandy path down the cliff where Nathan I had worn a walkway down to the beach, and out to its furthest point from the coven. As I suspected, right at the edge of the water, the feeling went away all together. It wasn't until that moment when it was gone that I had realized how painful it truly was. Now that we were in the clear, I spun up a portal, and the two of us stepped into my kitchen.

"Larissa, what the hell?" asked Jack. "You said you were going back for something, not someone."

"Something, someone, what is the difference?" I countered while Jack hugged Lisa and welcomed her.

"Hungry?" he asked.

"No, I already ate, but this explains where all the pop-tarts went." she pointed to the three pantry shelves stacked with boxes of every variety.

I smirked and looked all around the room. "We did a little shopping, yep."

"So, what about this curse?" Lisa asked.

Before we left the kitchen, I filled Lisa in on everything I knew about the curse. It was a real why, what, when, and how debrief. The what fascinated her, which I knew it would. She even felt she knew how Jean, or whatever dark magic witch he used, pulled it off. There were a couple of ways. One was just using what she called normal dark magic, which was what I had witnessed her use before. Where I used the energy and vibrations around me to create magic, she explained she used the reflection and after images of lives lost in that energy to resurrect or contact the dead. She could also do what I did, and Lisa had long thought I could do what she could. I hadn't attempted it yet. One of the other options was more likely she felt, which taught me something I didn't know. Where I knew the back story of every vampire in the coven, I really knew little about my sister witches.

"It's a good thing you came and got me. I can feel voodoo all around this place."

"In the house?" I asked, alarmed.

"The land, the air, the water. Everywhere. It sings to me like it did for my mother and her mother before her." She sat back and closed her eyes. "It's there. Can't you feel it?"

"Well, yea. I can feel the vibration."

"No, not that," she cooed. "The song. That sweet, sweet song. It doesn't sing to you?" She opened her eyes. For a moment, they were solid white, and then her irises returned.

I shook my head.

"Then you don't have it."

"So, there is no dark magic in me," I asked, assuming that was what she meant, and feeling a little disappointed.

"Oh no. Not that. I'm talking about the voodoo. I first started hearing it when I was six, a few years before my mother was murdered in Port-au-Prince. Someone blamed her for a curse not having the desired outcome and came back to take out his frustration." She held out her arms and let them wave with the world. "I haven't felt it this strong since then. It's like chicken soup for my soul."

"Think you can help?" asked Jack.

"I don't see why not. Not only could I possibly help with the curse, but I might also be able to turn it around."

"Then come with me. I have someone I want you to meet." I grabbed her hand and led her enthusiastically through the hall and toward the library. There was a collective gasp when we passed Laura and Mike.

"Hi guys," she waved with her free hand, and then followed us to the library.

From up above on the landing, I heard Martin ask, "Mike, what's going on?"

"You got to see this," he replied.

A parade of elephants pounded down the stairs and pushed down the hall into the door of the library behind us. I heard several whispers of "Lisa."

Nathan pushed through the crowd and walked halfway in, but seemed leery about coming any further, or maybe it was any closer to the mystery room and its occupants. He grabbed me by the shoulder, but didn't pull me around. I turned on my own to face his concerned expression. "Larissa, what.."

It was my turn to touch him, and this was a delicate touch. A hand on his arm that slowly traced from his bicep and to his forearm until I reached his hand. My fingers lightly traced across his palm and lightly interlocked with his. "I will explain later. You just have to trust me on this." There was no asking him for agreement. I didn't need it. I just needed him to trust me. My touch lingered for a tender moment before I let go and turned away to finish escorting Lisa to my father's library.

"Larissa," Jack called from the door. I turned around abruptly and glared back at this latest interruption. "His guest arrived. It's a Mr. Neven, or something like that." I spun back and around and ran to the hidden door. There he was. Sitting there at my father's desk with Master Thomas leaning over him, studying one of the many journals they had stacked next to them.

"Mr. Nevers," I said as I walked through the door.

"Larissa," he sprung up from the chair. "It's so good to see you." The hesitation he had the first time had melted away with time and familiarity. The short man embraced me in a friendly hug.

"What do you think of my father's journals?" I asked, curious about his take.

"Fascinating, to say the least." Behind him, Master Thomas gave me a disappointed shake of his head, and I knew neither of them could make anything of his notes. Even with what I felt was my ace in the hole, I still felt the disappointment. I had to remind myself, if none of this worked right now, my father was close, and in time I could learn to do what he did, and finish his work. As rational and mature as that thought sounded, there was still a bit of the impatient teenager in me, and it wanted to attack the curse now.

“Well, I brought someone who might help.” I reached back and pulled Lisa forward. She had stopped right at the door, frozen by the sight of two council members standing right in front of her. This was no time for her to go all fangirl on me. She needed to get in here and treat them as equals. “This is Lisa Baptista. Lisa, this is Master Thomas and Mr. Nevers.”

The two men stepped forward and shook her hand. She accepted the greetings, stiff and wide-eyed. “You’re from Mrs. Saxon’s Coven, correct?” asked Master Thomas with a very quizzical look on his face.

“She is,” I answered for the frozen and star struck Lisa. This answer caused an even more quizzical look from Master Thomas. “She has a very special skill that I thought would be helpful, so you could say I borrowed her.” Technically I had. I promised Mr. Markinson to take good care of her and to return her when I was done. Much like a book from Edward’s library. “She’s a Necromancer, skilled in both dark magic and voodoo.”

Now the light bulb went off in Master Thomas. He appeared to be thinking the same thing I was. We had a problem we didn’t have the tools to solve, at least not yet. I fully intended to work to become one of those tools, but that would take time. We didn’t have time. So, what do you do when you have the wrong tool for the job? You find the right tool.

“Ah, then you must be one of Leonard’s students,” realized Mr. Nevers.

Lisa looked confused, so I answered for her again. “She is.” Then I leaned toward my confused friend and whispered, “I’ll explain later.” I wondered if she would find hearing our master of the dark arts’ name was Leonard as odd as I did.

21

We spent the rest of the day going over my father's journals for any clues. Well, let me clarify. Master Thomas, Lisa, and I read through the journals. Amy sometimes sat in my lap and helped. Not that she understood anything I was reading to her, but I don't believe she cared either way. It was our activity. Mr. Nevers paced the room, thinking over and trying to interpret every new discovery we made. The one that didn't need any interpretation was the fact that my father was a genius. Lisa and I were impressed, if not intimidated, by what we had read. I knew I was, and even let a few moments of self-doubt occur, wondering if I could live up to his legacy. One of his old sayings seemed to resonate now more than ever. "Larissa, you need to be more calculated with your feelings." My father was absolutely calculated in everything he did, especially in what he felt where it came to magic.

Master Thomas and Mr. Nevers were impressed as well, and much to my disappointment, both felt it could take months, if not years, for even the most skilled witch to reach the level of understanding needed to replicate what my father was doing. That just meant my father was the right tool for the job, but he was gone. We just needed to find another equally as perfect tool, and I had, or I hoped I had.

We broke for a late lunch, probably around three or four in the afternoon, for those who needed such things. I could have kept reading, but I broke too. I needed a Nathan fix and pulled Lisa along with me, leaving the two council members to debate which of the two wise witches they could approach to help understand and learn what my father had. It was one that was unnecessary and unwanted. If there was anyone, it had to be me. Not because we were talking about my father here. Well, not entirely. I think I had finally gotten it. At least in my mind. I hadn't tried it yet. I thought about how two symbols felt when I conjured them. How the energy, that vibration, around me felt when I let it happen. Take the solar cross, for example. The vibrations became large. Not quick vibrations, but large peaks and valleys moving out away from me slowly, pushing whatever I focused away. The besom produced harsh, quick shock-waves that sped away. It made sense. That symbol was for protecting you against violent and evil forces, cleansing the surrounding area. One by one I ran through the symbols, and all but a few I could boil down to this. The movement of the vibrations, its speed, shape, and direction all did a job. Even something as simple as a push of someone or a throwing of a fireball or an object, evolved the energy, changed its shape around me in a way that matched the action.

My father had to have studied this, learned, and experimented to validate his thoughts, and that was what I was going to do.

When Lisa and I joined Nathan in the front parlor, we were an overwhelming flood of information that Nathan didn't understand, and probably didn't really want to know. His only break was when Lisa stopped talking long enough to take a bite, and in the second or two it took for me to realize there was an opening, which I quickly filled with my discoveries. His eyes ping-ponged back and forth between us until Lisa had finished her sandwich, and I finally noticed Nathan's eyes rolling back in his head. Then I laid the problem on him. All of this was going to take time, lots of time. I didn't doubt, at least not at that moment, that I could develop an understanding like that quickly. At least faster than anyone else. I was my father's daughter. But I couldn't avoid the fact that it wouldn't happen in the next two days. Which was why we had another idea that I needed to run past Lisa now that she had read my father's notes on this curse, without our two experts hearing. It was just us in the parlor. Amy came in from time to time, but at the moment she was outside in the field with Laura and Mike. The others were upstairs watching TV. If I had to guess something sports related based on the yells that echoed down the stairs from time to time.

"What are you thinking?"

"I'm not. I'm swimming in all this, and I'm way over my head." She pushed her hand up as high as she could above her head. I knew the feeling.

"Me too, but now that you read his notes on the curse, what are you thinking?"

"Definitely placed on by a witch doctor using voodoo. You described ghosts and spirits emerging all around town. Your father's notes mentioned a single place and reanimation. That's not ghosts or demons." She shook her head as she talked. If Lisa's head was swimming from all that we had read, there were no signs of it now. She was confident and clear. This was her element. "That's bodies coming out of graves and such. That's reanimation, and I think your father missed something, Larissa."

"Oh?" I asked, rather stunned. I had looked over these, and two members of the council had, and nothing jumped out to us. Lisa had just read through it once, and she believes my father made an error.

"This isn't a single spell that has lasted a century. There is nothing in the voodoo world that would last this long. Even something with a sacrifice. You would still need to go back to make offerings to those you are calling upon each time you did."

"You mean..."

"Every crescent moon, a witch doctor is out there in that one particular place making an offering of gifts and sacrifice to bring them back for that one night." She held her hand up before her mouth and blew on her nails and then rubbed them on her shirt. "Case closed." Then she sat back and crossed her arms and looked across at me rather smugly, and I didn't mind. I didn't mind one bit. I knew she was the right tool for the problem. What I hadn't realized until that moment, we were trying to solve the wrong problem.

Nathan sat forward on the settee, pulling his hand from mine while doing so. Something that at that moment felt like an unforgivable offense. I reached for it again, and he let me regain my grasp. Even though the angle of his arm couldn't have been very comfortable for him. The sacrifices he makes for me. "So, all we need to do is go out there and stop whoever it is, and then it's done."

"It's not quite that simple,"

"It never is," I sniped, before I could catch myself.

My comment drew an amused look from Lisa. She had obviously grown used to my smart mouth. With how often it went off, you didn't really have a choice. You could get used to it, or let it annoy you.

"If we can find them before they do it, yes, we can stop them, but just this time. There isn't anything to stop them from doing it again, unless we stop them each... and... every... time."

Just hearing Lisa say it sounded exhausting, though if we had to, we would be out there twice a month to put a stop to this. You would hope whoever was doing it would eventually tire of us showing up, and just stop all together. Hell, it surprised me they hadn't grown tired of just doing it as it was. This was a long-term commitment, and as I did the math, it most likely involved more than one person over time.

"Or you scare them," suggested Nathan.

Lisa and I both looked at him, puzzled. This was someone involved in voodoo. A witch doctor, of sorts. I can't imagine showing up in sheets or a mask would scare them enough to stop all together. It wouldn't even stop them the first time.

"Show them it would be more dangerous to defy you than defy Jean. Give them that threat as a motivation."

For once, his macho machismo had a purpose. It was an idea, and one with a lot of merit, which caused a shared look between Lisa and me. Our wheels were turning on what could we do to leave that kind of impression.

"First, we need to find out where. If we can't find where they do it, we can't ever stop it."

"Well, we know that, don't we?" I was fairly sure we did, and Lisa had already pointed out that my father's journal listed the place, which is why I found her statement very curious.

"We know the cemetery, Metairie Cemetery, but not the exact grave. We could be on one side, and whoever be on the other, and we miss them. We have to be right there and stop them from making the offerings of gifts and sacrifices. If we are late by even a second, it's too late. There is nothing I can do after it's done."

"Okay," I leaned forward toward who was now the dark arts master in the residence. "How do we find the grave?" I batted my eyes at my friend, which caused a little of a giggle. I felt validated for my choice to go back and get Lisa.

"I would want to look over your father's journal one more time to see if he mentions that, or even says it's the same one every time. If it is, then we could identify markings or signs of the past ceremonies."

"And if he wrote none of that down?" asked Nathan.

"It would be a bit more difficult..., but I think I might have an idea." She crinkled her forehead and sounded unsure. But I would take it. Having an idea was better than having no idea at all.

"Well, we have a few days to figure all that out."

"Two days," said Nathan, and then he corrected himself, "really one. It's tomorrow night."

"Two days?" choked Lisa

"One," I corrected.

When she finally cleared her throat, she asked, "You couldn't have come and gotten me before now? Like, oh, a few days ago?"

"I just found my father's library and journals late last night. My mother hadn't told me about them until then," I explained.

"Lisa, can you make this work?" Nathan asked, concerned. I reached over and patted the inside of his thigh. This was a lot to ask of our friend. She would do what she could. We didn't need to put any pressure on her.

"I think I can make it work," she answered, not exactly sounding like she had a mountain of confidence.

After the two council members finished lunch, Master Thomas and Lisa went back to their study of the journals. Lisa provided no more background on what her idea was, just that it was something she was working on in her head. We also didn't tell either of our two experts about our alternative idea. As far as they were concerned, what my father was trying was our only hope, and it was well out of reach, or at least somewhat out of our reach.

During one part of the afternoon's problem solving, or what I called throwing ideas at the wall and watching them slide down to the floor, I described to Mr. Nevers what I had worked out in my head as my interpretation of what my father had done. Surprised and proud weren't the words to describe his reaction. Maybe it was more astonished. He almost assumed I was recalling my father describing all this to me when I was younger. I assured him he hadn't. Whether he believed me, wasn't clear. What was clear, crystal clear, was that he wanted to see how well I understood my theory and if I could put it in to practice, so we headed to the safety of outside.

Our appearance in the field to the left of the driveway drew the attention of Nathan, Amy, Rob, and Martin, who, from a distance, looked like they were just running around like crazy people. The giggling I heard from Amy told me whatever it they were doing was fun, and it brought a smile to my face. That sound always did.

"Shall we test our little theory?" asked Mr. Nevers.

"I guess, but how?" I was all for testing it to find out if I was right, and to see if I could really pull it off as easy as I thought it might be. I just didn't know exactly how we would.

Mr. Nevers turned his back to me and then paced away. Was this one of those twenty paces duels? I readied myself as Mr. Helms had instructed and waited. How was this going to test our theory? I didn't understand. My natural reactions were faster than his, and every pace of distance he put between us added to my advantage. He paused a few times and looked back at me before he kept pacing. There were more than twenty paces between us, a lot more. It was probably closer to two hundred, and he was almost to where the others were standing and watching. When he finally stopped and turned, he yelled, "Ready?"

Ready for what? Was the question I had. From that distance, he wasn't much of a threat. Okay, he wasn't a threat at all. Even Mr. Helms from that distance wouldn't be able to touch me. By now, our presence had drawn a larger audience, with Clay and Jack out on the front porch. "Yep," I replied.

"What's he doing?" Jack asked.

All I could do was shrug. I didn't have a clue, and watching him flail his arms around wildly from this distance looked like the bugs were getting to him, even though they weren't really a problem this time of year. I watched curiously until a column of smoke rose from him, stretching up high in the sky. Now I was alarmed. I looked over at Jack, who returned my earlier shrug.

The column swirled, and looked like a tornado, causing me to wonder if I needed to tell Mr. Nevers I hadn't studied any of the weather or natural magic yet, except for a few growth potions. Then the first of several screaming masses of clouds spun out of the swirling mass right at me. Their form became clearer the closer they came. These were some kind of dark spirit, more Lisa's world than mine, but I felt I had seen them before, during her ascension. Empty eyes and all. I started trying to imagine symbols to combine, not to use together, but to make into one. I hadn't even thought of the first combination to try when the dark spirits knocked me on my ass and turned to come back around to finish me off. This was going to be easier said than done.

"Get up!" screamed Mr. Nevers.

I wanted to scream back, I am, but I held my tongue. Not really a show of maturity. It was more of a show of embarrassment, as my first attempt had failed royally. They came back around again, and I heard Amy yell, "look out!"

I screamed "Thanks", as I hit the ground again.

"What's the problem, Larissa?" Mr. Nevers asked. The floating evil creatures who had just bruised my ego and were now joining the cherubs on the list of things I needed to destroy returned to the swirling cloud above him.

"Speed," I replied. "It's taking me too long to think about what symbols to make one."

"Then don't. Just feel it," was the instruction from my mentor.

I was feeling something all right, and it wasn't what he meant. A little of the old Larissa's frustration was finding its way to the surface, and when I saw the bulge on the side of the swirl, I felt like launching a more traditional attack at my spiritual foes. But that would be cheating. I could do this, I thought to myself. Someone had to give me a pep talk, and maybe there was something to what he said. Though neither of us were skilled in this. This was something my father had done. If only he were here to tell me, or I could go visit him like I can my mother, but that isn't how any of this works.

The three of them emerged again and made a beeline right for me. For a second, I let myself ignore them. I had to. I needed to feel the vibration around me. It was flowing evenly, maybe a little erratically. Probably a disturbance I was causing with how I felt. What did I want that to feel like? That was the question. I wanted it to be harsh and jagged. This wasn't just about stopping them from getting to me. I wanted to fully destroy them. I imagined what I wanted, and much like when I first got a handle on pushing and pulling, there were small waves in the vibrations at first, but that was what I needed. A source of positive feedback. Getting knocked to my ass for a third time was negative feedback.

"Maybe we should stop," Mr. Nevers said.

"Once more. I got it this time," I replied.

"She's a stubborn one," Jack said with a wink from the porch. I was about to snap my fingers and send him inside until I saw the look on his face. He felt what I did, and he knew I had this.

The three spirits made a wide, sweeping turn and screeched as they headed back in for another shot. They were going to be screaming after this pass, that was for sure. I used that moment of feedback I had felt and expanded on it. Feeling the vibration of the energy around me shift with my thoughts. It first formed a bubble around me, which they wouldn't be able to get through, but then I sent a quick and jagged wave down it in their direction. There was a flash of blue glow in that direction, almost like lightning, but it was straight. When it hit each of the three, they disappeared instantly.

Applause exploded in the field and from the porch. Mr. Nevers stood there slack jawed at what he had just seen.

"Give me something else."

"Larissa, don't push it," cautioned Jack. I didn't have to tell him to mind his own business. He knew it. He also knew I was feeling pretty full of myself, probably too full, and that was where the caution came from. He was just looking out for my best interest.

"All right. Let's try this." Mr. Nevers started moving his hands around, clearing the swirling cloud that was above him. Two new ones replaced it. I readied myself for the demonic creatures, but none came. The two clouds touched down and moved across the field, sucking up everything they touched. He had just countered with two of nature's vacuum cleaners, tornadoes.

Maybe I should have reminded him earlier that I hadn't made it to that part of my classes, either at the coven, or with my mother? I hadn't even tried weather control on my own before. Even worse, and I wondered if that was why he did it, those two creations of his muddled the vibrations horribly. They were moving all over the place. Erratic peaks and valleys, lines crossing one another, others just stopping. It was a real mess.

"Nathan, get everyone inside. I'm..." I was about to tell everyone I wasn't sure I could do anything with this, but stopped. That was not something I was ready to admit to yet, and I hoped Mr. Nevers would jump in if anything became too dangerous. "Get everyone inside now."

"Need any help? I've had those classes," Jack offered.

"No," I snapped back. A new theory was developing inside. It was as if a giant light bulb had just gone off. Maybe one thrown by one of my ancestors. I reached out and searched the energy and felt the chaos. Then slowly, piece by piece, I brought that chaos into order. A nice flowing and peaceful order. A yellow glow projected from me and covered the sky, creating an amber hue everywhere. Slowly, the two twisting masses of clouds dissipated, as did every cloud in the sky.

23

"Did she say how many we are meeting with?" I asked as we walked up to Theodora's mansion. That was the only word for something so grand, and seeing it illuminated at night with old gas lanterns just added to its majesty.

"Four, plus her and John."

"So, six of them, and just two of us?" I questioned the math. I would have preferred a few more friendly faces with us. Maybe another vampire or two, or maybe Jack or Lisa.

"Yes, that was her stipulation."

"Stipulation?" I asked, wondering who actually used that word in conversation anymore.

"Her guests don't get out much, and she's worried about spooking them." We stepped up onto the porch. Moonlight bathed the front exterior. Master Thomas rang the bell, but quickly turned to me while it was still chiming inside. "These guys are really old... I mean old-fashioned. They come from the old world where there were things like manners. Try to resist saying everything that comes to your mind."

The door opened, and John stood there inside. "Master Thomas. Larissa."

Master Thomas entered, and I followed, still stinging from his last warning. He had said nothing about that to me before, and God knows he never hesitated to correct me on anything else before. I crossed over the threshold and followed the two men down the hall, wondering if I had been bothering or offending Master Thomas all along. How bad it disturbed me to have been a problem for my mentor surprised me.

John led us back to the library, or office. I wasn't really sure what it was yet, as it appeared to serve both purposes. Behind the antique French doors were Theodora and four other antiques, which explained the warning Master Thomas had given me. Each wore black suits and bow ties. Some of their suits were just waist coats, which had gone out of style probably just after the Revolutionary War if I remembered my history correctly. Their dark hair swept back straight, forming a harsh demarcation line where their hair stopped and their pale white flesh began. I glanced at the glass door for my reflection. I had been going back and forth so much lately; I forgot if I was me, or if I was the old me. What I saw was the comforting pale skin and dark eyes. I was *the me* they needed to see.

When we entered, all four of her visitors stood and faced us. They were tall and slender. Two of them sniffed quickly, and I knew they picked up the scent of Master Thomas. I realized they might not live in mixed company. Even Theodora had noticed and was watching them intently. I flicked my wrist, using glamour on all of them. They still thought they were in the room with us, but as each looked at Master Thomas, they saw, smelled, and felt one of us. Even I could see it. It would probably surprise him to hear he made a good-looking vampire. If only I could send a picture to Gwen with the caption—"I turned Master Thomas. Love Larissa."

"Benjamin, Larissa. I would like you to meet Harold Leeward, Jonathan Smith, Tobias Noel, and Keith Taylor."

The four men partially bowed as Theodora introduced each of them.

"Let's have a seat and chat," Theodora directed, and we all did as instructed. She sat in the same chair she had during our last visit. Master Thomas and I sat on the sofa on her right. The others sat in four high-back chairs with velvet cushions on her left. They sat vampire straight, as did Theodora, and I felt my body follow suit. My back no longer touched the cushion of the sofa.

"Larissa, I have discussed your situation with them. I wanted to give them a chance to tell you their response personally, as well to ask any questions they may have." She crossed her hands on her lap and turned to her left.

"Miss Dubois, we have heard your situation and discussed it." It was Tobias who spoke first. His voice was short and harsh, leaving out the softer syllables of the words he spoke. There was a hint of New Englander in his accent, but from an older time. He looked at the others, almost consulting them, before he continued. There were light nods from each of the three. "We understand the horrific acts committed by Jean St. Claire, and we truly apologize for their impact on you and your family. As Theodora said, we are here to discuss those and what you want to see done as a favor to her."

A favor to her? My heart sank hearing that. They weren't here out of concern or disgust at Jean's acts.

"What would you like to see done?"

I wanted to scream, "kill him", but I remembered Master Thomas' warning as we entered the door. I need to be more civil, more reserved, more respectful. "He needs to be dealt with. Removed from his coven at a minimum, but ideally destroyed to remove his threat." I tried and felt I had their attention right until the end, when I as respectfully and calmly as I could word my ultimate request. Each jerked back and responded with pained expressions at that point.

"Miss Dubois," Harold Leeward started, after a quick wipe of his face with his jewel adorned hand. "Understand, we can't just go around killing any vampire that attacked a human. It would be absurd to expect that, and being a vampire yourself, you should know that."

"I do..."

"It is obvious to me that you do not," he interrupted me. He didn't snap, he was reserved. "It is who we are. Some encounters between our kind and humans are more vile than others, but that is not enough to make it a death sentence. I am afraid the answer to that is a no. As to the request to remove him from his position in his coven, that would also be a no. While we may disagree with what he does, nothing Theodora has told us poses a danger or risk to our world."

I protested, but he held up a long, bony finger, and Master Thomas placed a firm hand on my arm.

"I understand you may share a different view and feel actions such as curses or establishing as Theodora described, a sense of fear in the human world is reprehensible, but it doesn't pose any risk to us or the safety of our community. That is what matters here, and us taking the very action you are asking us to do would destabilize this area, and may pose a danger." He regarded Tobias, who sat next to him. "In fact, it is in our best interest to take no action." Harold folded his hands under his chin and looked at us disgustingly smug.

"Our world is one of balance. We must maintain a balance between keeping our people content while either existing with or staying out of the way of humans. That is the only way to maintain a peaceful existence."

I leaned forward, abruptly. I wanted to say something, but I was at a loss, even though Master Thomas told me it was unlikely they would take actions, hearing it come from them was the gut punch of all gut punches. I searched Master Thomas for help, but he remained stoic. I turned my attention to Theodora next. She understood the threat here, or so I thought. Was she going to follow suit and join the party line? I looked at her in desperation, and she smiled.

"Perhaps you can explain to Larissa how things work. She isn't that familiar with our world, though she is one of us. Jean robbed her of a proper upbringing."

"Do you want to handle this, Tobias?" Harold asked.

"I can take it." Keith Taylor, the only one who wore a suit from this century, though the bow tie took that back a hundred years, offered. The man who appeared to be in his mid to late thirties stood up from his chair. He was taller than the others and sported a full beard that extended to his sideburns. I hadn't seen anyone with any facial hair in any of the books of pictures Edward found. "Larissa, we live in a delicate balance. Most of the human world doesn't really know we exist. We are just mythological creatures to them. Keeping that balance is our guiding rule. If something doesn't threaten that, or the peace between ourselves, it isn't worth the conflict that may arise."

"Unless, of course, it involves some of the other vile creatures, like witches and werewolves. Then we have no choice."

Jonathan looked like he just bit into something bitter, but Theodora was practically beaming as she pulled out a cigarette on the end of a quellazaire. With her beautiful features and lips that sported a dazzling color of red lipstick tonight, she looked like something out of the 1920s. I imagined she might have enjoyed the flapper lifestyle during that time in New Orleans. She held it just in front of her lips. "Larissa, be a doll and help me with a light." She had a mischievous glint in her eye. I didn't hesitate to oblige.

As soon as the flame started its dance in her direction, her four guests leaped out of their chairs. Two of them, Harold and Jonathan, retreated behind their chairs, as if that would really provide any protection. When the flame hit the end, she placed the end of the long black cigarette holder between her lips and took a quick but elegant drag to ensure it caught.

"Did I forget to mention Larissa's family were witches?" She took another drag and let the smoke exit out the side of her mouth. "They were pretty high in the coven here. Practically council members."

"Now, Theodora," stuttered Tobias. His eyes were enormous and locked on me the whole time he spoke. "You know that is a matter for their council. If there is any grievance, they have to approve..."

"Yes. Yes. I know." Theodora cut them off. "And if they approved any kind of action, we would take it as an attack by all witches, and feel the need to retaliate, and so on, and so on. If it were something that simple, I would have saved you and them the trip and just told Larissa no, or if she really wanted to, she could go after Jean herself, but then again, she is part witch and some of you," she waved the cigarette in their direction, "would try to make the argument she acted as a witch. So exhausting to just do the right thing."

She gave a faux yawn and then watched her guests silently at first, then moved her eye contact from one to the next, holding the cigarette off to her side. Her eyes begged for a response from them. After the third lap through the four men, she gave up, and let her free hand slap her lap. "Come now. None of you made the connection yet." She waited again, but this time only made it through them once. "If it was just a grievance, I wouldn't have even called you, yet alone asked you to come here. I know how you hate crawling out of your holes, but this involves you. It really involves all of us, and if we don't do something, we will all pay dearly. Sit, please."

Theodora pointed back at the chairs, and the four men retook their seats, but they were not exactly eager to do so. They watched me suspiciously as they moved the chairs around them and then sat. The tension in the room was thick, and even Master Thomas felt it. His pulse had elevated a few notches. Luckily for him, I was still controlling what the others saw.

"Let me lay it out for you. She is a vampire, and a witch. A witch that will live forever. What would happen if Jean became both?"

The four men regarded each other in some kind of silent conference until Harold spoke up. "That would be disturbing."

Understatement of the century there.

"How would he be able to do that?" Jonathan asked, his voice was full of worry.

I reached up and held out my charm.

"The last bit of blood that still has her blood and the venom," said Theodora. "Now, I have given a great bit of thought to that. At first, I thought he would just be able to drink the blood from her charm, but then I remembered her father. Jean took her father and tried that many times before finally killing him in frustration because of all his failures. Drinking never passes on anything. If we were to drink the blood of someone who was sick with cancer or something like that, we wouldn't take on the cancer then, but think about it the opposite way. If we have a specific ability, say we are a little faster than others, stronger, or those with some extra sensory abilities, when we turn someone, they take our trait."

"If he were to inject her blood into himself, it would work that way?" asked Harold.

"Possibly. Though I am not sure since he has already been turned, but that wouldn't stop him from finding someone who is loyal to him. He could turn them with her venom, giving them both abilities, with him pulling the strings. I think that might be more likely, but he will probably try himself first. There is so much unknown about this, but that hasn't stopped Jean from trying for decades. Can you imagine what he would be if he found a way?"

"I can see why you asked us to come. This is most disturbing," Keith responded. He seemed the surest of the four men as he sat there.

"Very disturbing indeed," added Tobias.

Harold shifted in his seat and turned to face everyone. I had seen this look before. This was that confident look of someone that felt they were about to make a very valid point. He all but sat there with a finger up to stress his point, as many did. I just hoped his point and contribution were going to be as earth shattering as he believed. "We need to consider his intentions before we decide. There is no need to be hasty and assume the worst."

"I wouldn't worry too much about that," crooned Theodora. "Larissa, why don't you tell them about Marie and all he has done to you?"

Over the next twenty minutes I recounted every way Jean St. Claire had terrorized me starting with the chase from our home, the killing of who I had thought of as my stepfather, the capture and torture of Marie—which seemed to bother Harold—all the way through every visit he paid me, the attack on the coven, and using Clay.

When I was done, they asked to be allowed to consult each other in private, and Theodora asked Master Thomas and me to join her out in her back courtyard. Holy Gone with the Wind. Her meager courtyard was massive. Complete with fountains, marble statues—Mrs. Saxon would approve, and rows of trellis covered in the most fragrant flowers I had ever experienced. She led us out to the square patch of walkway with a table. I believe she expected they would want time to talk alone. She already set a table with three glasses and two pitchers. Mint Julep for Master Thomas, and something she called her own version of a Bloody Mary for us. It was a typical Bloody Mary, with fresh blood instead of tomato juice and a little more vodka. I sipped at it slowly. This was my first alcoholic drink and I felt the little kick buried in with the other ingredients.

"Just because we are who we are doesn't mean we can't enjoy the finer parts of life. It is important that you remember that, Larissa."

"Yes ma'am."

"We are beautiful creatures, and we are gifted with the ability to enjoy an eternal life. Don't listen to those that call this a curse." She sat back in her chair and crossed her legs as she threw both arms up in the air. "This is a blessing, and we should bathe in fine wine and fine men."

It was hard to resist smiling at that, but I didn't feel it was the right time with the serious matter at hand. A small smile slipped out, and she pointed in my direction and smiled wildly. "You know exactly what I mean, don't you? What's his name?"

I said nothing and took another sip of my Bloody Mary.

"Come on. I can tell there is someone. You have that look about you." her eyes probed me from behind her pleasant, almost teasing expression. "Tell me this. Do you love him?"

"Yes," I shyly admitted.

"I knew it..." she said and then paused and stood up, looking behind us. I turned and saw John Milton standing there.

"They are ready," he announced. And the four of us headed back inside.

Just as they did when we entered the library the first time, the four men stood up and waited for us to take our seats before they sat back down. I searched their faces for some hint at what I was about to hear, but there was nothing. They were all stone-faced, which appeared to be a natural state on the four of them.

When we all sat, Tobias was the first to talk. When he did so, the other three remained focused on me. "Miss Dubois, we have discussed this matter, and agree with you regarding the danger that Jean St. Claire would pose should he obtain the ability you possess. We will discuss this with him tomorrow, with a stern warning that if..."

Master Thomas grabbed my elbow before I even twitched. It was more than a touch of assurance. He was attempting to hold me back. I hated to tell him, if I wanted to move, he wouldn't slow me up a second. I didn't. At least not externally. Internally, each word after the word warning grated on me.

"... he continues his pursuit of you and your abilities, we will remove him from leadership of a coven. Do you have any questions?"

I had a few questions and a ton of opinions. None of them were ones this crowd was going to appreciate it. That was one thing I was sure of. "No," I said, biting my tongue. Master Thomas' grip tightened. He was going to have to loosen it soon. With their verdict delivered, it was now time to leave, and I needed to get out of there before I exploded.

"There is something else," started Harold. Part of me wanted to scream back—I had heard enough. "That is our official stance. To do anything else would be disruptive, but if your paths were to cross and something happened to Jean, we would be inclined to look the other way if such events were to transpire in the case of defense. And, if something were to happen, we would ensure his followers wouldn't cause you any further problems." Harold actually cracked a smile when he finished.

Hope springs eternal, and in me it was full bloom.

"We assume this meets your satisfaction. It is all we can do in such matters." They didn't address this statement at me, but at their host instead.

"It does," she said, and then she asked, "Ben? Larissa? Is this okay?"

Master Thomas answered with a very shaky, "Yes."

I showed my gratitude a little more magnanimously. "Yes, thank you."

"Then we need to be off. We shall speak with Jean St. Claire before daybreak and give him the warning."

I pulled free of Master Thomas' grip, but stayed seated, right on the edge of the sofa. "You know where he is?" I asked.

"We do," confirmed Tobias.

"Take me to him," I spat, losing any of the respectful tone I had used most of the night.

"Absolutely not," declined Tobias. "That is not what we discussed."

My body was a spring, ready to leap. I was no longer seated, but I wasn't standing either. Master Thomas attempted to reach for me, but I easily shook him off. "I won't touch him, but I need to help Mrs. Norton."

"I'm afraid Mrs. Norton is not negotiable. Discipline of vampires is at the discretion of the coven itself."

"That's not fair!" The old Larissa slipped out, and I was now standing up, ready to rumble. My outburst earned a slight hiss from one of the four guests. Another hand grabbed hold of my arm. This one was more delicate than Master Thomas', but it held on like a steel clamp. Theodora whispered into my ear, "drop it, and I will help you." I didn't know until then, I had two blue flaming orbs glowing in both hands, ready to be launched.

24

"Completely out of the question," protested Master Thomas. "The council will never allow it. You both know that. No matter what the circumstances are, they will not permit you to take any action against Jean St. Claire." He looked frustrated and annoyed, still seated on the sofa in Theodora's library. Her guests had left an hour or more ago to deliver the message.

"It would work," agreed John.

"Ben, it would, and I don't see where the council would have any objections," added Theodora.

He shook his head wildly back and forth. Displeasure dripped from every pore. Every beat of his heart screamed it to the three of us. "Don't shortcut them. Mrs. Wintercrest and others have a past with Larissa and are well aware of her history with Jean St. Claire. They would see right through this."

"It's our only shot." I knew I was stating the obvious.

"Only shot now, yes, but who knows about the future? This is just such a bad idea."

"If we don't act now, what about what happens between now and whatever future point you are pointing to?" Theodora leaned against her chair from behind. "He won't stop just because they ask him nicely. That is a fact!" Her arms pointed wildly in a random direction, as if she were pointing right at him. She looked down at the floor, and appeared to sigh, which I found an odd reaction. A shadow of the person she once was. She walked around the chair and had a seat. "Jean has crossed the line of what should be accepted. They are just too afraid to stand up to him. Them talking to him won't cause him to even blink. I knew that before they arrived. I hoped, once they learned what he was really after, their own selfishness and desires to stay who they are in our community would drive them to take a further step, and they did. Agreeing to look the other way if you did something was the only step they could take. If they moved on him on their own, it would send ripples through our community. Some out of fear, which wouldn't be all that bad. Others would see it as an example and start contemplating their own moves to further their place." She sat back in frustration. "As I said about the thing with the witches, it is so exhausting. All the power plays. That is why I stay here."

"I get it. I truly do, but it just can't happen that way. Our world is just as complicated, if not more so, and again Larissa, don't forget you aren't exactly in the council's good graces. Remember Mrs. Wintercrest's warning just this morning?"

"She warned me about going after him and said nothing about defending myself and my friends. I bet if I didn't, and let Jack or Lisa get hurt, there would be hell to pay with the council, wouldn't there?"

Master Thomas said nothing. He just stared at the floor in front of him, contemplating. What was the question?

"Theodora, as always, it is a pleasure. Thank you for setting this up and helping to facilitate the meeting." Master Thomas stood up.

"My pleasure," Theodora reached out and shook his hand. As she reached out and took mine, she held on to it for a moment. "Larissa, if you plan to stay in this area, don't be a stranger. I love visitors, and I think we could be great friends."

I couldn't agree more. "I won't be one, and thank you for everything."

"My pleasure."

When I turned around, Master Thomas was already halfway to the door, and I quick-stepped to catch up with him. He was tired, I could tell. One benefit of being who I was, it being just after two in the morning, meant nothing to me. Outside, I offered to open the portal, and he didn't object. There were no objections when I offered that he just spend the night in one of the spare rooms upstairs. Not that he had to drive home tired or anything. He could just open a portal and walk right into his bedroom, but I could tell with how he kept looking back toward our library and the hidden library. That, more likely, my father's journals, called to him. Clay gave up his room without me even having to ask.

"It's not a bad idea," I said as I walked him to his room.

"I know. I just need some time to think it through."

"Good night, Master Thomas."

"'Night."

He went in and closed the door. I walked back toward the stairs, pausing at the door to my room. Nathan and Amy were in there, and a large part of me wanted to be in there with them, but at the moment there was too much on my mind. Was I thinking this through clearly? I needed to make sure, and there was a perfect sounding board of three people who were more than a little interested in how things went tonight, sitting right downstairs.

I went down to the parlor and explained to those that were still up, which were all vampires, what happened blow by blow. Clay seemed the most disappointed of all. He wanted revenge and didn't see any path to that with what I agreed to. Mike was working through every detail of the idea that Theodora and I hatched.

"It's risky," he said. "... but it could work." He paced a little further across the room, considering more details. When he reached the far corner, he stopped. "I'm in."

"Me too." Clay didn't hesitate.

Laura did, though, and I expected that. She was always the more calculated, less impulsive one of our crowd. The three of us put the spotlight on her, waiting for her decision. When she finally looked up at me, there was concern dripping from every inch of her face. "You know there is more of a risk to the others than to us. Are they going to be okay with it?"

"Well, I haven't really talked to anyone about it, except Lisa, that is. It was part her idea." Laura was right, and I hadn't really thought about that. Lisa and I would be exposed, and she would have to trust me. Now that we had three vampires to help, it should be a fair fight. It would probably be best to keep Jack and the others back here, far away from the action. I am sure several of them would protest and want to take part, especially Rob and Martin. They had a protective nature to them, which was a trait I intended to take full advantage of, if I needed to. "We will cross that bridge in the morning."

"I need to ask," Laura started hesitantly. "Do you think you guys can really do it?"

I nodded. I didn't dare try to verbalize it; my voice would have shown more than a few signs of the heavy doubt I felt. We had tried nothing like this before, and we were absolutely dealing with something we didn't fully understand. But the way I looked at it, my father stood on the same cliff many times and didn't hesitate to step off into the unknown. The best I could tell, he saw it as a win-win. Either it worked, or he learned something. Of course, this time we had a little more at stake. There were the lives of our friends, people I considered family, and that possibility shook me, and made me feel colder than normal.

When we finished talking about how it should go down, I suggested they head out for a feeding. If this was going to happen, they needed to be at top strength. When Laura asked, or pretty much begged that I join her, I told her I needed something else to replenish my strength, and dismissed myself and headed upstairs, where I promptly slid under the covers next to Amy and pulled her tight. I wanted... I needed the warmth of her love. When she was secured next to me, I reached over and grabbed Nathan's hand. I watched as his eyes opened in recognition of my presence. He didn't say a word, and just looked deeply, warmly into my eyes. Then he let go. I tried to hang on, but he pulled forcefully, and I reluctantly let go. My longing gaze followed him across the floor and around the foot of the bed. I lost sight of him, as he crossed back behind me, and the light I felt in my heart disappeared, leaving a cold dark place, but that was just momentarily. The mattress dipped behind me, and the covers rustled, then the warmth returned as Nathan slid in behind me, and wrapped his arms around Amy and me, and I lay there, basking in the comfort of my family. Hoping that would quell the doubts and fear I felt.

I sure hoped they fed well and felt renewed. I did.

25

I laid there all night. Just enjoying the feeling. Listening to their breaths. Where I had hoped it would renew me, it instead gave me a reminder of what I could lose if I failed. When the sun broke, I removed Nathan's arm from around me, but he wrapped it around me again, this time tighter. Another attempt, and this time I couldn't even move his arm.

"Nope," he silently mumbled, and his hand crept up and locked on to my shoulder. Who was I to fight it? I felt so safe there in his embrace. This was what I had needed all night, and while it didn't quell away all the worry and despair, it reduced it to a dull roar in my head. Outside in the hallway, I heard the first stirrings of the morning. A discussion about who would get the shower first. The hunt had gone well, it would seem. I heard two rounds of showers, and one was full of lots of giggling. The benefit, or curse, of hearing everything. When they were done, Nathan finally loosened up his grip, and slid out of bed, and started toward the door.

"I'm going to grab a shower before anyone else jumps in there."

I nodded, staring at his chiseled frame. The T-shirt he wore didn't stand a chance of fitting loosely. It hugged every ripple of his muscles. I think he saw me and knew what he was doing. I could see it in his eyes, and looked away.

"Want to join me? It will save on water."

I wanted to say yes. I wanted to bust him on how cheesy that line was. I wanted to do all of that, but instead I shook my head. Why? I couldn't really answer, besides the fact that there was so much on my mind. When it happened, I wanted to focus on him. No distracting thoughts. He left, and a little of me left, too.

Before he returned, I peeled myself away from Amy and made my way downstairs. Lisa and Master Thomas were already in my father's library looking over journals. I walked in the hidden door and leaned back against the wall with a thud. Any bliss left from earlier had left town, and fast. I thought I heard it slam the door on the way out. "The crescent moon is tonight."

Both looked up from the journals. "It's also Christmas Eve," said Master Thomas. "But it is indeed that."

"So, what's the plan?" I asked. It sounded funny to me. I had been the one telling everyone the plans for the last several days, and especially just in the last few hours. Now here I was, asking someone else what the plan was. Even funnier, I knew what the plan was. There was only one. Well, the only one they permitted us to do.

Master Thomas closed his journal and stood up from behind my father's desk. Both hands stayed planted on its top. "I still have reservations about all this, but I don't see another choice."

I sprung up away from the wall I was leaning against.

"Wait, there is more," he cautioned. "I can't be part of it. This has to be all you. If I am even around for it, it is a council action, and that has ramifications far beyond just going against what Mrs. Wintercrest has ordered, and... Lisa, I need to be really clear on this. You cannot attack Jean at all. If he attacks you, then you can defend your own life, but that is it. If you take up arms against Jean or any member of his coven, they will see it as an attack by a witch on a vampire. They gave Larissa a dispensation in that regard."

Lisa cast an odd look in my direction, but reluctantly agreed with his instructions. We walked through our plan with Master Thomas a few times. Each time, he pointed out a few areas where there could be problems and made suggestions to help. He also promised to stay with the others here at the house tonight, just in case. His instructions were explicit. If the worst happened, he was to take the others back to Mrs. Saxon and order her to take them back. She wouldn't dare defy an order from him. Though I honestly doubted she would say no either way.

As early afternoon arrived, Lisa went to go relax before we needed to leave, and I went to go find Nathan and Amy. I had neglected them the last few days, and I needed to remedy that. When I found them outside, I hid my hands behind my back and quietly walked up to them.

"Merry Christmas Eve," I yelled from behind them.

Both jumped, startled. Amy spun around, and I bent down so she could hug my neck. Then I stood up and gave Nathan a kiss with a little extra, prompting an "ooohhh" from Amy, and a gasp from Nathan. My next move produced two gasps. I pulled my hands from behind my back to show two ornately wrapped boxes. One for each.

"How about an early Christmas gift?"

Amy jumped for joy, and I sat right down there on the ground and pulled her down into my lap. My arms wrapped around her and held the box for her while she removed the bow. Tears threatened to invade the moment as I remembered this was probably her first Christmas gift ever.

After she removed the bow, she picked the box up, looking for a way to open it. I laughed, "Just rip it silly." She grabbed an edge and pulled. The paper ripped, and she looked back at me. "Exactly. Rip the rest of it." That encouragement was all it took. She had the paper shredded in just a few seconds. I had to help her with the box. My subconscious must be a taper. I knew what I had created for her, and even imagined it wrapped, but I didn't go into the detail of taping the box down. The top popped off after a light tug.

"Oh, my goodness!" She screamed, seeing the doll baby inside. It looked just like her, but younger. She pulled it out and clutched it against her. "I love it." I knew from how she held it, and how firmly she hugged me.

"Now your turn," I said to Nathan. He didn't have trouble with the bow or the paper on his small box. He had it opened quickly. I stood to help him with what was inside. "It was my father's." He pulled the onyx ring out and looked at it. Even under the overcast sky it glinted, and the light played in the jewel that was embedded in the center of the band. It was almost like there was magic running through it, which made sense. He told me it was.

"It's a protection band. It's charmed, and will keep the wearer safe." I took it and placed it on his finger. When I did, I felt a little charge, and so did Nathan. He couldn't take his eyes off of it. To be honest, I couldn't either. Green and deep blues raced around the ring.

I looked up into his eyes, and saw my now, my past, and my future all rolled up into one, and I was lost in the moment, lost in him. "I have something else for you. Follow me." I grabbed both him and Amy by the hand and led them inside.

"Laura, can you watch Amy for a moment?" It wasn't really a question. I had already directed Amy into the parlor, and she was already showing Laura her new doll before I even finished the statement. Nathan and I didn't even pause. It was straight up the stairs and to our room. The door flashed open and closed. I pinned him against the closed door and kissed him before he even knew we were in the room. He probably wasn't even aware we were inside the door when I pushed him on to the bed. I leaped on him like a prey, which he was, and kissed him while I pulled his shirt off. My hands roamed freely, and my lips consumed his. His hands fumbled around, trying to keep hold of me, and I slowed down. They found my waist, but did nothing else. Inside I screamed—come on, but I didn't wait. He was way too slow for me, and my own hands found the bottom of my shirt and ripped it up over my head, depositing it with his on the floor. The rest of our clothes joined them shortly.

26

Our plan went over like a lead balloon with the others. Nathan wasn't hearing it. He wanted to come along to help or provide protection. Martin and Rob didn't like being relegated to, as they called it, protecting the home front, and Jack wanted to go with us. I explained to him the same warning Master Thomas had given Lisa. Any action taken by a witch would be extremely problematic. Lisa was only involved because, well, she needed to be. The debate and protests continued long into the evening, so long I was about to grab Lisa by the hand and just transport ourselves where we needed to be while the others continued discussing it, but we ended with a compromise. Everyone would go along with my idea begrudgingly if we left a portal open so we could easily jump through to escape if things went sideways. I hated to tell everyone. I had a feeling things were going to go sideways, backwards, upside down and every other way, other than how I would have mapped out in a perfect scenario.

Nathan pulled me aside as Lisa went upstairs to prepare, whatever that really meant. She was the dark magic expert, and this time she was going to be getting in touch with her voodoo background. "You need to promise me you won't try to force anything. If things go bad, you and everyone else will come right through that portal, and we will all go back to the coven and face the music. You better promise me!" He demanded, and then kissed me deeply with more passion than I had ever felt.

"I promise..."

"No!" He cut me off. "Not a Larissa promise where you say it and then go do whatever you want to do. This is a dead serious promise. Not just for you, but for the others. There are a lot of lives at stake. I don't want to lose you... or anyone. Got it?" He grabbed my face with both hands and held it firm while glaring into my eyes.

"Got it." I said, holding his eyes with mine. "If anything goes wrong, we will be back here in a flash."

He pulled me in, tightly embracing me, almost squeezing as he whispered over and over to himself. "Oh god. Oh god." Then he pushed me back and yanked my father's ring off of his hand and forcibly grabbed my hand. "You wear this. It will protect you. Someone once told me it was charmed." I didn't argue as he slid it on my finger.

Lisa came back downstairs, looking the same as she had before, but this time she had a small bag slung over her shoulder. "We should go. I need to find it before midnight."

I slowly backed away from Nathan. Our fingers danced together until they could no longer reach one another. Then I followed Lisa and three vampires out into the dark night and through a spinning gold portal and into the oldest cemetery in New Orleans.

To say my tension increased when my foot first crossed into this place would be a major understatement. Everyone was on the defense as soon as we stepped through. I let my other senses feel around. There were no other humans in the vicinity, but that didn't mean there weren't vampires.

"One sec," I called to the others, to slow down our procession into the crypts. I needed to put step one of the plan into motion. I picked a small area that was clear of crypts and grave markers and spun open a portal. Through it was Theodora's library. She and John were standing there, waiting, just like we discussed. "We are here."

"Then we better get moving," responded Theodora.

"Thank you so much. I don't know how I am ever going to repay you."

"Just promise to be a good friend," she said, and I watched as they moved away from the portal, and I let it close.

"So, Lisa, what are we looking for?" asked Mike.

"Either signs of regular sacrifices at the bottom of a grave marker or a crypt door, or one with three X's scratched on it. One with lots of sets of three X's with circles drawn around them will be the jackpot."

"There are so many graves," sighed Clay.

"Yep," Lisa said as she was working the row. I was in the next row over, looking for the same.

"Are you sure this is how it works? They will use the same each time," Mike, the man of a dozen questions, asked. These would have been good questions to have asked earlier.

"Pretty sure. Contacting the same spirits over and over to rise would make sense. Once you know how to make them do what you want, you tend to stay with the same. Those spirits I pull out and let fly around from time to time in the coven are ones I am familiar with. There are thousands of spirits here, all unfriendly to me. I would have to start all over with one of them."

"But you can, can't you?"

"Should be able to."

Mike gave a big huff at that answer. "Doesn't really instill a lot of confidence here, Lisa."

"All right, enough chit chat, let's keep looking." He was right. It would have been nice if she had said yes, but she didn't, and we needed to stay focused.

"From what I read earlier, the older graves are here in this front section, and since this has been going on since the 1920s, it should be in this area."

We covered row after row and, just like Lisa had said, the older graves were at the front. We were in the 1700s, and so far, no X's, and no signs of anyone else walking around. I looked up at the massive size of this place and became a little worried that we waited too late to start our search. My best guess was we had another two hours to find what we needed to, and I felt a little relief when we reached the 1800s. Though it was no guarantee we were close, it just meant we had eliminated a lot and made progress, but we needed to move faster. We agreed to split up. Clay and Laura took one side, and Mike, Lisa, and I took another side. We agreed if anyone felt anyone's presence, we would hightail it back to the portal. This helped with our progress. We were moving through the 1800s rather quickly, despite the large amount in the mid-part of the century. From what I could gather from some of the engravings, there was a yellow fever outbreak around that time. It also explained why there were so many graves for children. Something that didn't occur in large numbers in any of the other areas we covered.

"I got one!" Laura yelled.

"Keep looking. I will go check," instructed Lisa. I might have kept looking, but that didn't mean I didn't keep glancing in that direction. From what I could tell, it appeared Laura had really found one. I watched Lisa examine the markings, and then she opened her bag and began applying something to the gravestone before making her own markings. Then she placed a yellow ribbon on top of the marker, before moving on.

Over the next twenty minutes, we found seven more. Which could have been all of them, or half of them, or some other percentage. We didn't know how many there were. Our goal was to find as many as we could before Jean's people arrived. From what Lisa had seen on the seven we had found; they had already been here earlier today and marked the graves with three X's meaning they were asking the spirit for a wish. If the wish was granted, they drew circles around the X's. Which explained all the rows of three X's in circles we found on the graves. What was disturbing was how each one we found had a fresh set with no circles. They had marked these graves for use tonight.

"How are we doing on time?" Lisa asked.

"11:28," replied Laura after a quick check of her phone.

"We can search for 20 minutes more, and then I need to get set up. If they are doing what I think they are doing, they will need a few minutes, too."

We kept searching and found four more marked graves. Each person who found one called Lisa over to do whatever she did to it. I didn't ask her any specifics of what she was going to do to each when we made this plan. She just said she would stop them.

As we progressed through the early 1900s, I saw Clay and Laura stop at one stone, and then look at the one next to it curiously. A call for Lisa was coming. I knew it, and I kept looking, but the name they called was not Lisa. It was Mike, who after he looked at the markers, made a curious, pitiful look in my direction, and I hated that look.

"Larissa, you might want to see this," Mike called.

I walked over, not knowing what he wanted me to see. They huddled around a single large concrete grave vault, with three distinct markers on top of them. As I approached, Laura and Mike moved, giving me a view that sent me stumbling backwards, falling back on my butt and landing on another grave. Even from there, I could clearly see the names. Susan Dubois and her date of death, June 19, 1939. On the other large stone was Maxwell Dubois, and a date almost a month later. In the middle, the smaller stone, Larissa Dubois, with a date of death of June 19, 1939.

A giant had just gut punched me, and while I didn't require air to breathe, I still felt life drain from me. I was locked on to the three markers, focusing more on my parents than my own. I felt a few hands on my shoulders. Then Laura bent down next to me and gave me a hug, but my focus was still on the markers. I knew they were dead. I knew everyone thought I was, too. Seeing something physical made it all real. Knowing that just six feet down in that concrete vault were the bodies of my parents, and what I had to assume was an empty spot for me, if they ever found my body, which they won't. I was still using it. I reached out first and touched the top of the vault on the side where my mother's name was.

"Let's give her a moment," Laura suggested. I heard the shuffling of their feet along the gravel path behind me as they resumed their search.

I wanted to say something prophetic, sitting here at my parent's grave, but all I could muster was, "Hi." I knew I could go talk to my mother anytime I wanted, which helped, but didn't ease the sadness I felt sitting here. When I shifted and touched the side my father was on, that was when the tears flowed. I couldn't talk to him. I couldn't go see or visit him. All I had left were the memories of the firm, but loving man who always took opportunities to teach me, but never let an opportunity to have fun, or a laugh, go by. That wasn't entirely true. He left me a lot. He left me a library of his life's work. A legacy I had every intention of living up to.

Time was working against us, and now that I knew where they were, I could come back to visit them. It was time to get up and finish this plan to take care of the person who did that to them. That was my focus and reminding myself of that didn't stop the tears from flowing, or the longing to stay sitting here longer with them. When I rejoined the search, each of the others regarded me with a look I hated, but I understood it. None of them said anything, but Lisa came and draped an arm around my shoulder as we walked down a row from the 1960s.

"Here's one," Clay called, and Lisa went over to it while we continued searching through the graves and crypts.

Had we missed any? That was entirely possible considering the sheer numbers of gravestones and crypts we had searched in the moonlight. Our eyesight helped fight through the shadows, but given how old and scratched up some of the older markers were, we could have walked right past a few. The hope was, we had the majority. If we didn't, this was going to be a problem.

"That's it," Mike declared as we reached the last of them. "How many was it?"

"Fifteen," answered Lisa. "They are mine now."

"Now what?"

"Well, we hide and wait."

That was exactly what we did. I had Jack shut off the portal to keep anyone from seeing it. There were more than a few protests from the other side as it went against our agreement for safety. I promised to reopen from our hiding spots, which I did, calming theirs and our nerves. The spot we chose was between two large family crypts that were as far away from any of the marked graves as we could. It kept us away from where those we were waiting on would go, and it was on a little rise in the path, giving us the best view.

Our wait wasn't long. Off in the distance, beyond the entrance, we spotted a series of lights, like lanterns, coming up the road. They turned in to the entrance, and the processional of four people made their way in. Three were holding lanterns and followed in a woman with long dark hair. She wore some kind of headdress and a long dress that dragged along the ground. She led them up the center path in our direction. Mike and Clay were both ready to pounce. I touched them on the shoulder and whispered. "Wait." They both relaxed a little.

Halfway up the path, she stopped, and the three dark cloaked individuals gathered around her, holding the lanterns.

"That's got to be her," whispered Lisa. She moved to the edge of the crypt for a better look, and I turned back to the portal and motioned for everyone to keep quiet. I considered putting a few runes around the portal to protect it, but what would I cast them against? Keeping witches and vampires out would keep us out as well.

Lisa moved back from the corner, and I took her place, staying in the shadow, even though my dark eyes wouldn't give me away in the darkness. "What's she doing?" I asked.

"The same thing I am doing."

I turned around and saw Lisa sitting down on the ground. She arranged the contents of the bag she brought on the ground around a bowl. One by one, she took something and deposited it in the bowl. First it was sage, which she ground up with a pestle, then it was a liquid on top of it, then green leaves from a bag she had labeled with the word nettle. She grabbed a handful of dirt from behind the crypt and sprinkled it around in a circular pattern. There was one bottle left, and when she opened it, it got all of our attention. I could taste it. It wasn't human, I could tell that from the smell, but there was no doubt it was blood. After dropping in two drops, she capped it quickly while looking up at the four vampires that were mesmerized by the smell of what was in the bottle. A panic hit me, and I spun around to the edge of the crypt to look.

"Crap. Crap. Crap." I whispered, turning back. "Lisa, you need to do it now. Those are vampires with the lanterns, and they smelled the blood."

Mike and Clay pulled me back from the corner and took up a crouch. Lisa re-stuffed her bag. Her hands moved fast and clumsily. I bent down and helped her put everything back.

"What's the next step?" I asked.

"Need to hurry. They are almost here," whispered Mike.

"Back up," Lisa said. She sat up and took a deep breath, then her eyes rolled white. Smoke rose from her bowl, and she passed her hands in and out of the smoke, causing it to take a shape, then multiple shapes.

"Oh shit," proclaimed Clay.

"Larissa..."

I joined Mike and Clay at the corner, and almost screamed "Oh shit," myself. Mists were rising from each of the graves we'd found, and Lisa marked. Right before our eyes, the mist took the shape of people. Men, women, and children floated up and then descended to the ground. The mystery woman stood up and almost appeared fearful. When the figures moved in her direction, there was no doubt she was fearful. She began backing toward the entrance.

Behind us, Lisa was directing the smoke figures over her bowl. The spirits that had risen followed her every movement. They surrounded the mystery woman, freezing her in her tracks. From the looks of things, we had them all, and tonight they would only terrorize one person in New Orleans.

Her escorts stopped and watched the scene unfold by the entrance. The spirits moved in closer and closer, and then stopped and held her there. Lisa floated up above the crypt and over the rows of mausoleums and grave markers until she was over her foe. Her vampire escorts dropped their lanterns and jumped for her as she floated overhead. Mike and Clay grabbed the first two. Laura grabbed the third, banging them down to the ground with a thud. They struggled, and then gave up, frozen by surprise.

I ran and checked them, one by one, for the one I wanted. The youthful faces that stared back up at me didn't match the one I was searching for. I stood there in the pathway between them and Lisa and announced, "He's not here." This put step three of our plan in jeopardy, but step two was going quite well. I only hoped step one was going as well. I ordered the others, "Hold them, but don't hurt them." I meant it too. They were only following Jean's orders, and I did not know what was truly in their hearts. They weren't struggling to get free or making any attempt to fight. They were just there.

Lisa had the woman suspended in midair. Her hands scratched for the ground, but she couldn't reach it. Only her long black skirt brushed the ground. Her dreadlocks hung down from her head, short of the ground, just like the multiple amulets and jewels she wore around her neck. The spirits were all around her, each taking a turn to plunge their hands deep inside her. She screamed with each intrusion.

"An atonement of your soul for disturbing these," said Lisa. The spirits continued until Lisa lowered her back to the ground. "You will never disturb them, or any spirits in this manner again." With that, the spirits shot up in the air, and once again became a mist that slowly fell to the ground, producing a rumble below our feet. "This ground is sanctified. You may never practice black magic or disturb these souls again." Lisa floated down and landed on the pathway leading to the entrance. She was smiling. Step two had worked. Thanks to her.

A figure emerged behind her in the shadows of the entry gate behind her, and I lunged, knocking Lisa out of the way. Step three still had a chance. Jean St. Claire stood there, dark suit, dark leather coat, top hat, and cane with his ghostly ivory skin glowing in the moonlight, none too pleased that we had not only ruined his fun for the night, but forever, at least not here and by the end of the week every cemetery in the city.

When he saw me, he hissed and charged into the cemetery, obviously not needing the cane. I stood my ground there on the gravel path. Stones ground together under my shoes as I dug in. We could do this one of two ways, and I was going to do it both ways. His hands reached for me, and I ducked down just out of his grasp, giving him a good shot from behind as he passed over me. He landed and slid along the ground, leaving an enormous dust cloud behind him. His perfect suit was now all smudged with dirt and pebbles. His fancy top hat was a crumbled mess on the ground.

"Want more?" I taunted.

Before he charged again, he looked back for help, but all he saw were three vampires on the ground, pinned by three others. Only one on the ground attempted to even move, and Mike quickly corrected that with several blows to the head and a foot on the throat while he stood over him.

Jean looked back at me and glared. "Finally!", then he charged me. I attempted to move out of the way, but I forgot about his cane, which he swung with lethal force. The impact with my ribs sent me flying backwards down a row until my head crashed into a grave marker.

Lisa was now up and throwing fireballs in his direction. He outran most of them, and the two that hit him forced him to discard the long coat he wore.

I leaned up, trying to shake the burning pain in the back of my head away, and watched as he charged Lisa, swinging the cane like a saber. There was no way she could get out of the way in time. Jean was way too fast for her. He was almost too fast for me. If she turned to run, she wouldn't even get turned around before he was on top of her, and with how hard he was swinging the cane, he would have broken bones if he connected. I pulled all I could together and sent a push in her direction. Mike and Clay beat me to it, tackling Jean to the ground. My push continued and found its mark, sending Lisa stumbling backwards off the path. I was going to have to apologize later for knocking her down twice.

I stood up, pain shooting through my ribs, and aches in several other areas on my arms and shoulders, where I must have hit other crypts and markers as I flew past them. There was a horrible sound coming from the path. I knew they had knocked Jean to the ground, but I didn't know Clay had hung on to him. He was ripping and pulling at every inch of Jean. He tried to shake him off, but Clay held on. After a few more attempts, he finally grabbed hold of Clay by the head and flipped him through the air, where Clay crashed into a crypt, cracking the marble wall of the structure.

Jean had moved on before Clay even landed. He had the mysterious woman held up by the throat. Her feet kicked furiously for the ground. "Do it! Now!"

"I can't," she croaked. "She sealed the ground."

"Who?" he asked, while leering right at me. Seeing her hand point in the opposite direction at Lisa caused his head to snap. He threw the old woman away like a sack of trash. "You should not have interfered."

Before I knew it, he kicked Lisa like an old dog, and I heard her scream in pain. Mike hit Jean first. A full-on tackle around his waist. The seemingly feeble man absorbed the hit. Then he grabbed Mike by the waistband of his jeans and slung him some fifty yards up the path. He faced me, glaring, and seething as I rushed at him. Having seen what he did to Mike, I wasn't going to play into his hands like that. I kept running, but as I did, I reached out and grabbed him, feeling the cold and evil vibration of his energy, and then hoisted him up in the air, and I spread my fingers, forcing his arms and legs out and stretched to the limits of his joints.

I felt immense pleasure in watching him squirm, and his screams were the sweetest music to my ears. In between guttural screams, he pleaded for help. Each time, I spread my fingers further, stretching the tendons that held his body together to their limit. All I had to do was twitch, and I would rip his body to shreds, but even that wouldn't kill him. It would give me intense pleasure and allow me to walk right over and finish all this with no resistance. That was now my plan. If only I could follow through with it, but life is funny about that. The best laid plans rarely ever come true. Two vampires tackled me to the ground, causing me to lose my focus, dropping Jean. I got back up to my feet, and the sight I saw was not a battle close to victory, as I had believed we were just moments ago. Lisa could barely stand up. Clay was standing, but that was about it. The impact with the wall had taken a lot out of him, and he seemed unaware of his surroundings. Mike rushed through like a bull, knocking the two vampires that had attacked me to the ground. His destination was Laura, who was lying flat on the ground with two other vampires standing over her.

Beyond the wrought-iron gates, hordes of vampires had gathered, watching the events that happened inside. They hopelessly outnumbered us.

"Larissa, we need to go!" Mike yelled. Laura was limp, cradled in his arms. "Grab Lisa!"

This couldn't end like this. He can't win. I was thinking of all the ways I could stop the assembly behind him from interfering. I was sure I could, but if I couldn't, I wouldn't stand a chance. It was a heartbreaking realization.

"Larissa!" Mike yelled at me again. I was going over my options again, unwilling to accept this was how it would end. Unwilling to accept the fact that Jean would live, and continue to terrorize me and those I loved.

"I got her," Clay grabbed Lisa and carried her back behind me.

I knew where they were going. NO! I couldn't accept this. He can't win. He just can't. There was so much of my future dependent on ending this here and now. So much of everyone's future. He just can't. Lines of pale faces had gathered behind him, and I felt the emptiness that was behind me. I was alone.

"Larissa, come on!" called Jack through the portal.

I knew what the agreement was, the plan, but my legs wouldn't make that step backward. Making that single step backward was giving up. Telling Jean, he won. Accepting a life of being hunted by him. I couldn't step forward either. The crowd had grown. I was stuck between a decision of living in hell and dying. What a decision?

Only when I felt an angel touch my arm did I finally make a move. "Come on Larissa. There will be other days." Nathan grabbed my arm and dragged me backward two steps before my legs started working on their own. Behind me, I heard a stampede of feet.

"Close it!" I screamed as we jumped through, and Jack let it close just in time. Nathan and I lay on the ground where we landed. Laura lay unconscious in Mike's arms. Master Thomas was attempting to check on her in between Mike's outbursts.

I looked right at Master Thomas, and he knew the question in my head. "She's still with us. Just knocked out. It will take time."

I spun around, looking for Lisa. She was sitting on the steps. "I'm okay. Bruised. Maybe a few broken ribs." Rob was helping to wrap bandages tightly around her chest. He stopped and dropped the roll, letting it bounce down the stairs and roll out onto the path. Then there was that deep hollow growl I had first heard when Mr. Markinson found me in the woods. Martin joined in.

I turned. How the hell did they get here so fast? We went through a magic portal. They... All of them, were just there at the entrance to the cemetery, and now they were here. Standing on my family's farm. I didn't wait until I was standing before I started throwing runes of the solar cross and any other symbol of protection at the ground in front of them. The flashes to the side of me had to be Master Thomas doing the same. Neither Jack nor Lisa would know how to do this.

The ground glowed an eerie purple, and I stood just on the other side of it, trying to look as defiant and dangerous as I could. Hoping to deter a few. Having two large werewolves on either side of me didn't hurt. There was a big problem. There were just three of us, and there were dozens upon dozens of them. Maybe even a hundred all circled behind one man, one man who had reshaped his top hat into something respectable and stood there causally leaning on his cane.

Master Thomas stood behind us, but was reluctant to step forward, and I understood why. He could protect us, but he couldn't attack them. Nathan and Mike came forward with Jack, who helped support a limping Lisa. She was in no shape for any of this. I turned back to Nathan and instructed him, "Take Lisa and Amy and get inside." At first, he didn't move, but when I screamed at him, "Nathan! Now!", he reluctantly turned and helped Lisa into the house with Amy.

Jean walked up and down the purple line, occasionally testing it with his cane and making a "tsk tsk" sound each time it smoked. He knew he was dealing with a powerful witch, just like my father and mother. That shouldn't surprise him, but I needed it to surprise the others. So, a bit of show wouldn't hurt, and might buy some time for an emergency exit.

I backed up to Jack. "Go inside and get everyone out of here. She will take you all back." Both Rob and Martin heard the suggestion and growled at it.

"Not a chance," said Mike. He had vengeance in his eyes. Jack understood. He knew what this was and turned around and asked Clay to help him with Laura. Now I had three other stubborn friends I needed to get to safety.

Jean continued to poke at the line, in some sort of hope it would dissipate, which I knew it wouldn't. Each time, he pushed his cane into it further and further. That was when I realized he wasn't testing to see if it was still there. He was testing to see how strong it was, and how much damage he would take if he forced his way through. Crap, I thought. I needed to ramp this up, and I did so.

My red hair flowed behind me, and one of the long robes, a green one with gold inlays, from my mother's closet that I saw her wear for special coven events appeared on me. I was now dressed for the part. Now it was time to act the part. With outstretched arms, I floated up high above the scene, riding the vibrations. I was up maybe twenty feet or more, and just hung there with large blue fireballs in both hands, just waiting for someone to test the line again.

Several of the vampires backed up. A few even retreated off into the woods. An action I was sure Jean St. Claire would consider treasonous. I let the fire grow in each hand just to see if I could encourage a few others to leave, and right on cue, another group disappeared back into the woods. Jean took no notice, but others did. There was actually an audible murmur behind him.

"Come on!" I dared them while looking right down at Jean. He toed up to the purple line. His body jerked as if to make another step forward, but he didn't, and his legs settled next to each other.

"What are you waiting for?" I asked. I reached over with my right hand and pulled my blood charm from under the robe and held it out for all to see, then I let it settle back down on my chest on top of the robe. That was almost it. He jerked again, but this time upward. He was showing a shocking level of control, being that close to the thing he has been after for almost a century. I needed to test that control, and I lowered myself until I was just on the other side of the line from him.

That was all it took. My feet hadn't even touched the ground before his hands bolted through and attempted to first grab the charm and second to grab me. Both attempts were unsuccessful. The flinching caused by the searing pain when he forced his arms through the line gave me just enough time to move out of the way, which I expected. When that went according to the plan I made just a few seconds ago, the rest of it backfired. Jean looked at his arms, and realized something I hadn't considered, and stepped right through the purple line with little more than a whimper.

"Rob! Martin! Get out of here. Get to the House." I screamed and unloaded on Jean. The first two fireballs didn't harm him, but the third had a little extra behind it and caught him right in the face. It was enough of a distraction to put some distance between him and me. From there, I could do real damage. I picked him up again, like I had in the cemetery, and instead of tearing him apart, I slammed him into the ground as hard as I could, then I raised him again before slamming him again. Once for Laura and once for Lisa. I had one more to deliver, and that was for Clay, but now several other adventurous vampires followed their leader right across the line of pain, screaming, and howling. One of them tackled me to the ground, causing me to lose my hold on Jean. Four other vampires grabbed me and pinned me to the ground. How stupid of them. I sent them flying high, landing somewhere I know not where, and didn't care. The others did, though. Everyone stopped to watch, allowing Mike to knock out the one he was fighting.

I had never heard a werewolf laugh. Until then, I didn't even know they could, but I can attest to the fact that they do. The sound was a very chuckle from deep inside Rob's chest. Almost like a forced sound with his breathing as he grabbed one vampire with his mouth and tossed him about as far as I threw my four. He gloated that his went further, which it didn't, but I wasn't going to argue the point right now. That would have to wait.

Some left again, but not enough. Others braved the line, rushing over, avoiding the two werewolves, and choosing to go after Mike and me. I gave ground, searching the crowd for Jean, who appeared to have disappeared in the masses. I wondered if he had retreated to the woods himself. Gone to survive another day. He was nowhere to be seen as I continued to give ground. Rob and Martin followed my lead but nosed forward, wanting to charge.

"Stay back! Behind me!" I ordered.

Then I focused on something a little larger than the handle of a closet door and shoved. The earth rumbled beneath my feet, then a shock wave radiated out along the vibrations of the world. It was a large violent wave, and when it reached the onrushing vampires, it threw them back along the ground in a cloud of dust. Only Mike, I, and two larger werewolves stood amongst the carnage.

"Next time, lead with that," remarked Mike.

One by one, the vampires pushed up from the ground, but they didn't stand up. They were hesitant, fearful.

"I don't want to hurt you, my brothers and sisters," I announced. "I only want him! Give him to me."

"I'm right here!" he growled from behind me. His long fingers on one hand grabbed and squeezed my throat. His other hand grabbed my head and attempted to twist. My hands flailed above my head for him, hoping to hit him and forcing him to release me. All I hit was air.

"I've got you now," he bragged. "Now to finish this." His hand released my head and grabbed my charm. I felt the impact of a great force from behind me and felt the chain of the charm yank against my neck. It didn't break, and it stayed with me when I landed face down on the ground.

I pushed up and saw a sight that made my blood flash boil. The anger of the scene forced my hand out away from me, and a column of flame projected out from it toward Jean, who was now sitting on top of Nathan.

"No!" I screamed, and the fire turned to lightning, knocking Jean off of Nathan with an echoing boom. From there, I could see the trail of blood coming from Nathan's neck, and he lay there lifeless. How I got to my feet, I didn't know. I didn't even remember running to Nathan. I just knew I was holding his head in my lap. His eyes were closed, and his breathing was growing shallow. I knew what was happening all too well. I could feel it. The slowing of the fluid in his body.

"Someone, give me your charm now," I demanded, and then added, "If you want to live." I laid Nathan down carefully. Tears streaming my eyes. "Now!"

Each of the remaining vampires stood up, pulling their shirts open to show no charm at all. A voice from the mass said, "He made us destroy them."

There was no doubt who the *he* was in that statement. It was that pile of crap to my left, still smoldering. He was still of this world, unfortunately, but I aimed to solve that problem for him shortly. I pulled him up again and suspended him in the air, stretching his extremities to their breaking point. I let one arm break free from its joint and took pleasure from the sound of the pop and Jean's scream. The anguish on his face was just icing on the cake.

"Give me a charm now!"

He cackled at my demand. "Miss Dubois, I wouldn't if I could, but I can't. My followers don't have any, and even Mrs. Norton already used hers on you."

I turned to Master Thomas, who was standing guard at the house. Pissed to hell that he let Nathan slip past him. "Find Theodora. Now! She and John both have one."

Master Thomas didn't move. He was frozen where he stood.

"Benjamin. Now!"

He still didn't move. He just stood there and stared right past me.

"Put him down Miss Dubois." I knew the voice, and it sent a chill down my spine. This was all I needed. My thoughts were on Nathan and how to help him. "Master Thomas, you will go nowhere except your home. You will be dealt with later."

"No!" I rejected Mrs. Wintercrest's demand. She stood there, just beyond where Jean St. Claire was suspended. By her side, my favorite person. Miss Roberts. She didn't seem to be any more a fan of me now than she did before.

"Your supreme ordered you to let him go."

I didn't grace her request with a response other than letting my fingers spread a little further. I should have spread them all the way. That was my chance, and I missed it. I took a shot in the chest from either Mrs. Wintercrest or Miss Roberts. I wasn't sure which. Jean fell to the ground. His left arm dangled freely, and I crumbled to the ground, feeling like a truck had hit me. Each attempt to stand felt like that truck backed over me again.

"It would appear you have become exactly what I predicted, and now you must be dealt with."

I pulled myself up to my knees and crawled toward Nathan. Each movement agonizing, physically and emotionally. Seeing him lifeless broke me into a million pieces. I sobbed, one tear for each piece. A few feet away from Nathan, I collapsed on the ground, unable to move any further, and I stretched as far as I could, but I still couldn't reach him. I screamed and then pleaded. "Do what you want with me, but help him." I pointed at Nathan.

"Miss Dubois, there is nothing we can do for him. His blood is on your hands."

"Help him!" I screamed.

Mrs. Wintercrest ignored me. "Master Thomas, come along."

The blank expression on his face snapped clear, and he straightened his bow tie and stood up, shoulders back. "I will be staying here."

"Suit yourself, but this ends your place on the council," she pronounced for all to hear. Then she did something that was the most shocking of all. Mrs. Wintercrest assisted Jean up to his feet. "Mr. St. Claire, let's get out of here." Seeing her treat that monster as a human was all it took to give me the energy for one more great strike. None of the three saw it coming, but they felt it. Oh, they felt it. Everyone for miles away heard it. Mrs. Wintercrest brushed herself off, and looked back over her shoulder before the three of them were gone with a flash, leaving behind nothing but silence.

I pulled myself the remaining few feet and spread myself across Nathan and cried. His heart still beat inside his chest, but it was slow, very slow, and his breathing was almost non-existent. I felt a hand on my shoulder and spun around, ready to attack. It was Master Thomas, standing over me.

"Let me help." He kneeled next to Nathan and began checking for a pulse and listening for his breath. The shock on his face changed to one of death. He knew the same thing I did. "Let's get him inside." He quickly gathered Nathan up in his arms and rushed up the stairs to the porch. We walked past Mike, who was lying flat on the ground. I regarded him as I passed, but he was not my primary concern now. It was Nathan. It was all of my hopes and dreams for the future. It was the one whose lifeless body produced screams and wails inside from Laura and Amy when they saw Master Thomas rushing up the stairs to the bedroom with him. I felt selfish in that moment, and of course I was. One hundred percent, with no question about it. My concern was my world, but I still paused and looked back at Mike.

"Go with Nathan," Martin said. "We will take care of Mike." Both were back to normal with the threat, or the perceived threat, gone. Behind us were still several dozens of vampires that were just as stunned as we were.

27

Master Thomas placed Nathan down on our bed just as he took his last breath, and I died at that moment along with him. I held him, almost crushing him, while my eyes beseeched everyone for help. Help that none of them could offer. I know that, but it didn't stop me from trying.

"Theodora," I said between weeps.

Master Thomas sat on the bed on the other side of Nathan and looked across at me. His eyes were apologetic. "I called; she isn't answering. She may not be back yet from her part in all this."

That wasn't good enough for me. I laid Nathan's head down and jumped up from the bed. My legs buckled at first, but then I found my strength. "I will find her," I announced defiantly and spun open a portal right to her office. I walked forward and screamed her name. "Theodora!"

There was no reply, nothing. No one was here, but I still tried again, this time as loud as I could. My voice strained to be heard and echoed through her home. Again, all I heard was the devastating sound of silence. I walked back through, resigned that there was nothing we could do, and collapsed to my knees next to the bed. My hand held Nathan's. He was cold, cold like me, and the rosy peach color of his flesh had all dissolved away.

I again searched everyone's faces, and where there were no answers before, there still weren't, but tears were common amongst everyone. Laura held Amy tightly as they both wept. Even Mike and Clay were shedding tears. Master Thomas continued to sit beside Nathan, and each time I looked up at him, he shook his head to answer the unasked question.

He and I stayed that way for most of the night. A vigil over Nathan, while many of the others had retired to other rooms to wallow in their own sorrow. The house was eerie, and many of the old noises I remembered as a kid reappeared. The odd creaks of the floors and walls as the house breathed with every gust of wind outside. The rattle of the window in the next room that my father said he was going to fix next weekend. It was the next weekend for about four months. Just like the squeak of the screen door, which he also said needed just a little oil. We only heard it when it opened. Someone probably needed some air to escape the dark cloud that was suffocating my home. I couldn't blame them. Then I heard steps coming up the stairs. Three sets of them at first, then others followed. I turned to watch the opening of the door. I saw the elongated shadows of them stretch down the hall when they topped the stairs.

When Theodora walked through the door, she gasped, and I threw myself at her feet. "Help him. Let him drink your charm!"

She put a hand over her mouth and then walked right around me to Nathan. She removed her charm and held a jewel filled with clear liquid in her hand and bent down over Nathan. Her free hand felt his skin, almost like a physician performing an evaluation. Then it returned to her mouth to cover another gasp. "When did this happen?"

"About six or seven hours ago," responded Master Thomas.

"That is what I feared. His skin has already changed. It's too late." She stood up from her examination and looked back at me, clutching her charm. "I'm sorry Larissa. There is nothing we can do. It's too late."

"No!" I wailed, collapsing on the floor.

"She's right," a voice said behind me in the door. It was weak, but warm and familiar. I sat up on my knees and spun around. She was there. She was standing right there, being held up by John Milton. Marie Norton was standing there in my home. She was weak and tattered from the torture. I lunged at her, draping my arms around her, yanking her from John's grasp to the floor with me. She embraced me as we fell. Something had gone right tonight, but that was little consolation compared to what all had gone wrong.

Marie and I held each other until the first glint of sun of the new day, Christmas day. The holidays were the last thing I wanted to think about as we sat there holding each other, and Nathan lay on that bed motionless. I stared at him, looking for any movement. This process could take hours to days, but there was also a more horrifying outcome. His body might not handle it, and he might not survive at all. Nothing I could do would help. I was helpless, just sitting, waiting, worrying, and dying inside. I told Marie how much he meant to me, and I also told her about everything else I had learned about myself. She apologized and wept about holding all of that back, but it was me, as weak as I felt, that was the strong one and told her not to feel bad for doing that. I knew she was doing it to protect me. That it was all in my best interest. I ended up thanking her for that. Thanking her for giving me a chance to escape my past and have a life. I even told her, if she hadn't, I would have never met Nathan. Which was the truth.

As the sun crept from the window across the floor, Amy crept into my lap and curled up, prompting a rather surprised look from Marie. "My, you have grown up."

I didn't deny it, and stroked Amy's hair. We sat there for a long time, while the others rustled below. There was the same chattery noise that filled the house every day for the last several days. It was the sounds of feet dragging on the floor, at the end of legs, that lacked the energy or motivation to lift them. Everyone felt what I did, but others were worse off, and I hadn't checked on them in some time. I picked up Amy and placed her on Marie's lap. The tired girl never woke.

"Can you watch her for a minute? I need to go check on the others."

"Of course," she said. Her hand still holding mine until I was too far away to maintain a grip. The first I checked in on was Lisa, who was in the next room over. She was in the bed, asleep, or was until I walked in.

"How you feeling?"

"Like a truck hit me, but okay. How's Nathan?" She groaned as she pushed herself up to her elbows.

"No change," I mumbled.

She reached out and rubbed the back of my hand. "He will be fine. I feel it."

I wish I did, and fine was relative. I knew what was happening. Most of the others did as well. Their perspective was a little different from the four of us who had been through it ourselves. Fine is not what I would call one's first moments like this. "Thanks."

I promised to bring her back an ice pack, which I would send Jack back up with, and left to head downstairs to check on those that took things even worse. Clay still looked out of it, sitting on the floor against the wall. Mike was pissed, obviously fully recovered from his injury, and looking for revenge.

"How's she doing?" I asked, pointing at Laura.

"Sore, but she will live. Nothing's broken," said Mike.

"I can talk for myself. I'm fine," she forced herself to sit up. Her movements were slow and cautious. She wasn't entirely fine. That much was obvious. "How's..." she pointed upstairs.

"You know," was the reply I chose.

"Really?" she responded, sounding shocked. "I was hoping it was just a bite."

I shook my head. "Master Thomas and Theodora both said they can feel the change in the skin already happening, and he is cold, like us."

"I..." she started, and then tried again, "I..."

It was then that I noticed the distracting sound that was stopping her mid phrase. It was a distant murmur. Like a large group of people talking. I opened the door and looked out. Off in the distance, in the shadows of the surrounding woods, lines of vampires stood. This wasn't good. I slammed the door shut and leaned against it. "Keep this closed at all times." I said to anyone that was listening.

Mike was looking out the window at them. "I think they'll wait until dark. That makes the most sense for any kind of attack."

I had to agree, and my instincts were to throw up some protection runes around the house. Those I placed last night were still there, but most of the vampires had seen others cross it, and the price they paid. I doubted those were going to be much of a deterrent beyond a momentary suffering. This would need to be stronger, a lot stronger. I wanted it to kill anything that dared to cross. Of course, I needed to be careful where I put them. There was enough suffering in the house, we didn't need any friendly fire.

The agonizing day passed feeling like the slowest day in my life, but I knew that wasn't possible. All days were the same length. It was a scientific fact, but an observable and universal fact was good days sped by, and the worst days of your life crept by with each second ticking loudly in your head. I spent the day going up and down the stairs. Most of my time was spent upstairs watching Nathan. He hadn't moved yet, but he hadn't shown signs that his body was giving up yet.

Marie had taken over the care of him, and of me. She calmed my nerves, which jumped on to every assumption or notion my mind threw up. Each time reminding me she had been through this before, with me. I knew that, but hearing it, knowing what it meant, and now seeing it hit me in the heart. Had she sat next to me, checking my skin, maintaining a watch over me? Of course, she had, and she would do it again over and over. That was in her eyes every time she looked at me.

I wanted to stay there with Nathan and never leave. There was no physical reason I needed to leave. There were no bodily functions, no need to eat, no need to sleep, nothing, but that didn't stop me from succumbing to the overwhelming need to run away in disgust at what I was, and what he was now cursed to be. Each time, running down the stairs, wanting to go out on the porch, but stopping because outside were more examples of what I now hated. I felt ill. Physically ill and I had to search for a space inside just to sit and cry. With people spread all around the house, that was an increasingly challenging task, but there was always one place, my father's library. With the door shut and light off, I was free to hate on myself with no interruptions. I cursed who I was, and what I was, until I was out of phrases to say. The sick feeling rolling inside stayed. It came in waves, and I felt lightheaded and once almost lost my balance, walking down the stairs. After that, I held on to the railing going up and down. That was something I hadn't done since I was probably six years old. Each time, eventually, the desire to check on Nathan overcame my hatred for what I was, and the sick feeling, and I headed back upstairs to sit on the other side of him and hold his hand.

Night had fallen, and I was deep into my self-hatred, almost to the point of making another dash downstairs. I couldn't even stand to hold Nathan's hand anymore, not wanting to expose someone so pure to something like me. My kind had already stained him. I heard the door downstairs open and heard voices. I looked out the window at the clear moon lit night and remembered I had forgotten to set more runes. Theodora poked her head in through our bedroom door. "Larissa, you should probably come down here."

"The vampires?" I asked, and stood up. The world around me moved, and the vibrations waved around me erratically.

"No," she said, and motioned with her hand for me to follow.

I followed her out and froze at the top of the landing. Below there was a reunion of friends. The world shook for me again, and I grabbed the rail as I walked down. I made it three steps before Apryl sprinted up the stairs and hugged me around my neck. "How is he?" she whispered.

"It's still happening."

"Oh god," she whispered back, letting go of the embrace. "It's going to be okay. It is," she insisted, looking into my eyes.

Right behind her, next in line for a hug, was Jennifer Bolden. "What happened? Why are you here?" I asked.

She didn't reply, and just held on.

"Jen, what happened?"

"She knows. Rebecca knows, and she kicked us all out."

That lightning bolt hit me right in the soul, and I pushed back from her and looked down the stairs. They were all here. All of them. Everyone who wasn't a witch at the coven was now here, in my house. All of them. I kept repeating that to myself over and over again. Each time the world spun around me, and the sick feeling came back stronger than before.

"Oh god," I gasped, and fell down to the step.

"Don't," Jen warned me sternly. "Don't do this to yourself."

"I cost them their home. I fucked up their lives." No one could debate that. The spinning increased and the sick feeling deep inside intensified. I leaned my head against the railing for stability.

"Larissa, don't you dare think that." She reached over and rubbed my shoulders, but didn't offer any argument about why I shouldn't think that, or why I hadn't just completely screwed up everyone's life unbelievably. "Where is he?"

"Up there," I motioned toward the bedroom, "with Marie."

"Marie.. Marie Norton? You found her?" There was actual joy in Jen's voice.

I nodded, now afraid to open my mouth for what I felt inside. Something stirred, and I couldn't control it. The longer I looked at what I would call the official gathering of everyone whose life I destroyed, it grew deep to the point I could no longer contain it, and rushed down the stairs, pushing Jeremy and Steve out of the way to get out the front door. I hit the railing, and it spewed out, a mixture of colors and textures. Then I collapsed right there on the wooden deck.

"Larissa, what have you been up to?" Jeremy asked.

I looked up and was about to give him a rather obscene gesture, when I noticed he wasn't looking at me. He was looking out. I pulled at the railing to turn around and saw it. Dozens of vampires all kneeled down in front of my home and looking at me.

"I don't know," I replied. Using the banister for support, which I absolutely needed, I walked to the other end, and they stayed locked on me, creepy.

Then, out of the tree line, emerged another large group of people. I watched as they circled around behind the vampires and stood there facing the house. These were not vampires. These were witches.

The screen door creaked open. "Larissa," Theodora said rushed. Master Thomas and Jennifer Bolden followed her out on to the porch.

"What the hell is this?" I asked, hoping she would know.

"Oh my god," said Jen.

"Well, I'll be. Those are rogue witches, Larissa," announced Master Thomas.

Theodora walked slowly down the front porch and studied the crowd.

"Why are they here? Why are they..." I was about to ask why they were kneeling there, staring at me, when she interrupted me.

"Jean's gone, and you are their new leader," Theodora said. She moved to my side and grabbed both of my shoulders, turning me around. "You are the new head of the coven because of what you did."

"I don't..." This time, the sickness interrupted me, and I spewed again over the railing.

"Are you all right?" Jen asked.

"That's the second time she has done that," reported Jeremy. "She did it just a few minutes ago, over there." He pointed to the other side of the porch.

Theodora let go of my shoulders and grabbed my face firmly and studied my face. She smirked with a sparkle in her eye as she moved one hand down to my stomach. It pressed against me firmly, and I felt my insides jump. "She's fine. She's pregnant."

Up Next – Coven Cove Book 4 – The House of the Rising Son

Available for pre-order at the links below:

For the US Store, tap here.
UK, tap here.
Canada, tap here.
Australia, tap here.
Everywhere else, tap here.

1

"Just have a seat."

Several sets of hands ushered me inside to the closest chair. I fought each of them away. Despite the room spinning, I felt I was more than capable to find my way to the chair on my own. I was wrong, and would have completely landed on the floor if Jen hadn't caught me and moved me a few feet to the right to the chair that I never sat in as a child. It was one of those things that was nice to look at, but not something you sat on. A fact that made it a constant joke between my mother and father, but now I was sitting there, and the joke was on me. "How?"

The room was full of silent stares, but I felt a few struggling to withhold their sarcasm.

"If any one of you starts with the birds and the bees, I am throwing you in to the next state, and trust me I could do it." I held up a hand, showing one of my newest tricks. There wasn't just a glow. There were lines forming patterns and runes.

"I have heard of this before, and it is not that uncommon," said Theodora. She strutted across the room and sat on the loveseat that was next to the chair I sat on. She crossed her legs elegantly and leaned as close as she could to me. "The father is human, correct?"

I gave her a 'duh' look, and then I shot a warning at the rest of the room before anyone clarified he was human at the time. Nathan was no longer a member of the human species and was well on his way to becoming a vampire.

"That's a yes," assumed Theodora.

"I've heard about it too, but I've never seen it before," Marie said curiously. "It usually reversed, though. A human female carrying the child of a male vampire."

"That's true," agreed Theodora. She leaned back away from me and then looked at Marie Norton. The glance had a shared understanding between the two women. It reminded me of the days sitting in Mrs. Saxon's residence back in the coven, watching her and Jen or Mrs. Tenderschott carry on a conversation about me, but without me. Oh, to be back there. Those were simpler times.

"Everyone out," ordered Marie. "Everyone but Theodora, Jen, and Larissa. Everyone else get out now!" I had never seen or heard her this forceful before. She walked around and ushered a few stragglers out. Apryl tried to linger just outside the door, but Marie put a stop to that, and gave her a little shove from behind to move her down the hall.

"Larissa, I want you to relax."

That wasn't going to happen. I guess Theodora didn't know that I wasn't a relaxing type. Especially not with the world exploding around me, witches and vampires assembled outside, and the love of my life upstairs becoming a monster. Yep, there were plenty of reasons to relax.

"Can you feel it?" Marie asked.

Jen Bolden stepped into the center of the room and nodded.

Theodora nodded as well.

"What?" I screamed at them all.

Marie Norton walked over and kneeled in front of me. She laid her hands on my legs and looked up into my eyes the way she had for years. The look on my mother's face, or foster mother's face, was one of concern. Seeing it just added to my own. She then moved her hands up and over my stomach. I flinched backwards when she yanked her hands away from me and gasped. "It's there. I feel it. It has a pulse, but how?"

"Dhampir pregnancies have an accelerated gestation period. Some as short as a month," said Theodora. "But this is not one of those."

"Dhamp-what?" I asked. All I knew was that the word sounded both funny and terrifying at the same time.

Theodora leaned toward me again, and reached over with her long slender hands, taking mine in hers. "Forgive us Larissa. As strange as all this is for you to hear, it is also new to us. A Dhampir is what we call a child that comes from the union of a vampire and a human. No one knows why, at least not medically, but those pregnancies have a much shorter term. I have heard of ones as short as a month, and others a few months. I have never witnessed one personally, but..."

The three women exchanged looks again. I was beyond tired of this little unspoken language they had, and I leaned forward in my chair and allowed my head to drop into my hands. "But what?" I exclaimed. "Will someone tell me what is going on?"

"Larissa honey," started Marie Norton. "The problem is this is a little different. In those, the woman is human, not the other way around. That is a crucial difference. When we become vampires, our bodies stop changing. We stop aging. We stop growing. We stop everything. And... well, our bodies can't adapt to carry a child."

Maybe it was the stress of the situation, or the bizarre situation with everything else going on around us playing in my mind, but my first thought wasn't about what she had said and what it meant about my situation. My first thought was about the conversation I had had up on the rooftop one night, and I looked right at Jennifer Bolden and said, "Well, we have our answer." The last word passed my lips at the same time as the realization of what that answer meant entered my brain. The answer converted into a question. "Wait! If my body can't change. How can I give birth?"

"Yes," started Marie. "This leads to a ton of questions, and I don't have any answers," she finished, looking around at the others.

"I could try to ask around, but I'm not even sure who to start with," remarked Theodora. "It is possible this is a miracle of sorts."

Right then another wave hit me, and I leaped out of the chair and ran across the parlor and back out to the front porch, where again I heaved nothing more than a few strings of yellow foam.

"Dry heaves are the worst," Jen commented from behind me. I turned around and gave her the look from hell. She didn't know the half of it. I remembered dry heaves from when I was sick as a child once. The feeling of the gagging, and the constant rolling and squeezing of your stomach as it tries to empty whatever contents it had left. This was worse, way worse. The squeezing was there, with an enormous cramping that followed, almost paralyzing. Then came the heaving that felt like my stomach was being ripped from my insides.

"So, if everything happens faster, how long will this morning sickness last?" I asked, hoping to hear it would only be minutes, but then I heaved again in front of the large audience still gathered in front of the house.

Marie reached down and helped me gather myself, and then walked me back into the house with a supportive arm around my shoulders. We didn't stop at the parlor, and I let her guide me down the hallway to the kitchen where most of our new house guests were. A bit of dread set in. Was she wanting to make some grand announcement to everyone? I wasn't ready for this yet, not that most hadn't already heard Theodora's announcement on the porch earlier.

Amy pounced on me and grabbed me around my waist as soon as I entered the door. "Larissa, are you okay?" She squeezed me firmly, and I stroked her hair.

"I'm fine."

"You sure?" she asked, looking at me with her big blue eyes.

I nodded while I smiled and tried to be more convincing than I felt.

"I want to do a test," Marie said as she approached me with a glass of water in her hand. Apryl and Brad stared at the glass like the Wicked Witch of the West, fearful of melting. "Take a sip."

"What?" I asked in disbelief. "I've been dry heaving, and you want me to drink this?"

"Yes, I want to see something." She handed it to me.

"No thank you." I put the glass down on the table. "Are you trying to get me to vomit even more?"

"Larissa, trust me on this." Marie reached down and picked up the glass and gave me that look that only parents seem to have mastered. The type that told you they would not take no for an answer and would stand there until the end of time until you finally did what they wanted. For most, that wouldn't last more than a few minutes or maybe an hour at the most, if the parents were persistent. We were immortal, so that timeframe would be a little different.

I had done this a few times before. Some as an experiment when I was, I guess, what you would call–younger. Another when I made the mistake of swallowing after I brushed my teeth to freshen my breath. Just a few drops of water in my stomach caused a tossing and turning unlike anything I had ever felt, and then it rolled back up faster than the speed of sound, bringing up blood and anything else that might have been in there. I braced myself and took the glass, while looking at Marie for confirmation.

"Go on," she urged.

I tipped my head back, but stopped. My stomach was already turning. Either it was another dry heave coming or the anticipation of what was about to happen. To be on the safe side, I moved close to the backdoor. Pamela moved out of my way.

"What's going on?" asked Jack from the door.

"Larissa is about to spew," announced Apryl.

I didn't even bother with a dirty look or any comment. She was right. I was about to spew, but there had to be a point to this, or Marie wouldn't make such a request. I knew she wouldn't ask me anything that would be dangerous. She basically gave her own life to protect me. It was that trust that allowed me to raise the glass to my lips. It took a little more than that to tip it far enough for a few drops to pass over them.

Maybe it was curiosity. Maybe it was a lapse in judgment, but I did it. First a drop, then a second, and then what I guess most would consider a sip passed over my lips and into my mouth.

My lips clamped shut instinctively, and Pamela moved away even further from the back door.

"She's about blow!" Apryl warned, and everyone scattered.

It was cool and moist. A feeling of comfort flowed over and around my tongue on its way through my mouth, and a quenching of a thirst, that I didn't know I had, exploded when it hit my throat. That was it. After that, the feeling disappeared, and I braced myself for the rolling. My hands grabbed at my stomach, ready to hang on, but the loud gurgling I expected wasn't there. It was silent, really silent. It hadn't been that silent in almost a day. Then, amidst a room full of gasps and horrified looks, I took another sip, and after another uneventful reaction, I drank the entire glass, and then sat it down on the table.

Stay In Touch

Dear Reader,

Thank you for taking a chance on this book. I hope you enjoyed it. If you did, I'd be more than grateful if you could leave a review on Amazon (even if it is just a rating and a sentence or two). Every review makes a difference to an author and helps other readers discover the book.

To stay up to date on everything in the Coven Cove world, click here to join my mailing list and I will send you a **free bonus chapter** from "The Secret of the Blood Charm".

As always, thank you for reading,
David

ALSO FROM DAVID CLARK

The Miller's Crossing Series

The Origins of Miller's Crossing
Amazon US
Amazon UK
There are six known places in the world that are more "paranormal" than anywhere else. The Vatican has taken care to assign "sensitives" and "keepers" to each of those to protect the realm of the living from the realm of the dead. With the colonization of the New World, a seventh location has been found, and time for a new recruit.

William Miller is a simple farmer in the 18th century coastal town of St. Margaret's Hope Scotland. His life is ordinary and mundane, mostly. He does possess one unique skill. He sees ghosts.

A chance discovery of his special ability exposes him to an organization that needs people like him. An offer is made, he can stay an ordinary farmer, or come to the Vatican for training to join a league of "sensitives" and "keepers" to watch over and care for the areas where the realm of the living and the dead interaction. Will he turn it down, or will he accept and prove he has what it takes to become one of the true legends of their order? It is a decision that can't be made lightly, as there is a cost to pay for generations to come.

The Ghosts of Miller's Crossing
Amazon US
Amazon UK
Ghosts and demons openly wander around the small town of Miller's Crossing. Over 250 years ago, the Vatican assigned a family to be this town's "keeper" to protect the realm of the living from their "visitors". There is just one problem. Edward Meyer doesn't know that is his family, yet.

Tragedy struck Edward twice. The first robbed him of his childhood and the truth behind who and what he is. The second, cost him his wife, sending him back to Miller's Crossing to start over with his two children.

What he finds when he returns is anything but what he expected. He is thrust into a world that is shocking and mysterious, while also answering and great many questions. With the help of two old friends, he rediscovers who and what he is, but he also discovers another truth, a dark truth. The truth behind the very tragedy that took so much from him. Edward faces a choice. Stay, and take his place in what destiny had planned for him, or run, leaving it and his family's legacy behind.

The Demon of Miller's Crossing

Amazon US

Amazon UK

The people of Miller's Crossing believed the worst of the "Dark Period" they had suffered through was behind them, and life had returned to normal. Or, as normal as life can be in a place where it is normal to see ghosts walking around. What they didn't know was the evil entity that tormented them was merely lying in wait.

After a period of thirty dark years, Miller's Crossing had now enjoyed eight years of peace and calm, allowing the scars of the past to heal. What no one realizes is under the surface the evil entity that caused their pain and suffering is just waiting to rip those wounds open again. Its instrument for destruction will be an unexpected, familiar, and powerful force in the community.

The Exorcism of Miller's Crossing

Amazon US

Amazon UK

The "Dark Period" the people of Miller's Crossing suffered through before was nothing compared to life as a hostage to a malevolent demon that is after revenge. Worst of all, those assigned to protect them from such evils are not only helpless, but they are tools in the creatures plan. Extreme measures will be needed, but at what cost.

The rest of the "keepers" from the remaining 6 paranormal places in the world are called in to help free the people of Miller's Crossing from a demon that has exacted its revenge on the very family assigned to protect them. Action must be taken to avoid losing the town, and allowing the world of the dead to roam free to take over the dominion of the living. This demon took Edward's parents from him while he was a child. What will it take now?

The Jordan Blake Paranormal Mysteries

Sinful Silence (Book #1)

Amazon US

Amazon UK

He is the FBI's only paranormalist...
...She is america's favorite television medium.
Together they are more than the supernatural world bargained for.

Jordan Blake is the FBI's only paranormalist, a position that costs him more than a little credibility with the other agents. Throw in his girlfriend Megan Tolliver, the darling, and impulsive, host of the top cable paranormal show, "America's Medium", and he doesn't stand a chance of ever being taken seriously. But that doesn't stop them from turning to him when they come across something that the natural world can't explain, such as the mysterious death of a coed in Richmond Virginia. They sent Jordan up to just consult on her autopsy, but her spirit begs him to dig further. With Megan's help, they uncover a ring of evil that spreads up to the highest reaches of government, and cost several young women their lives to keep them silent. What is the old saying, dead men tell no tales? Well that is true, unless you have someone who can speak to the dead now isn't it? Together the hunt down those responsible and try to stay out of the way of their only true adversary, an entity who says he is the source of all Evil in the world.

The Dark Angel Mysteries

The Blood Dahlia (The Dark Angel Mysteries Book #1)

Amazon US

Amazon UK

Meet Lynch, he is a private detective that is a bit of a jerk. Okay, let's face it he is a big jerk who is despised by most, feared by those who cross him, and barely tolerated by those who really know him. He smokes, drinks, cusses, and could care less what anyone else thinks about him, and that is exactly how the metropolis of New Metro needs him as their protector against the supernatural scum that lurk around in the shadows. He is "The Dark Angel."

The year is 2053, and the daughters of the town's well-to-do families are disappearing without a trace. No witnesses. No evidence. No ransom notes. No leads at all until they find a few, dead and drained of all their blood by an unknown, but seemingly unnatural assailant. The only person suited for this investigation is Lynch, a surly ex-cop turned private detective with an on-again-off-again 'its complicated' girlfriend, and a secret. He can't die, he can't feel pain, and he sees the world in a way no one ever should. He sees all that is there, both natural and supernatural. His exploits have earned him the name Dark Angel among those that have crossed him. His only problem, no one told him how to truly use this *ability*. Time is running out for missing girls, and Lynch is the only one who can find and save them. Will he figure out the mystery in time and will he know what to do when he finds them?

Ghost Storm – Available Now

Amazon US

Amazon UK

There is nothing natural about this hurricane. An evil shaman unleashes a super-storm powered by an ancient Amazon spirit to enslave to humanity. Can one man realize what is important in time to protect his family from this danger?

Successful attorney Jim Preston hates living in his late father's shadow. Eager to leave his stress behind and validate his hard work, he takes his family on a lavish Florida vacation. But his plan turns to dust when a malicious shaman summons a hurricane of soul-stealing spirits.

Though his skeptical lawyer mind disbelieves at first, Jim can't ignore the warnings when the violent wraiths forge a path of destruction. But after numerous unsuccessful escape attempts, his only hope of protecting his wife and children is to confront an ancient demonic force head-on... or become its prisoner.

Can Jim prove he's worth more than a fancy house or car and stop a brutal spectral horde from killing everything he holds dear?

Game Master Series

Book One - Game Master – Game On

This fast-paced adrenaline filled series follows Robert Deluiz and his friends behind the veil of 1's and 0's and into the underbelly of the online universe where they are trapped as pawns in a sadistic game show for their very lives. Lose a challenge, and you die a horrible death to the cheers and profit of the viewers. Win them all, and you are changed forever.

Can Robert out play, outsmart, and outlast his friends to survive and be crowned Game Master?

Buy book one, Game Master: Game On and see if you have what it takes to be the Game Master.

Available now on Amazon and Kindle Unlimited

Book Two - Game Master – Playing for Keeps

The fast-paced horror for Robert and his new wife, Amy, continue. They think they have the game mastered when new players enter with their own set of rules, and they have no intention of playing fair. Motivated by anger and money, the root of all evil, these individuals devise a plan for the Robert and his friends to repay them. The price... is their lives.

Game Master Play On is a fast-paced sequel ripped from today's headlines. If you like thriller stories with a touch of realism and a stunning twist that goes back to the origins of the Game Master show itself, then you will love this entry in David Clark's dark web trilogy, Game Master.

Buy book two, Game Master: Playing for Keeps to find out if the SanSquad survives.

Available now on Amazon and Kindle Unlimited

Book Three - Game Master – Reboot

With one of their own in danger, Robert and Doug reach out to a few of the games earliest players to mount a rescue. During their efforts, Robert finds himself immersed in a Cold War battle to save their friend. Their adversary... an ex-KGB super spy, now turned arms dealer, who is considered one of the most dangerous men walking the planet. Will the skills Robert has learned playing the game help him in this real world raid? There is no trick CGI or trap doors here, the threats are all real.

Buy book three, Game Master: Reboot to read the thrilling conclusion of the Game Master series.

Available now on Amazon and Kindle Unlimited

Highway 666 Series

Book One – Highway 666

A collection of four tales straight from the depths of hell itself. These four tales will take you on a high-speed chase down Highway 666, rip your heart out, burn you in a hell, and then leave you feeling lonely and cold at the end.

Stories Include:

- Highway 666 - The fate of three teenagers hooked into a demonic ride-share.
- Till Death – A new spin on the wedding vows
- Demon Apocalypse - It is the end of days, but not how the Bible described it.
- Eternal Journey - A young girl is forever condemned to her last walk, her journey will never end

Available now on Amazon and Kindle Unlimited

Book Two – The Splurge

A collection of short stories that follows one family through a dysfunctional Holiday Season that makes the Griswold's look like a Norman Rockwell painting.

Stories included:

- Trick or Treat – The annual neighborhood Halloween decorating contest is taken a bit too far and elicits some unwilling volunteers.
- Family Dinner – When your immediate family abandons you on Thanksgiving, what do you do? Well, you dig down deep on the family tree.
- The Splurge – This is a "Purge" parody focused around the First Black Friday Sale.
- Christmas Eve Nightmare – The family finds more than a Yule log in the fireplace on Christmas Eve

Available now on Amazon and Kindle Unlimited

A big thank you to my beta reading team. Without all your feedback, books like this one would not be possible. Thank you for all your hard work.

David Clark
Visit my website at www.authordavidclark.com

Printed in the United States of America

First Printing: September 2022
Frightening Future Publishing

Printed in Great Britain
by Amazon

37629264R00106